For Eddie and Kurt,

Sweet friends,

kind hearts —

with much

love through the years.

Tony

7/6/91

THE MEMBER-GUEST

Novels by Anthony Robinson

A Departure From the Rules
The Easy Way
Home Again, Home Again
The Whole Truth
The Member-Guest

THE MEMBER-GUEST

A NOVEL BY

ANTHONY ROBINSON

DONALD I. FINE, INC.
New York

For my daughter and son,
Jennifer and Henry

All rights reserved, including the right of reproduction in whole or in part in any form. Published in the United States of America by Donald I. Fine, Inc. and in Canada by General Publishing Company Limited.

Library of Congress Cataloging-in-Publication Data

Robinson, Anthony.
    The member-guest / Anthony Robinson.
        p.   cm.
    ISBN 1-55611-268-8
    I. Title.
PS3568.O279M4   1991
813'.54—dc20   90-56082
                                                                            CIP

Manufactured in the United States of America

10   9   8   7   6   5   4   3   2   1

Designed by Irving Perkins Associates

CONTENTS

PART I

THE PRACTICE ROUND

C H A P T E R   1

H E HAD ARRIVED, if not quite at Gordon McSweeney's house at least in the town where Gordon McSweeney lived. Augie checked his scribbled directions and made a right at the next intersection. *Beach Boulevard.* Wide, tree-shaded, lined with magnificent colonial-style houses. He continued along, weary, stressed out, but glad to be here—at last. It had been a very long day.

Up ahead, some twenty cars were parked at the curb. Drawing closer, he noticed an outdoor party in progress. He couldn't see all that well because of a thick, neatly clipped hedge, but the house was huge; it had half-a-dozen gables, a wide veranda and a grand lawn. As he drove by, a couple in their mid-thirties—he in white linen trousers and blue polo shirt, she in a green cotton print—were approaching the house on the sidewalk, hand in hand.

He turned right when he hit Old Forge Road, almost immediately coming to a golf course. No one appeared to be playing. That was understandable; it was the cocktail hour in Easthelmsford. He gave the course a careful look. The rough was high, thick, not something you'd use a 3-iron to get out of; maybe a 6. The fairway appeared superbly maintained. Then he saw the green. It had two large sand traps guarding the front and a smaller one on the left—as many traps on this hole as the sum total on his course at home. Augie had a quick kind of hollow feeling in his stomach. Maybe he was out of his league.

3

Then he told himself to relax. If he didn't fold completely, he'd do OK. The houses started getting smaller. He kept on Old Forge for another half-mile, at last coming to a rusty, dented mailbox—719; he braked and drove in.

The house was little more than a cottage—shingled sides, white several years ago but now dingy, with a minuscule front deck. The grass was overgrown. The driveway wasn't blacktop or gravel—just packed grass and dirt. On one side of it sat a Chevy coupe. His car had some years on it; this one had seen service on D-Day. He picked up the envelope on which he'd scrawled information, and the last line read: "White shingle sides, black roof—719 Old Forge." Augie turned off his ignition and stepped out.

He was of medium height, no excess weight on him, in his early forties, with dark curly hair partially covering his ears and starting to recede, bluish green eyes and a small, straight nose. He had an open, boyish look and was fair skinned, a smattering of freckles on his nose and cheeks. His arms were very tan. He stretched, trying to get a kink out of his back, when the house door opened and a terrier-type dog streaked down the steps leading from the deck, barking furiously. He deferred to the dog's less-than-friendly behavior by standing perfectly still.

"Rainbow!"

He looked up; a man with a full head of silvery gray hair and a substantial gut was standing on the deck. Augie seemed to recall that Gordon had mentioned the new shade of his hair on a recent phone conversation, but the stomach was a surprise. Gordon started down the deck steps. The dog wouldn't stop barking.

"Rainbow!"

It stopped but only because it had to scratch. As it was sitting on its ratty haunches, raking its ribs, Gordon extended his hand. "Augie! You old son-of-a-bitch!"

"Hello, Gordon."

"You made it!"

"I think so."

The two shook hands, then bear-hugged each other. Augie picked up a clean, shaving-cream scent on his friend's cheek; and a touch of gin, generally. "How are you, Gordon?"

"Just great. You look terrific!"

"So do you."

"Bullshit. I'm up to two-forty-five."

The animal, finished with its scratching, began barking again and running around. "Rainbow, knock it off!" Gordon yelled. Then he said, "He's a friendly old dog, she picked him up at our local ASPCA—he was scheduled for the oven that afternoon. Hey, I'm sorry about your troubles today."

"These things happen."

Gordon had on a pair of white trousers and a light blue dress shirt, open at the neck, gapping at the midriff. He put his hands affectionately on Augie's shoulders. "Why have we let so many years go by?"

"Who the hell knows?"

"By the way, you're already invited for next year."

"I am?"

"We're making this an annual event, Wittenbecher!"

Augie moved around to the back of his station wagon, opened the tailgate and pulled out two pieces of luggage. Gordon relieved him of the garment bag. "Any problem with the directions?"

"None. They were perfect."

They walked toward the house. Gordon yanked open a screen door and they were in the kitchen. It was small, cluttered, reminding Augie of a kitchen you might find in a hunting lodge—open shelves, a few small cupboards with plain plywood doors, a chipped enamel sink with ancient spigots, a crummy gas range and a noisy old refrigerator. The sink itself was empty, but the drainboard was stacked with pots, glasses, dishes and coffee mugs. Remove one item, the whole structure would collapse.

"Is Catherine here?"

"She's taking Kelly to a friend's house for the night, she'll be back in a minute. How about a brew?"

5

"How about a brew? I've been on the road for eleven goddamn hours and the man says how about a brew!"

Gordon grinned, reached into the refrigerator and pulled
out a couple of St. Pauli Girls. He snapped the caps with an
opener and ambled over. They sat down at a small formica-
topped table. Gordon lifted his bottle. "To having you here,
Augie. I'm really looking forward to this."

"Me too."

"So, was it the fuel pump?"

"It was the fuel pump." He took a double pull on his beer.
"That was only part of it. First off, I was seventh in line for
service. Two-bay garage, everyone's having major work—
brakes, transmission. Then when they finally took me in, the
pump they installed malfunctioned. They had to start all over.
That meant calling out, waiting for delivery—"

"What did you do all day?"

"I followed your advice and looked for a friendly bar—
there are no friendly bars in Newburgh. So I practiced some
wedge shots in the empty lot next to the garage. Cop came
along and wanted to bust me; said I was endangering the safety
of motorists and pedestrians. Article 17, Paragraph B, City Or-
dinance."

Gordon started to laugh. "What kind of wedge shots were
you hitting, for Christ's sake!"

"Little pops, from one beer can to another. Except I topped
one and it bounced across the street and smacked someone's
front door. That brought the heat."

"What else?"

"Well, after my brush with the law, I sat in the waiting
room. This woman took a shine to me."

Gordon perked up a little. "Was she nice?"

"She was pleasant, very friendly—a little heavy."

"How heavy?"

"Maybe three hundred fifty pounds."

"This woman who weighed three hundred fifty pounds
took a shine to you, is that correct?"

"Lost her husband in a hay-baling accident two years ago. Thelma Quick. She gave me her number."

"Jesus Christ, Wittenbecher!"

"You asked me what I did all day."

"Who else was in this waiting room?"

"Five Hasidic Jews."

"What were they doing there?"

"Waiting, like the rest of us. Engine on their van seized."

"Those guys wrote the book on male chauvinism," Gordon said.

"Two of them were Mets fans."

"That's verboten."

"What can I tell you?"

There was a scratching at the back door. Gordon got up, walked down the little hall and opened it; Rainbow came scooting in and Augie lifted his feet. But the dog ignored him, and Augie assumed he was now part of the family.

"How about another beer?" Gordon asked before coming back.

"Sounds good."

He brought over two frosty bottles and sat down. Augie inquired about his public relations job. "I've told so many lies in the past five years," Gordon said, "I don't know what the truth is anymore. What they want *said,* I say."

"Ever think of quitting? Doing something else?"

"What could I do? It's a lousy job, but it beats commuting, working in the City."

They were quiet for a moment. "When will I get to see Kelly?"

"Tomorrow. She's a great kid, Augie. She likes boys but she's not your typical fourteen-year-old. Do you know how many times she went to Communion in May?"

"No."

"Every morning, didn't miss a day. But her mother's *convinced* she's having sex."

"What do you think?"

"No way."

7

Rainbow set about to attack his fleas; he took a sitting position and went to work with his rear leg. "How'd you play today?" Augie asked his friend.

"I bagged it."

"Didn't we have a practice match scheduled?"

"I called Dr. Flannery, told him what happened."

"You were free to play," Augie said.

"It was a good opportunity to take her to the beach. It's been rough-going for us these past two years, Augie. If it wasn't for Kelly, we'd be finished."

"I'm sorry to hear that," Augie said.

"These things happen. Hell, you know."

"Sure."

"So I do what I can to keep it together."

"What's the problem?"

"She's moody. Bitchy. You know how a woman gets just before her period. When they hit menopause it's like that every day—only worse."

"Is that what it is?"

"I'm almost positive that's it."

"Did you ever mention it—I mean, ask her?"

"Fuck no—she'd kill me."

"She would?"

"For Christ's sake, you don't say that to a woman. You don't say, 'Are you going through menopause?' "

Gordon lifted his bottle of beer, had a healthy slug. "Enough of that shit. Thanks for kicking in."

"I was glad to."

Gordon's hand dropped; he stroked the dog's short leathery ears. "I never told her, so don't say anything. She's very big on 'form.' It wouldn't be good form having a guest help with expenses."

"I understand," Augie said.

"Each year it's always the same, can we really afford to belong? This year dues are a cool four grand. Of course, she likes it for the social and business reasons—she thinks it's important we keep up the membership. And now that I'm playing golf, it's a better deal—more for the money."

Augie felt himself relaxing; after a good shower he'd be like new. "I think it's great you've taken it up, Gordon."

"It's too bad you missed the practice round!"

"Tomorrow you'll have to club me," Augie said.

"Club you?"

"Give me the distances."

"To the greens, that kind of thing?"

"Yeah."

"I'll do the best I can. I never paid that much attention—"

"No big deal. Who do you suppose called my pro yesterday?"

"The tournament chairman, Steve McMahon," Gordon said.

"Right. Checking on my handicap!"

"They're doing that this year. Last year they had a situation develop, so they're watching out for sandbaggers."

"What made him think I was a sandbagger?"

"No, no," Gordon said, laughing. "They called *everyone's* guest. You weren't singled out."

"Oh."

Gordon glanced at his watch. "The Flannerys said seven for cocktails. I don't know what's taking her so long. Come on, I'll show you the guesthouse."

"You have a guesthouse?"

"Fixed it all up for you," Gordon McSweeney said.

THEY EACH PICKED up a piece of luggage and
went out the back door, walking across a large yard that had a
rusted barbecue kettle in it, along with four blue-and-green-
webbed A&P lawn chairs and a badly pitted aluminum folding
table. A power mower, draped with a sheet of black plastic,
was parked near a rear window; for a moment Augie thought a
nun was on bent knee, praying in the yellow grass behind the
McSweeneys' house.

At the end of the plot, opposite the shed-like structure
(which Augie feared was the guesthouse), was a vegetable garden—except even an eye untrained in matters agrarian could
see it was, or had become, a weed garden. Gordon had the
shoulder strap of the garment bag on his shoulder; its bulging
sides had a resemblance to his middle. He set it down outside
the shed's screen door, which squeaked when he opened it; the
door proper was a warped, ungainly thing made of reinforced
plywood.

"The latch has a way of snagging on the inside, so you
have to"—Gordon was using force—*"lift up.* Wait a minute."
The door wouldn't open.

He applied both hands to the latch and lifted again, simul-
taneously kicking the bottom. "There. You'll get the knack."
He picked up the garment bag and Augie followed him in.

It was a rat's nest. Crowded and piled here and there in the
room were several pairs of old skis, three old bicycles, a num-

ber of old television sets, an old push-type lawn mower, hundreds of old books, two old fans with broken cords, racks of old clothing, an old loveseat with springs popping out, some old standing lamps and several old bureaus and chests. That Augie immediately noticed. Gouged out of the middle of this Salvation Army mini-warehouse was a little circle in which a narrow steel-framed cot rested. It was (to give credit where due) neatly made up. On the battered two-drawer file cabinet serving as a night stand sat a white vase filled with wild flowers, pretty though wilting. The temperature in the room was unbearable.

"Let me open the window," Gordon offered.

It was directly behind the cot. He tried to raise the lower half but it didn't budge. To give himself a better purchase he shoved the bed aside and now, directly in front of the window, struggled to lift it.

"Seems stuck," he said.

"No big deal."

"There's a knack to it."

"Right."

Sweat broke from Gordon's forehead. His hair, though gray, was thick as the first day they'd met—Augie a nineteen-year-old sophomore, Gordon older by some five years—in a pick-up game of touch football on South Field. When the game ended some of the players headed for a local establishment called the West End, and there Augie and the tall, slender, good-looking player who'd done the passing for their team had started talking. Gordon McSweeney was an ex-Air Force pilot, Augie soon found out, who had flown forty-one missions in Korea and was now going after a graduate degree in business administration. He was also (Augie was to discover) intelligent, humorous, easygoing; a lady's man; and partyer without peer.

Finally, using the heels of both hands to jar the window, Gordon succeeded in loosening it. He slid up the lower panel and inserted a handy wooden stick lying on the sill.

"There's a second window—well, behind those clothes,"

11

he said. "Unfortunately there's no screen, so I wouldn't advise opening it."

"Who picked the flowers?"

"Kelly. Like a robe?"

Before Augie could answer, Gordon went to one of the racks, pushing and pulling at the old clothing, and lifted out a short, yellowish, terry-cloth garment. "Here you go."

"Thanks."

"Anything else, give a yell."

"Then I, ah, should use the bathroom in the house."

"No problem. Kelly's the only one who hogs it."

"OK. See you later."

Gordon gave him a grin and went out, and Augie stood in his little circle—an island in a very confused sea. He took off his shoes; next—struggling like an escape artist shedding a straitjacket—his shirt; and finally he tugged off his khaki pants. Exhausted, dripping wet, he sat down on the cot. It groaned and squeaked. Mercifully a little breeze was playing at the window. Augie stretched out, thinking at least he had his own four walls—to look at the bright side. He closed his eyes. As he was about to doze off, a thin, whining noise, as of a low-flying missile, sounded in his ear. Suddenly it stopped. There was a moment's silence. Then he felt a needle-like sting. Augie lifted his hand and slapped himself, hard, on the neck.

He twisted about and examined the screen. One whole edge was loose. Thinking to tuck it in, or somehow secure it, he reached for the loose corner, and the screening disintegrated in his fingers, like dust. He poked his head out; just beneath the window were wet leaves, a couple of old tires and a tot's discarded plastic pool. Even as he looked, two new mosquitoes flew inside, smelling good upstate blood, so he pulled out the support and let the window down; at once his room became dead still. Augie stripped off his shorts, slipped on the robe, then opened his bag, grabbed his toilet kit and trudged to the door.

The robe, securely enough belted, came only to his thighs, and the neck was very loose, collarless, to facilitate a comfortable, leisurely shave. He went up the rickety back steps of the house—and stopped dead; in the kitchen, putting together some hors d'oeuvres, was Catherine. He wanted to backtrack but she looked over and saw him before he had the chance.

"Augie!"

"Catherine."

"Come in!"

With his hairy legs hanging out, he felt like a human tarantula; but did he frighten Mrs. McSweeney away? She came up without hesitation or shyness, embraced him and gave him a kiss—on his lips. As she did, her pelvis slid forward, in a way that made the contact seem accidental. Augie wasn't sure it was accidental. "It's wonderful to *see* you again!" she continued in a shrill, somewhat grating voice.

"Forgive my appearance—"

"Your appearance couldn't be nicer."

Catherine McSweeney laughed gaily. She was wearing a champagne-colored cocktail dress, hemline above her knees, with a lacy top, and she had on a pair of matching silk heels. Her perfume, if evocative, was overpowering.

"I feel terrible about your trip, Augie. How awful to waste such a beautiful day!"

"I made it, I'm here."

"That's the important part, you're here." She put her hands on his forearms. "I do want to apologize for the condition of the guesthouse."

"Not necessary, Catherine. Really."

Her hair fell in a single glazed wave just below her ears. He remembered her as a dirty blond, seven years ago when they had last met, when she and Gordon and their daughter Kelly had spent a weekend with him and his ex-wife Abby in Shufferville; now Catherine was a blonde blonde. She was quite tall, perhaps five feet eight inches, with small hazel eyes and faintly grainy skin. Above her thin upper lip was a growth of hair, carefully bleached. Her nose was longish and the tip of it perfectly round, like a marble; her body was hard, sinewy—

"It's a crime after all these years we don't have anything

13

nicer," she said in a quieter tone, "but would he *do anything?* He kept promising me he'd have it ready by the time you got here. Yesterday after work he went out and pushed around some boxes!"

"Please—it's fine," Augie said.

She was now talking in a distinct whisper. "The truth is, he *likes* living like this; that's what it comes down to."

"I—"

"He's a pig."

Augie was shocked; more, he felt disturbed. "But you want to take a shower," Catherine said with sudden brightness.

"If it's not too inconvenient—"

"Please, Augie. Make yourself at home!"

"Thank you."

"He'll want to have a drink before we go, so join us when you're ready."

"Sounds good."

She gave him a second kiss, this one merely on the cheek. For a moment he looked after her as she walked back to the kitchen. She had a small waist and round hips—and one pair of thoroughbred legs. The bathroom was right off the little hallway, and Augie opened the door. It was in keeping, at least, with the rest of the house—small, crowded, disorderly. Combs, shaving creams, razors, soaps, lotions, tampons, deodorants, bath powders, lipsticks, and dental floss were scattered about on two open shelves to the left of the basin; on the edges of the basin lay toothpaste, a cake of soap, a bottle of aspirin and several toothbrushes. He almost thought he was at summer camp, including that smell in the air of dampness, mildew. He looked around, finally setting his kit on top of the toilet seat as the only empty spot.

There was hot water, at least. While he was shaving he heard faint conversation through the bathroom wall, nothing he could make out; but by Catherine's tone it seemed she was on Gordon's case. He dried his face on a towel, then stood, staring at the shower. It was in the tub: a ring at top, the size of a barrel hoop, holding up a plastic curtain; and a hand-held spray nozzle attached to a rubber hose, other end connected to the tub spigot.

Augie didn't have to push aside the curtain because it only went two-thirds of the way around. He reached in and twisted the hot and cold handles; then, inside the tub, he picked up the nozzle. Only, no matter how he fiddled and played with the archaic goddamn thing, water wouldn't come out. Frustrated, becoming careless, he slipped—catching himself but inadvertently yanking hose from spigot.

"Fuck."

"Everything OK in there?" It was Gordon, just outside the door.

"Actually I'm having a little problem with the shower."

"There's a valve under the spigot," he said. "You have to push it *in.*"

"Oh, thanks."

First he had to reattach the hose.

"See it?"

He was on his knees in the tub, working like a plumber's assistant. The hose was wet and slimy.

"Augie?"

"Yeah?"

"That valve. Sometimes it pops out if you press the button on the shower nozzle too fast."

"OK."

"You'll get the knack," said Gordon.

DRESSING was one of the unhappiest experiences of Augie's life. By the time he opened his bag, pulled out shorts and socks, shirt, tie, jacket and pants—and put them all on—he needed another shower. He went out, sweaty and cranky, closed the door and crossed the yard. Rainbow came yipping and yapping down the back steps, his different clothes no doubt confusing the beast. Augie was in no mood for a second round of "Scare Off the Terrorist." Fortunately (for the dog) Rainbow veered

15

off just in time, as if knowing the precise distance a man's foot could reach. Augie went inside the house.

Catherine and Gordon were in the living room. "Don't you look nice!" she said as he walked in.

"Thank you."

She was sitting in a loveseat, upholstered in a gold fabric with a light blue floral design. Of all the rooms he had seen so far, this was the only one that had a pulled-together, finished look, even if its dimensions were odd. It was long and narrow, something like a railroad car. It had blue, wall-to-wall carpeting, two windows with white filmy curtains, a pair of dull gold easy chairs, plus the loveseat. Gordon, in one of the chairs, asked Augie to name his poison.

"What are you having?" Augie asked.

"Little silver bullet here."

"I'll stay with beer."

"That's my partner. One of us has to be sober in the morning."

"When is our tee-off time, by the way?"

"7:17."

"Maybe we should just stay up all night, Gordon."

"Now there's the Augie I love and know!"

Gordon stood and padded into the kitchen. Catherine wasn't crowding the loveseat but she still moved over slightly —it wasn't anything more than a wiggle of her hips, as if she were trying to rearrange her slip. He might have sat beside her anyway, but now he had to. As he joined her, he smelled her perfume again. On her carefully bleached mustache clung minute beads of sweat. In the kitchen something fell, making a crashing noise. Gordon swore and Catherine took Augie's hand —a gesture, he seemed to feel, that had conspiratorial overtones.

"They're all alcoholics," she whispered.

Both Catherine and Gordon were so loose with their pronouns, Augie wasn't sure whom she meant; maybe she meant everyone at the Easthelmsford Country Club. Or was she referring to the entire McSweeney clan, Gordon's three brothers in particular? Or was he thinking too much like the lawyer he was by training? Augie did notice that his hostess wasn't sipping a Shirley Temple. Her drink, in a rocks glass, had a serious cast to it. Augie steered clear of the subject and asked her about her job.

"Last year was fabulous," she said. Then in a lower voice, "I made *twice* what he did doing p.r. for Shore Gas and Electric. But this year's been slow. Interest rates mostly. Even the well-to-do don't want that kind of burden. Then there's so much luck in real estate—like being at your desk when the call comes. Otherwise it's routed to someone else."

She touched his arm. "Just last May I had a house *sold*, Augie. Going price, eight hundred seventy-five thousand! Do you realize the commission I would've made? All I needed was the couple's signatures. We had a meeting set for the morning; that night the man had a heart attack and died."

"Oh, boy."

"I still wake up in the middle of the night thinking about it."

Catherine took a taste of her cocktail, as if to kill a lingering pain. Just then Gordon came in with a St. Pauli Girl, a glass over the top. His trouser legs were spattered. "What happened?" Catherine asked.

"Pepsi bottle fell out of the fridge. Here you go, partner."

Once Gordon was seated, Augie made a toast, to the effect that he appreciated the McSweeneys' hospitality; he was anticipating a wonderful stay.

"It's such a great pleasure having you," Catherine said to her guest.

They tasted their drinks. Catherine sat with her legs slightly apart, no doubt an idiosyncrasy. A man's fist would just fit between her knees. Gordon had put on a red knit tie and a blue blazer. He lifted his cocktail and offered a salute of his own. "To making this a great tradition, Augie."

"Next year we'll have *real* accommodations for you," Catherine said.

17

Augie smiled and picked up a cracker with two smoked oysters on it.

To her husband she said, "Let's show Augie the plans."

Gordon had just settled back in his chair, holding his martini glass like an object d'art—or, more closely, as if it contained one. He had a quick sip, then stood and disappeared into a room off the living room. Catherine again touched Augie's arm. "Of course, he's just going along," she said. "He has no real interest in this."

Augie tried another hors d'oeuvre.

"Bathroom, kitchen, guesthouse—we're tearing everything out and starting from scratch."

"Ah, ha."

From the next room came another crashing sound, but heavier, like from a falling body. Augie looked over his shoulder. "Don't worry. For him to hurt himself is a contradiction in terms," Catherine said.

Gordon, in fact, came out five seconds later—he wasn't limping, holding his arm or grimacing in any way. Catherine extended her hand without looking and he placed in it a cardboard tube, considerably thicker and longer than a runner's baton; the transfer, in any case, was clean. She positioned her glass on one side of the low table and, sliding blueprints from the tube, spread them out.

She talked. She knew every detail—the type of sink, of dishwasher, of shower; of shingle, of window, of flooring. She was a realtor, after all; she knew all this. And terms too, percentages, costs. Gordon sat in the matching easy chair sipping his martini, tuned out. Augie, trying to stay tuned in, was following Catherine's long bony finger as it scratched here and there over the architect's plans.

"It's really going to improve your property," he said politely.

"Well, we'll have a *house,*" she said.

"When do you plan to start?"

"Hopefully by September 1."

"That's pushing it," Gordon said.

18

"We really should have started this spring," Catherine said, "but he kept dragging his feet—"

"I wasn't satisfied with what I saw."

"You're uncommitted. That's the bottom line."

"Do you have a contractor lined up?" Augie asked, stepping in like a referee.

"We have two or three who're interested," Catherine said. She rolled and tucked the plans away, then faced Augie more directly, her hand grasping her ankle. "How about you, Augie? What's new in your life?"

"Not a hell of a lot."

"I can't believe that—after all these years!"

"If there was anything exciting to tell you I'd tell you."

"Are you involved with anyone?"

He didn't like the expression but he responded, regardless. "Not right now."

"So you're available for some lucky lady."

"I'm available—I don't know how lucky she'd be."

"I was thinking maybe we should have a little party tomorrow night," Catherine said to her husband. "Do you think Augie would like Betty McKeon?"

"I'm not sure she's his type."

"What's your type, Augie?" Catherine asked.

"I don't have any, so far as I know."

"I think he'd be happier with Rose Trippico," Gordon said.

"You're disgusting," Catherine said.

"What's disgusting about that?"

"Rose Trippico is cheap, she sleeps around."

"I'd call her sexy," Gordon said with a laugh.

"You would. Because it's all you think about. There are other things in this world—and I think Betty McKeon has lovely qualities. She has good values and Augie might like her —for *herself.*"

Gordon's hands went up, as if to signify a truce. "It was just an idea."

Augie sat quietly, looking down at his frothy-sided glass. Catherine asked him how his children were.

19

"They're doing fine, they're good kids."

"Heather must be fifteen by now."

"Next month. Brian was twelve in March."

"Do you have someone staying with them?"

"My neighbor's daughter. She'll be coming in every day about five to spend the night."

"That's convenient."

"Yes."

The next moment Catherine was making a judgmental face. "I still can't believe Abby left like that. You, her house, the kids—and just ran off."

"Well, that was what she did."

"I've never understood how any woman could put herself before her children and family."

"Abby wasn't happy with our lives together so she decided to do something about it."

"I'm really surprised to hear you defend her," Catherine said.

"Sometimes I do, sometimes I don't."

"Do you ever hear from her?"

"The kids do." Augie gave his hostess a little smile, changed topics. "I'm looking forward to seeing Kelly. I hear she's quite the young woman."

"That's the problem—she's quite the 'young woman' and she's only fourteen! It's the same with all of them around here. All her and her friends talk about is boys! Everything is sex. Sex, sex, sex! And their mouths! You'd think they were truck drivers!"

Across the room Gordon threw Augie a look, as if to say, Take it with a grain of salt. Then, perhaps to minimize his wife's accusation, he said, "Kelly started an organization at school called L.I.F.E. Living In a Fulfilled Environment. The recycling they do is unbelievable."

"You do not know or understand your own daughter," Catherine said to her husband.

"Sex isn't the only thing they talk about, I know that."

"You encourage it in her," Catherine said.

"I don't encourage it. I believe a boy or girl, growing up, should see life honestly."

"Honestly, like in *Playboy*."

"They have good articles," Gordon said. "They interview interesting people—"

"*Which* is why you always read it in the bathroom?"

Maybe, it crossed Augie's mind, Gordon would like to strangle his wife but decided, wisely, to laugh instead. No one spoke. Augie wondered if this was the way it was going to be. He felt like a correspondent at the front. The shells had stopped whizzing. Did that mean the fighting was over, or was it only a lull?

"What do you say?" It was Gordon who broke the silence. "It's getting pretty late, I think we should go."

Catherine suddenly seemed fine. "Augie, you're going to love this house. It's a classic."

"I like classic houses."

"And the Flannerys are such super people!"

C H A P T E R 3

I T WAS STILL broad daylight when they parked in front of the big house on Sycamore Lane, directly on the golf course. Gordon, at the wheel of his wife's beige, late-model Buick, said the hole was the fifteenth, one of the few "reasonable" par-4s at the E.C.C. He slapped the shift into park and put the keys above the visor.

"I don't like how you do that," Catherine said. "It's the first place a person looks."

"You're right."

He reached for the keys, slipped them into his jacket pocket. Augie opened his rear door, then held the passenger door for Catherine. She smiled up at him as she swung out her legs; he offered his hand.

"Thank you, Augie."

They walked up the broad flagstone path to the house, Catherine between the men, and Augie could only think she must've thought he was interested in buying the place, how she carried on. Eighty-year-old colonial, she was saying. Frame, white wood siding, black roof and shutters, brick chimneys at either end—as if he couldn't see. *Her* kind of house, she said. The contemporaries out on Ocean Drive were architecturally stunning, stylistically dramatic, and the beach was *the* place to live, no question about it; but for pure comfort *and* value, you were getting the most house for your real-estate dollar with a traditional beauty like this one.

"How'd you like living on a golf course, Augie?" Gordon asked.

"I could get used to it."

"I wouldn't be able to hack it."

"Why not?"

"Temptation would be too great."

"You have no discipline," Catherine said.

They were at the door. Gordon lifted the brass knocker, in the shape of a fairway wood, and let it drop on a dimpled brass ball. Catherine had her hand on Augie's elbow. The intimacy made him uncomfortable but he stood beside her like a dog imperfectly at heel (he wasn't sitting), waiting for the door to open. In another moment, it did; standing in the doorway, greeting them, was a woman in a flowery silk dress with gray hair and a charming smile, maybe sixty-three. Both Gordon and Catherine offered pleasantries; then Catherine said, "This is Augie Wittenbecher, our weekend guest. Augie, Mrs. Flannery."

"How do you do," the woman said, extending her hand.

"It's a pleasure, Mrs. Flannery."

"Please, come in. Catherine, Gordon—"

They entered a vestibule, only two steps across but deep, the shape of a cribbage board. At one end three golf bags, each filled with matched sets, rested against the wall, as did a couple of umbrellas, two loaded shag-bags and a telescopic ball scoop; in a varnished keg two dozen loose clubs were fanned out like giant-sized pickup sticks. At the other end of the vestibule were a clothes bar and several hooks holding visors, hats, sweaters, jackets and rain suits. Several pairs of spiked shoes were on the floor, along with a bushel basket filled with used, but playable, balls.

Once across, they entered a central hall with a grand, crown-shaped chandelier overhead and a curving set of green-carpeted stairs leading to upper stories. The floor was a rich, dark oak, highly polished, but for all that, badly chewed up. Especially in the area leading from the front door to the stairs.

Wearing one's golf spikes in the house, Augie had always assumed, was grounds for divorce. If not murder.

In the hall were a man in his mid-thirties—dark hair, athletic physique, good-looking—and a young attractive blonde about twenty-two. Augie sensed the young woman was upset. She was speaking earnestly to the man, who, as he listened—if he was listening—had his hands joined at belt level, or just below belt level. Not *idly* joined. He was experimenting with different grips even as the pretty blonde talked to him: now making to interlock, now to overlap his fingers.

He gave the new arrivals a glance, and that was all he gave them—they were no one he should, or wanted to, meet; his disinterest was, in Augie's opinion, rude. Unless he was far more wrapped up in the young woman's problems than seemed apparent. Off the hallway, twelve or fifteen people were standing or sitting in a large sunny room. French doors, thrown wide, opened to the outside, where still other guests were moving about on a terrace.

"Jack, you know Catherine and Gordon McSweeney," Mrs. Flannery said to the man gripping an imaginary golf club.

He turned again, not having any say in the matter now. He had incredibly blue eyes. "Of course," he said, and walked over with the young woman.

Gordon and he shook hands, exchanged niceties; then Jack said, "Mrs. McSweeney, how are you this evening?"

"Please—*Catherine,*" she said, smiling fiercely. "Fine, just fine."

"This is my fiancée, Janet O'Roehrs," Jack said.

"Yes, I heard. Congratulations!"

Jack acknowledged with a small nod.

"How do you do," said Janet. She was wearing a little cotton dress with a scoop neckline, and was even prettier, close up, than Augie had first thought.

"Our guest, Augie Wittenbecher," Gordon said. "Augie, Jack Flannery. And Janet O'Roehrs."

Augie shook hands with the couple.

"When are you getting married?" Catherine asked Janet.

24

"Next May."

"Oh, how wonderful. In Easthelmsford, of course."

"Yes."

"What flight are you in?" Jack asked Augie.

"Twelve."

"That's my dad's flight."

"Gordon told me. Are you playing?"

"Yes, I am," Jack said. "Championship Flight."

There was a brief silence. "I drove by your house last week," Catherine said to the couple. "Without question, it's going to be *the* most exciting place on Ocean Drive."

"If we ever get it finished," Jack said.

"Do you like O'Malley and Son?"

"They're great. Just, you know, building has its headaches."

"Tell me about it," Catherine said, as if she had two or three projects underway.

"Here's John now," Mrs. Flannery said.

Dr. Flannery crossed the living room floor, coming out to the central hall, where they were all standing beneath the chandelier. He was a tall spare man in his mid-sixties with neatly trimmed gray hair, dressed in white flannel trousers and a double-breasted blue blazer with gold buttons. He greeted Gordon and Catherine with an easy enthusiasm.

"This is our guest, Augie Wittenbecher," Gordon said.

"Yes, of course. Sorry you missed the practice round. I was looking forward to it," John Flannery said.

"So was I."

"Gordon tells me you're a good player."

"That's interesting—Gordon has never seen me play."

"You have a ten handicap," Gordon said.

"Anyone who's a ten is a golfer, in my opinion," Dr. Flannery said. "Above that, you just play the game."

"That makes you a damn good player of the game, then," Jack Flannery said to his father.

"You should've seen me today."

"He only hit fifteen fairways," Jack said to Gordon.

25

"I'm happy if I hit the rough," Gordon said.

"Darling, I'm sure the McSweeneys and Mr. Wittenbecher would all like a drink," Mrs. Flannery said.

Catherine wished the engaged couple the best of luck. Then, with her husband and Augie, they walked into a spacious, airy living room; the furniture, white wicker, had pale green-and-yellow cushions. Augie didn't know if he were developing a sudden paranoia, but the people in the room looked at them with a certain disinterest, much as Jack Flannery had when they'd first come in. Dr. Flannery went through the open French doors, and then they were all outside on the terrace, which was made of brick and extended the full length of the house.

Off the terrace a great lawn, level for about sixty feet, fell away into a gentle recess, at the bottom of which a flagstick was planted. Guests were taking turns shooting at it from the level area of the lawn that served as a tee. Augie sized up the distance as an 8- or 9-iron, though stronger players would use a wedge. Even while he, Gordon and Catherine watched, a high, cleanly hit ball landed ten feet from the hole. Everyone clapped. The man who had made the shot described its flight with a motion of his arm—how the ball had moved left to right, dropping in softly. Now the other way, he said with a different arm motion. The draw. He addressed a new ball. He had on a striped silk necktie, lightweight gray flannels and white bucks. He made an effortless swing and the ball, sailing away, curved right to left; it hit, bounced and rolled to within six feet of the pin.

"Dennis, stop showing off," Dr. Flannery shouted.

The man on the tee looked over, grinning. He bore a strong resemblance to Jack Flannery—the dark hair, the good looks, the trim body. Maybe a couple of years older. "Another son," Gordon said privately to Augie.

Dr. Flannery escorted them to a linen-draped bar on the terrace. The man behind it, who tried to conceal his baldness by the old sweep technique, came up and gave the new arrivals a pleasant greeting. Dr. Flannery introduced him as Jason.

Catherine wanted a ⌐
tini, and Augie stayed with⌐
he had ever played the Easth⌐
said no, he hadn't. "Well, I ho⌐
the doctor said.

"I'm not."

"Where are you from?"

"Shufferville."

"I don't know where that is," Dr. ⌐

"No one does," Gordon said.

John Flannery laughed. "Who are you ⌐
round?"

"Al Keegan and Bob Quinn," said Gordon⌐

"They're a solid team," said Dr. Flannery. "⌐
and me a darn good run for our money in last y⌐
Well, enjoy yourselves." He gave Catherine a cor⌐
then turned and walked away.

"What a charming man," she said.

"He'll charm you into whipping your ass 6 and 5," Go⌐
said.

"What do the sons do?" Augie wanted to know.

"They're both downtown," Gordon said. "One's a law
partner, the other's an investment banker. I'm not sure, I think
Dennis is the banker."

"He is, he's with Morgan Stanley," Catherine said.

"When do they get time to play golf?" Augie asked
Gordon.

"Weekends. They fly out Fridays, get in nine holes before
dinner—then play all day Saturday and most of Sunday."
Gordon nudged Augie's arm. "Watch this guy hit the ball."

"Who is he?"

"Dennis Flannery's guest for the tournament. Frank Gildersleeve."

He was a tall gangling man of twenty-eight—with a big,
loose, go-at-it swing. The ball sailed out high and straight, then
started to fall—and plugged four feet from the stick.

27

guys in the Championship Flight play like pros,"
id.

e nodded absently; among the people on the lawn was
in her early to mid-thirties—whom he was looking at
tly would be staring at, because he was finding it diffi-
top looking. She had short dark hair and large beautiful
nd she was wearing an off-the-shoulder lavender dress,
h-fitting, with matching heels. She was standing with
or eight people to one side of the tee, and everyone in the
l gathering was listening intently as a man talked—and
ed. He seemed to be telling a story, perhaps a joke. He was
y animated and obviously liked the attention.

"Last year they lost in a sudden-death playoff," Gordon
aid.

"Excuse me?"

"Dennis Flannery and his guest, last year they lost the
Championship Flight in a playoff."

"Oh. Right."

The man doing the talking was in his middle forties, with
close-cropped sandy-colored hair; he wore a pair of tan slacks
and a green blazer. Whether it was a Masters blazer, Augie
couldn't tell, but it was meant to resemble one. Then, at once,
he stopped talking, and the people around him broke into
laughter, and Augie watched the woman in the lavender dress.
She laughed too but not so loudly; either she'd heard the story
before or didn't think it was that funny. She glanced around a
little, perhaps—Augie found himself fantasizing—bored.

"Isn't this a divine piece of property?" Catherine said,
coming a little closer.

"It's very nice," Augie said.

"They own to the wall."

Augie looked toward the flagstick; just past it ran a stone-
wall, and on the other side was a large field crowded with
bushes and weeds; in the middle of it grew a couple of tall
oaks.

"It's such a waste," Catherine said.

"Excuse me?"

"All that land, right now, is no good to anyone."

"You'll have to explain that to me, Catherine."

"Birds—some kind of endangered species—nest there."

"Oh."

"Twelve homes, that's what the parcel would accommodate. It's been a bone of contention in the community for years."

Catherine brought her rob roy to her lips; as she did, almost finishing the drink, she looked left and right, as if to see who might be within earshot, then continued in a secretive tone. "Each year there are new charges and countercharges. Did he tell you about the Donohues?"

"Gordon?"

"I shouldn't even mention that name around here!"

"What name?"

"Get me a new drink, Augie. Would you, like a dear?"

He looked around for Gordon, saw him with an elderly gentleman just off the terrace, and went to the bar—grateful for the respite. While Jason of the swept fleece was fixing a rob roy, Augie watched the golfers on the Flannerys' tee. A man wearing black trousers and a pink shirt was knocking out pitching wedges to the flag. He had a good-looking swing; what was unfortunate was that he knew it. At the completion of each shot he would pose with the club draped over his left shoulder until the ball landed. The woman in lavender was still with her group, and watching her, Augie felt a pleasurable sensation in his chest. Masters blazer was at it again, jawing away—

"Here you are, sir."

"Thank you."

He delivered the cocktail. Catherine took it eagerly and brought it to her lips. Rob roys were straight stuff, on the order of martinis, and he wondered why she wasn't showing any effects. "Let's move around a little," she said.

She introduced him to a few people but no one said anything that wasn't a commonplace, and even the commonplaces were brief. They continued mingling, Catherine's hand forever on his elbow. Augie had the feeling that people were scattering before them, like trout in a stream when the caster advances clumsily. Then Catherine bumped into someone she really knew—another woman in real estate. Franny DiCosta. Evidently she was one of the more important people in Catherine's office, a bony-shouldered horse-faced woman about forty-seven. Augie stayed for a few minutes as Catherine and her fellow realtor discussed the variances needed for the new minimall on Jeffrey Street; then he said he was going to the bar to get another beer. Catherine patted Augie's hand; he understood, didn't he? This was business. He got a new beer from Jason, then moved off the terrace and mingled with the group of people on the Flannerys' tee.

"COME on, Gil," Dennis Flannery said.

The man with the close-cut hair and green blazer said he didn't want to, he might fall down if he swung—he was working on his third gin-and-tonic; but that made Dennis Flannery and several others push him all the more and finally, by popular demand, he took off his jacket, handed it to Dennis Flannery and chose a club from the canvas golf bag in the arms of a chrome rack. He positioned a ball on the grass. Everyone seemed to know him; there was constant back and forth banter as he took a couple of practice swings. He was strongly built; his arms, shoulders, stomach were solid, and he had a barrel chest. Perhaps the man competed in arm-wrestling competitions, Augie thought; champ in the over-forty, one hundred seventy-two-pound division. Then he was ready to hit. His swing was tight, short, ungraceful; he swung just about the way Augie thought he would. The ball went too far and bounced off the stone wall.

It was cause for great joking. From the terrace Dr. Flannery shouted, "Gil, you're a year older, OK. But a *5-iron?*"

"That was a *9!*"

"Gil's not getting older, he's getting stronger," said Dennis Flannery.

"Next year he'll be shooting his age," said Frank Gildersleeve.

"For nine holes," someone put in.

"Where's the wedge?"

"You reach with a wedge, Gil, I'll caddy for you tomorrow!"

Gil stowed the 9-iron and clinked through the clubs until he found the one he wanted, and Augie, watching all the while, felt himself suddenly frowning; sensed his heartbeat pick up. Could it be . . . ?

Before taking his stance to hit a new ball, the thick-chested man tucked his silk paisley tie into his shirt; that brought a few more comments. Then he drew the pitching wedge back and muscled it down. The swing wasn't pretty but the ball was smartly struck and landed twenty feet to the left of the flag. "Now who's caddying for me tomorrow?" he asked, looking about. More laughter.

Augie saw him full-faced. It could be—and it *was*. His impulse was to leave the party right then and there.

"OK, Azy, show us how it's really done," the man said.

The woman wearing the lavender dress balked, but people urged her on and finally she kicked off her heels. As uncomfortable as Augie felt, he watched her with interest and pleasure. She was a good sport. Dennis Flannery handed her a club as if knowing what iron she used for the shot. She took an easy practice swing, then hit the ball—it went straight but landed fifty feet short.

"More *ooomph,* Azy!"

One of her shoulder straps had fallen down and she tugged it back in place, looking at Gil. "You might wish you hadn't said that."

Everyone laughed. She hit a second ball. Augie didn't follow its flight, choosing to keep his eyes on her face and figure. In a moment there was a lot of clapping and Gil shouted, "You sellin' that, Azy? I'll take two dozen."

Just then Jack Flannery breezed through the French doors, crossed the brick terrace four steps ahead of his fiancée and

31

strode out to the tee. "Enough of this kid stuff," he announced. "Who's for 'Shooting the Gap'?"

Whatever it meant, several people were for it. Not Azy. She stowed her iron and left the tee, but instead of returning to the side Gil and Dennis Flannery were standing on, she walked to the opposite side, where Augie was standing. He liked the proximity—were their elbows touching?—but didn't make anything out of it. The whole area was crowded. He did notice, however, Gil looking over, as if keeping tabs. A new wave of uneasiness—of anger that Gil Plumber was here, the lousy luck of it—swept over Augie.

A tow-headed man about twenty-four, in topsiders and rust-colored pants, selected a wood from the bag of clubs and teed up a ball. He stretched his back muscles, then commenced to hit a couple of big drives, each 250 plus, and Augie quickly saw that the idea was to power a ball between the tops of the two oaks in the sanctuary. On his third drive the young man nicked a branch, even if his ball didn't quite "shoot the gap." People gave him a big hand nevertheless.

"Isn't that a pretty swing?"

Augie wasn't sure the question, spoken by Azy, was meant for him; or for anyone really. Perhaps it was rhetorical. But her head *was* turned a little, his way, and he risked an answer. "Sure is. Who is he?"

"Larry Bisell. Jack's guest."

There was a pause. "You have a pretty swing too," Augie ventured.

"It's misleading."

"A pretty swing can't be misleading, it's what it is."

Her eyes were an amazing, captivating blue, and she had clear lovely skin. She asked him if he was in the tournament.

"Yes, I am."

"What do you think of the course?"

"I arrived too late to play. Everyone tells me the greens are fast."

"If you're not used to fast greens, they're extremely fast."

"I'm used to slow greens."

"Then you've got an experience coming," she said with a smile.

Now it was Jack Flannery's turn, and he hit a tee shot that started out low, almost as if he'd topped it, but then—*zoom*—it kicked in. The ball rose, whistled past the pair of trees, wide to the right.

"Left that one out there, Jack," said Frank Gildersleeve.

He teed a new ball, made a shoulder turn that put his back squarely to the trees, held the club motionless for a fraction of a second, then: *crack.* Whether the ball still missed a few yards to the right, no one seemed to care.

Dennis Flannery took the driver from his brother; for a few moments they pretended to jostle each other. Augie noticed Dr. Flannery on the terrace saying something to one of his guests. This, it occurred to Augie, was what it was all about, kids making their parents proud; handsome, successful, gifted sons making their parents proud. Dennis had an easier, freer swing than his brother (less "schooled," Augie thought), and his first shot—a truly awesome drive—split the gap. Match over. He tossed the club aside and everyone laughed and cheered. People started moving toward the terrace and French doors.

"Where are you from?"

Augie was surprised, and equally delighted, that she was continuing the conversation. "Upstate. Shufferville."

"I've never heard of it."

"It's on the map, that's about it. How about you?"

"Here. I grew up here anyway."

"Then you're a native."

"I grew up here but I didn't go to school here."

"OK, so you're a quasi-native."

She laughed. Her mouth was full, expressive—she wore some makeup but not much. Lipstick and eyeshadow. "I'm Azy," she said.

"Augie."

"Hi, Augie."

But that was it; that was all they would get to say. Gil

33

Plumber was coming up and handing Azy her shoes. "Everyone's going," he said.

"Fine."

He looked at Augie. "I'm Gil Plumber."

"Augie Wittenbecher," he said.

"Son-of-a-gun, *Augie Wittenbecher*. Sure. *Sure.*"

"You know each other?" Azy asked.

"We went to prep school together," Plumber said. Then to Augie, "We missed you at the twenty-fifth. Where in hell were you?"

"At home."

"We had a blast," Plumber said. "So, you're here to play a little golf."

"Yes, I am."

"Who're you a guest of?"

"Gordon McSweeney."

"Damn—you guys were supposed to have a practice round with us today. I'm Dr. Flannery's guest."

"My car broke down," Augie said.

"Well, better your car than your swing," said Plumber. "Hey, you were always a smart guy—English major, right? Why did they name golf, 'golf'?"

"I don't know."

"Because 'shit' had already been used."

Plumber laughed. He winked at Azy. "Who you playing tomorrow, Augie?"

"Al Keegan and his partner."

"Well, we're all in the same flight—we might play yet."

"We might."

Plumber extended his hand and Augie put out his, unprepared for the pressure Plumber applied. He came close to saying something, in anger. Then Plumber made to lead Azy away; as she left she gave Augie a smile, very warm, it seemed to him, mostly with her eyes.

He stayed on the lawn, made happy by the smile; but then different thoughts, emotions crowded in, pushing out the pleasant ones . . . Of a boy from Chicago. A solid, thick-

34

armed boy who always had a joke to tell—popular with class leaders, on the wrestling team, tenor in the school's harmony group. Who made life miserable for an upstate New York kid who had never wanted to go to the damn school in the first place . . .

"Augie, come on, we're leaving."

He was rubbing a spot with his thumb, dead in the center of his hand—and looked up. Gordon was waving to him from the terrace.

CHAPTER 4

FIVE MINUTES LATER they were getting into Catherine's Buick for the drive to the club; in another three minutes Gordon was saying something about a flag pole—it was the highest on the entire South Shore. Augie, in the back, lifted his eyes and saw an American flag on top of the pole; beneath it was a smaller flag of green-and-white, which he gathered were the Easthelmsford Country Club's official colors.

Catherine's foot stomped the floor on the passenger's side. "Watch *out.*"

"What?"

"That boy on the *bike.*"

"I see him."

"You're weaving all over the place."

"I'm not. Relax, will you?"

"You're drunk already."

Augie tried not to listen. Peering through the side window he saw a long black roof. The main portion of the clubhouse was concealed behind a thick hedge at street level. All he could immediately say was that the E.C.C. looked huge. It had white siding, which showed faintly through the hedge, like a green canvas where the paint is thin. Gordon pulled into the main entrance, marked by two stone columns, just behind a gunmetal gray Mercedes-Benz.

An elderly couple, man in a light blue jacket, woman in a dazzling white cocktail dress, got out; immediately a club employee wearing a green-and-white vest drove the car away. Gordon eased forward and braked. Doors were held, and once the three were out, another carhop slid behind the wheel.

They walked down a long wide corridor; on their left the main dining room was set up—fifty glittering tables. So far no one was seated. Talking and laughing and the bright clinking of glasses kept getting louder; then they were in the main bar. Augie said he'd get drinks but Gordon said no, thanks anyway —the club didn't take cash.

People were standing and mingling about, lots of them— the room, no small area, was packed. By and large, Augie saw it as a somewhat older crowd—forty-five, fifty, though the twenty-seven and thirty-three-year-olds were certainly in attendance. Affluent, good-looking, upwardly geared white America. The bar area was particularly mobbed. Gordon lifted his hand to gain a bartender's attention; old veteran of the scene that he was, it was still going to take a while.

Augie and Catherine talked, though it seemed to him more interview, with her asking the questions, than conversation. First she wanted to know what he thought of Easthelmsford— so far; then she wanted to know what he thought of the Flannery party. He answered her questions for politeness' sake, wishing she'd shut up. Then she *sincerely* wanted to know if he'd enjoy having a date for tomorrow evening. Betty McKeon was a "really lovely girl." The way she said it, Augie got the impression that Betty McKeon was sixteen. But before he could impress upon his hostess that a date wasn't necessary, as he thought he had earlier, Catherine gave Augie's lapel a quick little tug. "Don't look now," she said in hushed tones, "but just behind you—in the dark-blue jacket—is Kevin Donohue."

"Who's Kevin Donohue?"

"Didn't I tell you?"

"I don't recall—"

"He was engaged to Elizabeth Flannery."

She was speaking in a tense whisper. "Poor boy—so handsome! He tried to kill himself . . ."

"Why?"

"She dumped him."

"Oh."

Catherine's eyes darted left, then right. Augie had the impression that she was about to hand him a roll of top-secret microfilm. "I just thought you should have a little background on her," she said. "Before you go and make a fool of yourself."

"Before I *what?*"

"Make a fool of yourself with Elizabeth Flannery."

"What am I missing here, Catherine?"

"She plays up to men, leads them on—"

"OK, but where do I fit in?"

"She wasn't coming on to you? Augie, you *are* naive."

He was trying to get some traction under his wheels; they were slipping badly. Then he said, "You mean *Azy?*"

"Yes, Azy. I think of her as Elizabeth."

"Azy is a Flannery?"

"Of course. What did you think?"

"I didn't think anything."

"She's engaged to Gil Plumber."

"Azy—is—engaged—to—"

"Such a charming man—and so rich! He's good for her— stable, well-established, he keeps her on the straight and narrow. She needs that kind of man. Prior to Gil, Elizabeth Flannery was *not* to be trusted."

"Why not?"

"She had a terrible reputation for playing with men's emotions."

"Leading them on—"

"Yes!"

"Maybe she's leading Gil Plumber on."

"Augie! Last year he was named Mid-West Businessman of the Year. And he *owns* the Chicago Blackhawks."

It wasn't news to Augie. Hardly an issue of the Reddon Bulletin came out—it went to all living alumni—without mentioning Gil Plumber and his successes. "Plus he's funny," Augie said.

Catherine looked quickly about, as if to spot any operatives in the room. "Just be careful, that's all I want to say, Augie. I wouldn't want to see you getting hurt."

He wanted to ask her if she meant by Azy or Plumber, but Gordon appeared with the drinks. "It's a zoo in here," he said. "Let's go out to the patio."

Catherine smiled at Augie and took his arm. As they turned to leave, he gave Kevin Donohue a glance. He had a huskier build than Jack or Dennis Flannery, and his features weren't so fine; there was something about him that Augie thought appealing—a quiet manner and look. He was talking with an elderly woman who had an enchanting smile and blue-dusted hair.

THEY walked through the main part of the bar, then pushed open glass doors and moved onto a large terrace covered by a green-and-white awning. Glass-topped tables were every-where, all taken. Off the terrace was an actual tent, like you might see at a wedding; in it, for reasons Augie didn't know, some fifteen tables—not dining tables—were set up. Then came open space, great open space—the famed E.C.C. course. Cocktail waitresses were bringing drinks and carrying around trays of sumptuous hors d'oeuvres. Gordon snagged a waitress, grabbed a chilled jumbo shrimp, devoured it, then snatched a second. A sliver of his white belly was showing through his shirt. Catherine asked Augie to hold her drink while she lighted a cigarette.

She inhaled, blew out smoke. "Thank you."

"See that guy who just stood up?" Gordon said.

"That tall guy?"

"That's Dick DeVoe. Played for the Knicks."

Augie didn't follow basketball that closely but he knew the name. "Is he a guest?"

"Oh, no. He's a member," Catherine said.

"Let's go get some clams," Gordon said.

They angled across the patio toward a solid but movable bar; two men, one a burly fellow about thirty and the other older and thinner, were standing behind it in heavy rubber aprons shucking clams and placing them on large silver plates. Gordon picked up a clam, spooned on a little cocktail sauce and put the shell in his mouth; the clam slid off and disappeared. Augie did the same but Catherine didn't seem interested. She was happy drinking and smoking. Gordon and Augie did the routine again, and Gordon did it a third time and a fourth.

"There's someone else you might know," he said. "Just walked through the door—André Gilliam, skates for the Islanders. Is his wife a knockout or what?"

Gilliam didn't have the height of DeVoe but he was certainly a big man—about six feet two inches and two hundred twenty pounds. His wife was a voluptuous blonde. "He's in our flight," Gordon said casually.

"That's nice," Augie said, with a kind of sinking sensation.

"He's only been playing three years," Gordon said. "He hits the ball a mile but it doesn't always go where he wants it to."

"I have that same trouble hitting it two hundred yards," Augie said.

"I have that trouble just hitting it."

Gordon had another clam, chased it with his martini. Augie had the sudden, uncomfortable image of his friend and himself as a pair of sacrificial lambs; part of him just wanted to get the killing over with. The next moment loud laughter erupted across the patio. Gordon, Catherine, Augie, and people generally, looked over. Standing near the wide glass doors were Dr. Flannery and his wife; Jack Flannery and his fiancée; Jack's guest, Larry Bisell, and Gil Plumber and Azy. Plumber's hands were raised to the level of his shoulders in a disclamatory gesture. "Who, me? I said that?"

"What a fun, fun time everyone's having!" Catherine said.

IT wasn't as if Gordon and Catherine McSweeney didn't know anyone; by the time they finished their drinks and a cocktail waitress delivered a new round, they had chitchatted with three or four couples. First it was the Fredericksons, Sandy and Steve; then it was Peg and Joe Maguire; next they talked to Phil Brand and his wife, Rita. Everyone was charming, polite, gracious. No one ever said anything—that is, everyone said the same thing. What flight were Gordon and Augie in? Was Augie used to fast greens? Where was Shufferville?

Catherine continued coming in close whenever she spoke to Augie, as if sharing great secrets with him, and he began picking up a scent: not her perfume. Under, beneath her perfume. And it wasn't body odor—at least not your ordinary body odor. They all had another drink. Gordon was guffawing with a club member, and Catherine leaned in to tell Augie that Franny DiCosta—the woman at the Flannerys' party?—was a lesbian; it was a real problem for Catherine because Franny wanted to "do things."

"Why is it a problem? Can't you just say, 'Not interested'?"

"Well, she knows that."

"Then I don't see—"

"A woman wants to be held, caressed!"

"I understand, but you *are* married."

"Our marriage is dead. We haven't done anything for *two* years."

Augie scratched his left eye. "Catherine, I feel I'm on thin ice here. I just—I don't know what to say."

Gordon suddenly broke in. "Let's go do it, partner."

"Do what?"

"Come on, I'll show you."

Augie hesitated, looking at Catherine. He wanted to get away from her but didn't want to be rude. "It's OK. You *boys* run along," she said, glass empty.

OFF the patio, under the big tent—sides of which were rolled all the way up—people were moving from table to table, stopping, looking, putting down money as if making purchases; but purchasing what? If this was a fund-raiser for the local church

41

or PTA (Augie didn't believe it was but it looked like one), where were the cakes and homemade jams? Behind each table, stapled to a stand that resembled an easel, was a large sheet of lined paper. On the left side of each sheet ran a list of names, arranged in groups of two. At the very top of each sheet were the bold words: FLIGHT 3, or FLIGHT 6, or FLIGHT 11.

"Let's see how we're doing," Gordon said.

They walked over to the table where a twenty-one-year-old redhead wearing an E.C.C. vest over a white shirt was sitting. Behind her, fastened to a stand, was the FLIGHT 12 roster.

Halfway down the column Augie saw their names: Gordon McSweeney (22) and Augie Wittenbecher (10)—*Shufferville.* Just above were their opponents for tomorrow: Al Keegan (12) and Bob Quinn (19)—*Wingfoot.* He kept looking, recognizing André Gilliam (17); his partner in the tournament was Tom Hrazanek (11)—*Wiltwyck.* Augie knew Wiltwyck; it was in Kingston. At the very top, as the defending champions of FLIGHT 12: John Flannery (18) and Gil Plumber (12)—*Butler National.*

After the teams were a number of marks—vertical lines—then a diagonal slash through the vertical lines to indicate 5. Flannery and Plumber had six complete units plus two lines. Keegan and Quinn had four units and one line. As for McSweeney and Wittenbecher, they had nothing. Zero.

As Gordon and Augie were observing the roster a middle-aged woman in a shocking pink dress, tucked in below her knees like an inverted duffel, handed the young woman fifty dollars. "Five on Team One," she said.

The young redhead wrote out a slip, handed it to the woman who had placed the bet, then completed the last unit and began a new one after the team of Flannery and Plumber. The sheet of paper on the wall was a tote board, Augie realized; he and Gordon, and everyone else, were the horses.

"I don't know if I can stand the pressure," Augie commented. "All that money on us!"

"Let's change that right now."

Gordon took twenty dollars from his wallet and put it down. "Two on Team Five," he said to the young woman.

"Same," Augie said.

She wrote out slips, then stood and put four lines after their names. She had skinny legs but full hips. "Thank you, gentlemen," she said, coming back to the table.

"We wouldn't want people thinking nobody believed in us," Gordon said.

"Oh, I believe in you!"

It gave Gordon and Augie a good laugh and they made their way through the throng of bettors, stopping in front of the tote sheet that read: CHAMPIONSHIP FLIGHT. On top was the defending team of Tim Donohue (2) and Andy Mulligan (3)—*Round Hill.* Then came Dennis Flannery (1) and Frank Gildersleeve (4)—*Shinnecock.* Several teams down were Jack Flannery (2) and Larry Bisell (2)—*Wykagyl.* Also in the Championship Flight was another Donohue, Bob (3), and his guest, Ed Sargent (1)—*Pine Valley.* Here the heaviest betting was taking place; people were throwing down twenties by the fours and fives.

"Who are the Donohues anyway?" Augie said.

"They're the *other* golfing family in Easthelmsford," Gordon said. "Some people say, player for player, they're better than the Flannerys."

"What do they do, besides play golf?"

"They're all in construction. It's said that whenever any concrete is poured on the South Shore, the Donohues get a piece of it."

"Legally?"

"There's a big Irish Mafia out here—probably not."

"So they're local boys," Augie said.

"Born and raised. All of them went to Easthelmsford High."

Augie took another look at the tote sheet. "How about Kevin Donohue? Is he playing?"

"Not in the Championship Flight."

Gordon moved slowly down the row of tables. "Here he is, Flight 4."

Augie saw the name, an (8) after it.

"Kevin Donohue used to be the hottest golfer at the club," Gordon said.

"What happened?"

"The night Elizabeth Flannery broke off their engagement, they found him in his garage—dead drunk, engine running. He's just coming back."

"How long ago was that?"

"Three, three and a half years."

"Why did she break up with him?"

"Family pressure."

"Can you explain that?"

"There's an old Irish saying. 'Want the sister, win the brothers.' "

"So Kevin Donohue never won her brothers."

"You kidding? The Flannerys and Donohues hate each other."

"That's interesting," Augie said.

"It's a real down-to-earth feud. Old Tim Donohue did everything he could to change the status of the land behind the Flannery house so they could build on it. That was twenty-five years ago, and it's still going on."

FIRST off were the lobsters. Tray after tray of steamed Maine beauties. Then roasts—beef, pork, lamb. All kinds of chicken dishes. A huge whole salmon. Salads—green, macaroni, tomato, cucumber, shredded carrot, fruit. Vegetables, all sorts; potatoes, all varieties; and breads and rolls. It was buffet style and people walked down one line, up another, then down a third. One plate wasn't nearly big enough, especially if the first thing you put on it was a pound and a half lobster. Augie and Gordon both started with one, a baked potato and green salad. Catherine's cocktail glass had somehow got full again; she came back to their table with a few slices of beef, some carrot salad and a small helping of wild rice.

Two other couples were at their table—Fletcher Davenport and his guest, Alex Hemsworth, were in Flight 9. Hemsworth and wife Paula were from Nashville; he was fifty, bald, and designed military hardware. His wife, a prim little woman in navy blue who was drinking diet Pepsi, worked with retarded children. Fletcher Davenport was an attorney. He had a long fierce jaw and considered the three people across the table intruders; but he was kind—only xenophobic at heart—and willing to share important information with Augie, as proof. "Greens here are lightning fast." "Thanks." Davenport's wife Christine didn't engage in conversation, letting her stones do the talking. Fingers, ears, neck, bosom—the woman was a veritable Demosthenes. The main dining room was now full and everyone was partaking earnestly. For those having lobster, disposable bibs with a picture of the E.C.C. clubhouse were on the tables, and almost everyone in the dining room was wearing one. A waitress served drinks on request. Gordon said he'd had his quota of silver bullets, and Augie and he ordered a carafe of chilled white wine. Catherine saw no reason to change; a rob roy for her. In time Gordon and Augie went back for some Southern-style chicken, fresh green beans served with almonds, and corn on the cob. That was it for Augie. But Gordon, by now well into the second carafe, said he wanted to sample the lamb curry and salmon.

"It's disgusting how much he eats," Catherine said, lighting a cigarette.

"The great things they're serving, it's hard to stop," Augie said.

"You stopped."

"I'm smaller. I get full easier."

She leaned in. That smell—an incipient blaze of paper, dry twigs, smoke—seemed suddenly stronger. "You have discipline, Augie. Does he have discipline? Is he a good example for Kelly? Don't you think she knows what he's doing in the bathroom with *Playboy!*"

"Catherine, you're trying to make me say something—to agree with you. I don't—"

"You can *hear* him in there."

"Maybe he's humming an old Irish ballad while shaving."

"He used to have values," Catherine said, "when he worked on Madison Avenue and believed in himself. Now he hates what he's doing!"

"Jobs are hard to come by when you're fifty."

"Especially when you're a dirty old man."

"That's kind of rough," Augie said.

"He'd do it to a woodchuck if it stayed still long enough! What kind of message does that give to Kelly?"

"Some men are just hornier than others."

She took a huge drag on her cigarette. "He's consumed; all he thinks about is sex. Sex, sex, sex!"

"Catherine, could we talk about something else?"

"I'm sorry, I just get so keyed up. Tell me about your children."

She was sitting with her legs crossed; not at the ankles but at the thighs, and her thighs kept pushing against one another rhythmically—going tight, loosening, going tight, loosening. Augie was starting to feel warm, in part, he told himself, because he'd eaten much more than usual. He wanted to get up and get some fresh air.

"They're pretty well-adjusted," he said, on automatic pilot. "They haven't given me a hard time, so far."

"I'm glad—it was such a terrible thing Abby did, deserting them like that. I only met her those few times but she always struck me as an extremely selfish woman. Beautiful, yes—I'll say that. But I never sensed her *soul?*"

He didn't respond, in no mind to have a conversation with Catherine McSweeney about his ex-wife.

"Especially having the abortion," Catherine said. "She left two children and took the life of a third. What gives any woman the right to *do* that?"

"It was her decision and she's lived with it," he said.

46

"Augie, I know how hurt you were—you wanted the baby. Why pretend?"

"I wanted the baby but Abby had reasons—"

"Reasons! She destroyed your family! Without the family, where are we?"

He began making little fists, then caught himself doing it and stopped. Gordon suddenly reappeared, setting down his loaded tray. Augie folded his napkin. Would Catherine excuse him? He wanted a breath of air. She touched his hand intimately.

Augie walked down the wide hall and into the main lounge; several men and a couple of women were at the bar proper, but most people were still at their tables. He continued onto the patio, fairly empty at the moment. Not the pari-mutuel tent, however; it was still hopping. He angled toward the course, only stopping when he was in the middle of the first fairway. Then he loosened his tie and took a deep breath and continued at a slower pace. It was a beautiful night. He could see the flagstick on the first green. Or was it a skinny old woman standing motionless in a bonnet?

He continued walking, breathing in the mild night air, his shadow following faithfully along. He wanted to get back whatever it was he'd lost—a kind of equilibrium. But he didn't know if he could. That Gil Plumber was here, in the tournament, had thrown him for a loop. Then there was Catherine. Maybe he should just leave, get the hell out of Easthelmsford and go home, before—

Before what?

I don't know, thought Augie. Or at least wouldn't answer.

He continued on, taking occasional deep breaths. Fifty yards shy of the green he stopped walking, turned and looked back. A great ocean liner lay at anchor in a dark bay, ablaze with lights. He was tired, that was probably it, just dog-tired from an enormously long day. In the morning he'd have a better outlook; be more himself again.

Augie started back. As he was entering the patio he took a tug at his tie—and someone called his name. He turned. Just leaving the pari-mutuel tent was Azy Flannery. "What a nice surprise," she said, coming up.

He was stunned. "Hi."

"How are you?"

"Better," he said. "All that food, I needed some air. Were you placing a bet?"

"I was sitting at our table and got this great hunch."

"I hope it turns out for you."

"It's on McSweeney and Wittenbecher."

He gave her an incredulous look. "I would imagine you'd be betting on your dad and your fiancé."

"I have money on them too."

He laughed.

"Not as much," she said.

He was looking at her, thinking how lovely she was—how absolutely gorgeous. She asked him if he had ever played night golf.

"No . . . but I've always wanted to."

People were starting to come out of the clubhouse, sitting down for after-dinner drinks on the patio. "How about tonight?" she said.

Augie frowned. He wasn't sure he had heard her correctly. "Tonight?"

"At twelve-thirty."

"Twelve-thirty, *tonight?*"

"Everybody needs a practice round, Augie."

"That's true. I just—"

"So—"

"Well, fine. Wonderful. Sure!"

"Meet me in the middle of the first fairway."

"OK."

"See you later."

Azy crossed to the wide door; her brother and his fiancée, Janet O'Roehrs, were at a table near it and she stopped and spoke with them for a moment before continuing inside. Then Augie walked across. He offered the couple a greeting and received a subdued one from Janet; she was a subdued woman.

Jack moved his lips. Whether it was a pleasantry, Augie didn't know. He doubted it.

Inside the bar, he followed the hallway to the dining room. Catherine had a new rob roy in front of her on the table. "Augie! Come *sit,*" she said.

CHAPTER 5

They were standing in the club entrance with two other parties waiting for their car. When it appeared, Gordon opened the rear door and tumbled in and Catherine slid her narrow hips into the front passenger seat, bringing her legs in with a delicate lift-and-sweep motion. Augie thought it pretty amazing. She'd been doing rob roys since six-thirty and here she gave the impression that all she'd had all night was a single brandy Alexander. Her husband at least showed he'd had half-a-dozen martinis, a carafe or two of wine and an after-dinner rusty nail. Gordon was drunk. No problem. Here, Augie, you drive. Catherine—except for her eyes—might've been leaving the Thursday night bingo game at St. Jude's. Augie put a dollar into the carhop's hand, got behind the wheel and drove away.

"What time do you have to get up?" she asked him when they were moving along the street.

"Five-thirty, thereabouts."

"I'll have breakfast for you."

Augie seemed to feel she was speaking to him alone; her ox of a husband could forage for himself. "That's thoughtful of you, Catherine," he said, "but really—"

"Serve bre'fas' at club," Gordon offered from the back. "Part've the package."

"I'll be happy to make you something," she said, ignoring her husband.

Augie glanced over; she wasn't sitting in the seat so much as reclining against the door, looking at him with fiery gray eyes. "There's no reason for you to get up so early," he said.

"Oh, I'll go back to bed."

"We'll jus' go to club, bre'fas' part've the package."

Augie turned on Old Forge Road. A full moon hung over the roadway like a streetlamp. On the left they followed the E.C.C. course for the full length of one hole. He imagined by tomorrow he'd know which hole it was—or maybe by tonight. It seemed an incredible thing that Azy had asked him to play. At the McSweeneys' rural mailbox he pulled into the unpaved driveway and parked behind Gordon's rattletrap. He went to open his door and Catherine reached across and took his hand. Gordon was snoring in back. Her dress was a third of the way up her thighs, and her knees were separated, more than normal. Two fists.

"I want to make you happy, Augie," she said, her lips barely moving.

He gave a glance over his shoulder. The ex-Air Force captain with forty-one missions over Korea was out cold; his mouth was open, head way to one side. "I'm happy already, Catherine," Augie said. "Ha-ha."

"I mean really happy!"

She smiled wickedly, then opened her door and kicked out her legs; outside, she opened the rear door and tried dragging her husband off the seat—the way one might a roll of jammed-in carpet. Augie assisted Catherine in her efforts. "Wake up! Gordon, come on!" he said.

Nothing.

"Gordon!"

"Whhaaa? Bre'fas' club—part've package."

"Easy now."

Gordon, once on his feet, was steady enough, but Augie still walked with him toward the house, taking his arm. Catherine went ahead and opened the front door and the Mongrel of Easthelmsford came streaking out, yapping at Augie's heels.

"Know sum'pin?" Gordon said.

51

"What's that?"

"Nev' bark wom'n, on'y man."

"Rainbow's a prince."

"Likes wom'n, on'y bark man."

They took the steps up to the little deck; then they were inside the kitchen and Gordon shuffled into the bathroom and let go a cascade without closing the door. He came out and announced he was hitting the sack. "G'night, Wim'besher," he said lovingly.

Augie was standing by one of the filmy-curtained windows in the living room. "Sleep well, Gordon."

"You too, par'ner."

He took the doorway into the bedroom, closed the door, and seconds later all the windows in the house rattled. "Like a little nightcap?" Catherine asked.

"No, thanks."

"I'm having one."

"I'm dead tired, Catherine."

"Oh, stay with me for a while."

She went out. Gordon lurched to get comfortable; then all was quiet. Augie stayed at the window, looking out at the clear night, wondering if Azy would really show up. He glanced at his watch. Then the toilet flushed and Catherine came back out holding a brandy snifter; her feet and legs were bare.

"Talk to me," she said.

He went over and sat beside her in the loveseat. "It's always so good to get home, isn't it?" she said.

"Sure is."

"Take your shoes off, get comfortable."

"I'm very comfortable already."

"Did you have enough to eat?"

"God, I'm stuffed."

"He can't *wait* for breakfast."

"Gordon has always had healthy appetites."

Her legs were drawn up and the space between her knees seemed like the mouth of a burrow, into which a little creature might crawl. From behind the wall came deep steady snoring.

"Every night it's the same," she said. "He passes out, and that's that."

"If he didn't, would it make any difference?"

"No! It's over, I told you. There's nothing there, nothing between us!"

"How about professional counseling? Have you ever considered it?" Keep talking, he thought.

"I know what I need, I don't need *counseling.*"

Augie loosened his tie, then pulled it off entirely, slipping it into his side pocket. How Catherine interpreted the gesture, he couldn't say. Yes, he could. Her knees—including hips and thighs—trained several degrees to port, as if toward a target.

"It's not healthy for a woman to live like this!" she said.

"I guess not."

"Touching is very important!"

"Sure."

"Will you touch me, Augie?"

"Catherine, I don't see how—I mean—"

"Hold me for a minute, can't you just do that?"

It seemed fair. What was she asking? He raised his arms and she slid in closer, but her legs, instead of moving down to facilitate the embrace, separated and came up—really facilitating it. He had his arms around her back, harmlessly; but without doing too much, without radically shifting or changing positions, they could have sex. Like this. Right here on the loveseat.

"You might not believe this," Catherine said. "But you've kept me going. Thinking about you, Augie."

"I never—I didn't know—I—"

"Oh, yes!"

She took one of his hands and placed it on the inside of her thigh. The skin was damp; it wasn't perspiration. It had a slicker feel than sweat. Then she reached down and took hold of his zipper. The snoring, behind the wall, suddenly ceased.

"Catherine," he said, restraining her hand.

"Let me, please!"

"I don't feel right about this."

53

"How can we stop now?"

"We have to."

"Go to the guesthouse, if you're worried. I'll come out."

"Catherine, I want you to understand—"

"Don't do this to me, Augie!"

"I'm sorry, Gordon is too close a friend—"

"All *right*, then."

It was brusque; she pulled away. Augie held his head for a moment, then stood, awkwardly adjusting himself. Her dress was all the way up and, with her legs apart, he felt himself losing control after all. But then—somehow—he got it back. He pressed against the sides of his neck, said good-night, walked through the kitchen and out the back door.

The nun was still kneeling outside the McSweeneys' window and he was beginning to understand why—they needed all the praying they could get. In the bright night sky bats were darting about. When he reached the guesthouse he lifted the latch and pushed but didn't have the knack and at last just plain kicked the miserable goddamn door and it opened. The heat inside was oppressive. He picked his way through the jumbled mess of bicycles, skis and old furniture to the little opening and turned on the lamp on the file cabinet, the wild flowers in the vase wilted, dead. By his watch, it was ten to twelve.

He sat on the bed, leaned forward and held his head, but Catherine's smell—the slickness on her thighs—made him bring his hands down. A mosquito whined, attempted a landing, and Augie slapped his ear. Fuck. He was sweating and he thought of Gordon, out cold, and of his sex-starved wife pouring herself a second brandy.

He took off his clothes. Fortunately the towel he had used earlier was still faintly damp and he wiped down his chest, arms, hands. He pulled on fresh clothes from his suitcase— slacks and shirt—and the tennis shoes he'd worn on the drive. He was early but he'd rather wait in the club parking lot than here. He turned out the light and moved to the door.

The lights were still on in the main part of the house and

54

he saw Catherine moving around in the kitchen. Then Augie realized he'd be unable to start his car and drive off without upsetting her even further; he didn't want to add insult to injury. When he got to his station wagon he opened the door and closed it carefully, afraid of alerting Rainbow.

He checked his watch every few minutes; just when he thought he'd have to start his engine, regardless, the house lights went out. Augie allowed another minute to pass, then twisted the ignition key, backed out of the McSweeneys' drive and, on Old Forge Road, turned on his lights.

HE parked a good distance from the front doorway of the E.C.C., in the club's main lot. Straight through his windshield was the eighteenth green. He went to the back of his wagon, opened it and pulled out his bag, removing nine clubs from it and a dozen balls. As Augie hoisted the lightened bag to his shoulder he saw that the betting tent and patio were deserted; except for a few security lights, the clubhouse was dark. He imagined all the players were sleeping by now, resting up for their first-round matches. All except Augie Wittenbecher, out for a little night golf. He walked over a grassy hillock and was on the course.

As before, his shadow followed him along, this time with a bag over its shoulder, like a small, faithful caddy. Augie could see the first green but not the old bonneted woman; evidently she'd grown tired of standing around and had wended her way home. He continued walking, remembering as a boy how he would always feel a certain spookiness when he would play after supper on the old Woodbridge course, and sometimes he would look around, on the fifth, sixth and seventh holes particularly, and think someone was watching him from the darkening woods. He walked farther out onto the first fairway, then stopped and glanced about—no Azy. Behind him, the great ship still lay at anchor; the party aboard her had ended.

He set his bag down and took out a 9-iron and swung it. His back felt like an ironing board. He stretched, took a few

55

more practice swings, feeling his body was telling him something: this wasn't the time for anyone to play golf! Go to bed and sleep, yes.

Augie fished a ball from his bag and dropped it onto the grass, to see how it would look. The ball was visible but he felt as if he needed glasses. He made to hit a chip shot and topped the ball, scooting it along the ground; he tossed down another, swung—this time taking too much of a divot; the ball moved five feet.

He swore quietly. He wasn't angry; he felt stupid. He retrieved the divot and stamped it down with his foot, then picked up the ball and walked ahead to look for the first. It had disappeared. He hadn't knocked it thirty feet and he couldn't find the goddamn thing. And the grass wasn't long; it was neatly clipped, ready for morning play. He kept searching, beginning to see that perceptions at night were altogether different; distances were very difficult to judge—

"Augie?"

He glanced up. A woman was walking toward him. "Azy?"

"Yes."

She came closer, wearing jeans and a sweater; a lightweight nylon golf bag was on her shoulder. "Have you been here long?"

"Couple of minutes."

In the moonlight she looked so altogether beautiful, Augie felt disoriented. Her crew-neck sweater was either dark blue or gray, the collar of her shirt, distinctly white. "Did you only bring one club?" she asked.

"I hit a chip—ball's somewhere around here. I was looking for it."

"Do you want to keep looking?"

"No, no. It's OK."

They walked back; his bag looked like a big dog lying on the grass. Azy told him there was a pond just before the green; the pin was one hundred seventy yards away from where they were standing. Normally she'd go for the green, she said, but this wasn't normal.

True, thought Augie.

She reached in the pocket of her bag and came out with four balls—that glowed. "Here," she said, handing him two.

"I'll be damned."

"They're a necessity for night golf."

"Where did you get them?"

"My parents' house is an annex of Nevada Bob's."

Azy dropped a ball. She took a couple of practice swings, stepped up and made an easy pass at the ball. It flew away like a single tracer, curving gracefully. "Nice shot," Augie said.

"Are you going for it?"

"I'll lay up too."

His 9-iron was off line but he felt glad to have hit the ball halfway decently. He picked up his bag.

"I have bug spray if you need any," Azy said as they began walking. "We used to play night golf a lot when I was a kid."

"Here?"

"Right here. The golf committee finally put their foot down."

"How come?"

"They claimed we weren't golfing."

"Was that so?"

"To a degree."

"Who would you play with?"

"Sometimes my brothers. Mostly with boyfriends."

"Like two or three at one time?"

"That might've been fun too! There's my ball."

It was just short of the pond. Azy made a neat little pitch to the green. He knew she had a good swing from watching her at the cocktail party, but now he saw she could really play. His ball lay in the rough; when they got to it he observed a glowing blur, Mars through a home telescope. He choked down on a wedge, swung poorly—barely cleared the pond; but his ball took a member's bounce and made the left corner of the green.

They started across a small bridge. The water was an ebony mirror; he could see the sky and moon and a single fleecy cloud. They walked onto the green. Augie's ball was away, so Azy went to the flagstick and tended it. He had a long, down-sloping putt. Before he took his stance, he glanced over his left shoulder, then his right. Was that a rustling in the bushes?

"Just get it going," Azy said.

He lined up the putt—guessing at the break—and gave the ball a light stroke. It rolled and rolled and kept on rolling and ended up on the opposite fringe. Augie crossed the green, stood over his ball again and heard another sound, like someone walking through rough. His putter blade scuffed the green before hitting the ball, which went eight feet and stopped. He was now at least close enough to see the hole, and Azy pulled the flag.

He tried again, missed right and picked up. Azy lagged her putt to within eighteen inches and tapped in. They walked off the green. She led the way to the second tee along a dark, narrow path. The tee itself was brighter, thankfully. Azy pointed out the troubles: out-of-bound right, heavy rough left. They were standing by the white markers. It wasn't a long hole but it was the tightest on the course, she said. "Go ahead, Augie."

"No, I four-putted."

"Who's counting?"

He pulled a 3-wood from his bag but didn't immediately tee a ball. "I guess I'm a little nervous, Azy."

"About what?"

He didn't answer right away. "Being out here with you."

"I'm not so dangerous."

He had to laugh. Then, seriously, "I keep hearing sounds. It's in my mind Gil's out looking for you."

The moonlight flickered on her face. "He was dead to the world when I left . . . This should help."

She reached into the side pocket of her bag and pulled out a sterling flask. "Here."

"You thought of everything."

"I'm a little nervous too," Azy said.

A PARK bench was on the edge of every tee, and on the third tee they sat down and had another nip of brandy. The hole was one hundred sixty-five yards to a sunken, invisible green, she said, Easthelmsford players called "the saucer." Augie nodded. A rabbit hopped around on the tee, up by the red markers.

"The thing to remember here is everything between you and the green spells disaster," Azy said. "There's no fairway, everything is sand and gorse."

"OK."

"What do you have?"

"A 5-iron."

"Give it a whack."

He walked to the markers and the rabbit scooted away, disappearing into the brush. His shot was OK, but he knew he hadn't got all of it—he'd be short. She teed a ball, swung. It flew away and they began walking toward the green. "The McSweeneys call you Elizabeth," Augie said.

"Some people do. My mother does. The nuns always did at Mt. Saint Agnes. But now I'm pretty much Azy."

"How did the name come about?"

"Jack started it," she said. "My mother would say Elizabeth and somehow he got Azy out of it when he was five. He doesn't remember, but it stuck."

They were walking along a sandy path, approaching a helter-skelter patchwork of bunkers, some shallow, others very deep; past the bunkers the terrain dropped off sharply. "How about you?" she asked.

"Me?"

"Are you by chance Augustus?" She smiled warmly.

"Augustus Terrence Wittenbecher, God help me."

"And I thought Elizabeth McGrenaghan Flannery was a mouthful!"

Only one ball shone on the green. The gorse all around the

perimeter was so thick that, glow as Augie's ball might, they couldn't find it. Azy suggested they move on. She picked up her ball and they walked to the fourth tee. Again they sat on a bench. Augie asked her what she did and where she lived when she wasn't in Easthelmsford, and she said she had an apartment in the city on East 66th Street and worked for Leslie Neher, a graphic design studio.

"Do you actually do designing?"

"I'm not a partner but I design. I helped create the 'bonus pack' for Top Flight golf balls."

"Fifteen for the price of twelve," Augie said.

"The free sleeve you can see? That was my brilliant idea."

"That's really terrific," he said.

Azy teed a ball and it drifted into the lake on the right side of the hole. Augie's drive was straight but too high. She played another from the rough. Then, going into the green, he hit a 5-iron—perfectly. His best shot of the night. Crisp, pure. So crisp and pure the ball sailed over pin, green, bunker—and ended up in an area of impenetrable brush.

"That finishes me," he said.

Azy's ball was on the apron of the green, and she picked it up.

"You can go on," Augie said.

"No, let's just walk."

They went past the bench on the fifth tee and out onto the fairway. It was a glorious night, soft, bright, warm. The hole was a long par-5 and you had to have two good woods to set up a third shot in; the land sloped to the right and a fade rolled into the woods. The idea on the hole was to stay left. Augie wished he had a notebook. Then they were on the sixth. "This hole is like the second," Azy said. "It's not long but it's very tight. Most players drive with an iron."

"On six, drive with an iron."

"On your approach, stay right. If you miss left you end up in thick, lush grass below the green. It's an impossible up-and-down."

"Got it."

"Let's cut over to seven."

They went through a grove of evergreens and emerged in tall yellow rough, but soon they were on a new fairway. Azy said the hole was one hundred seventy-eight yards but it played longer. "Something like three," he said.

"Except the third green is in a hollow, this one's elevated."

They walked toward the green. The fairway, rising, crested exactly where the putting surface began; the green itself sloped down and away. Azy said it was the toughest green on the course.

"To hit or to putt?"

"Both. Even experienced players usually don't take enough club from the tee. And remember on the first green, how your ball just kept rolling and rolling? This is lots worse."

"Thanks."

"Take a look at this bunker."

They walked a few steps and stood on the lip of what appeared to be a major excavation. "This is the deepest trap I've ever seen," Augie said.

"One time my father was blasting out of it," she said, "and an old ankle joint flew up with his ball."

"Human?"

"Aye, to be sure," she said, putting on a brogue. "Patrick O'Toole, a famous old Easthelmsford golfer at the turn of the century, ventured forth one day and never came back."

He gave her a little push. Azy dropped her bag and sat down, stretching out her legs. Augie sat beside her. The green, and the shadow of the flagstick slanting across it, resembled a great sundial—or moondial. "Where's your house from here?" he asked.

She twisted about and pointed toward the tee. "That way. You cross the road, walk down twelve, cut over to fifteen—and you're there. How about yours?"

"Mine?"

"Your house—in Shufferville."

The stars were dim; he managed to locate the Big Dipper,

however, then the North Star. "That way—a hundred and eighty-one miles."

"Driver, 5-iron."

He laughed, really enjoying himself. The brandy had worked wonders too. "What's it like?" she asked.

"It's an old nineteenth-century farmhouse—it sits on an oxbow."

"An oxbow?"

"It's where a river once ran before changing its course a hundred and seventy years ago. Or whenever. Now the *old* riverbed's a kind of swamp or wetlands—all kinds of wildlife in it. Once or twice a year it floods—you wake up and think you live on a bayou."

"Is your house ever in danger?"

"No. It sits pretty high up."

Azy reached inside her golf bag for the insect repellent, gave the applicator a few pumps and smoothed the spray on her arms and neck. "Want some?"

"Thanks."

She passed him the applicator. "Tell me something else about your house."

He squirted his wrists. "It has a big old cistern in the basement. Years ago—last century—they used it to hold rain water for washing and cooking. The house has a rear deck overlooking the oxbow. Standing on it gives you the feeling you're on the bridge of a ship, but the deck's not in the greatest shape— half the boards have to be replaced. Inside the house, some of the floor boards are sixteen inches wide. It's drafty, in summer the upstairs gets very hot. Red squirrels live in the rafters and scurry around, usually at night. The house stands east and west so you have a lot of morning sun and evenings you get some beautiful sunsets. In the tool shed there's an old dug well with twenty-five feet of water in it. Deer walk on the property and behind the shutters you can sometimes hear these little squeaking noises—bats. But they only come out at night and they keep the insects down. The house has a brick walk leading to the street, except the grass is shouldering its way in so the walk's only half as wide as it might be. When I get home I have to start painting, the exterior's beginning to peel. My son wants to keep it gray but my daughter favors white. If you look at early pictures, the house was white, so I'm leaning toward white—but it's going to take twice the work because it'll need two coats. That'll mean twice the cost. The house has thirteen rooms and a full attic and it's surrounded by locust trees and maples. It's got a huge brick fireplace, a shake roof that has a few years left on it and a detached garage—used to be the carriage house—that kind of tilts to one side. The whole place needs work."

"That's the fun of owning an old house."

"And the headache," Augie said.

Azy smiled. "How often do you play golf?"

"I go out every day, sometimes with my son—sometimes alone."

"You play golf every day?"

A dark cloud passed across the face of the moon; the flag-stick's shadow disappeared. "Nine holes. It's a nine-hole course."

"What do you do, Augie?"

"I'm a lawyer. Have an office in town. Local stuff, some-times I go to court—pays the bills and gives me time. The time is what I like best."

"Are you single?"

"Divorced," he said.

"What happened?"

"Flask handy?"

She laughed and pulled it from her bag, uncapped it and handed it to Augie. He had a taste.

"What happened? Abby, my wife—ex-wife—loved New York. When we were first married we had an apartment in the City, I was with a good firm, junior partner. New York was great for four or five years. But then we had a couple of kids—it just wasn't what I wanted any longer. I was raised in the country, seventeen miles from where I live now. Abby told me I was running away. Almost left me right then, but she said

63

she'd give country living a try. It didn't last long. She missed what she loved. Then one day she just left. She wanted to start over and the kids—our two kids—would be better off with me, she said. That was it. She just left . . ."

Azy shook her head. "Where is she now?"

"In Paris, with her third husband."

A chill was coming to the night air and he put his arm around her and she leaned her head against his shoulder. "Do you ever get bored in Shufferville?"

"It's more loneliness," he said. "I have that. But I'm never bored. There's too much to do. Four or five hours in my office, I love fly fishing, and I like tools. I make things—cabinets, shelves, boxes. I'm always working on golf clubs, refinishing, repairing them—maybe an old set I've picked up at a garage sale. In the evenings the kids and I usually have dinner together, talk, maybe play something, then I'll read until twelve or one . . ." Was she laughing at him?

No. She was just looking at him. A doe and two fawns were browsing on the fairway near the tee. Instead of white, the fawns' spots had a golden hue. Augie uncapped the flask. "This is good brandy," he said.

"House gift from Gil."

"Be sure to thank him for me."

She gave a little laugh. After a moment: "What was it with you and him at Reddon?"

"We were two kids who didn't get along. The old black-ant/red-ant syndrome. Our signs clashed, I guess. I don't know . . ." He picked up some loose clippings of grass. "It confused me, because I didn't hate Gil at first sight. I didn't say 'I hate that kid.' But *he* saw me and said, 'I hate *that* kid.' "

"Was he mean?"

"Azy, you're going to marry the man. I can't—"

"No. Tell me."

Augie stared straight ahead, remembering. "He was a husky kid, wrestled in the one hundred thirty-five pound class, I weighed one hundred seven—this was when we were four-teen, our first year at Reddon. He got to me. If I was playing

64

pool in the rec room he'd come along and mess up the balls. Kid stuff, but at the time . . . He was always daring me to do something. I'd tell myself tomorrow, tomorrow when he came up the stairs in the physics building I'd punch him out. Then one time—I guess this is what really stays with me—he erased my name on a sign-up sheet for the Friday night dance at our sister school in the same town. Taylor Hall. By then we were both sixteen, and I liked this girl a whole lot—still remember her name, Melissa Brown. I didn't know he'd erased my name until that evening when the headmistress of the girls' school read Melissa's name from the list and the name of her date from Reddon—all very formal. The name she read was Gil Plumber, and he and Melissa walked together into the main hall where couples were dancing. I was so mad I couldn't speak. After all the names were called I looked at the list—and there it was, my name erased and his written right over it. I wanted to go in there and kill him and I actually started in but then I saw them dancing close and it looked like Melissa wasn't exactly suffering. I turned around and walked back to the campus. I was going to pack up and run away. Come back another day to get even. Kill him, kill her, kill myself. As you can see, I didn't. Which concludes the saga of Augie and Gil and teenage heartbreak. Well, you asked for it."

"I'm glad you told me . . ." They sat, silently, on the edge of the huge bunker. "Were you happy there at all?"

"I had some friends, I played on the golf team. The truth? I was never happy at Reddon."

"Why did you go?"

"My father wanted to get me out of upstate New York—to 'expose you to boys from the finest families in America.' That's a direct quote. I was his only son and he had big ambitions for me. What was I going to say, no? Well, I could have, I should have. I never wanted to go."

"Did he go there?"

"No, he went to a high school outside of Boston, then to college and law school."

"So he was a lawyer too."

65

"At one point in his career he was chief counsel to the Secretary of State."

"The Secretary of State, like in Washington, D.C.?"

Augie nodded. "We hardly ever saw him. Maybe he'd come home four times a year. He liked having his family away —safe, comfortable, but away. We lived in a little town called Woodbridge New York."

"Which is seventeen miles from Shufferville."

"Yes."

"So really when you left the City, you went home."

"Abby said I was looking for something I could never have again, a 'lost youth'—lost when I was sent away to school. Hell, Azy, I don't know. I'm still looking for answers. At this late date."

She put her hand over the back of his, gently rubbing his knuckles. "But you love living on the oxbow. From everything you've said, that's clear. No question about that."

"I do, there are plenty of questions about other things. When I left the law firm it wasn't just my wife who said I was running away. It was my father too, just before he died. He said I was 'ducking life's challenges,' another direct quote. He lived for challenges. By going to Shufferville I was admitting I couldn't hack the real world, he said. I told him he was wrong but—"

"What's the real world, anyway? Is it downtown? Is it Washington? That's it? Everything else is the *unreal* world?"

"He meant where the power is. There's not too damn much power in Shufferville."

"Maybe it's just a different kind."

He was liking that she saw what *he* saw most of the time. "How about you? How did you and Gil meet?"

She didn't start in right away, then said, "It goes back eight years. At the time his wife had a brain tumor—their doctor in Chicago called it inoperable. Gil wanted a second opinion. So they came east for a conference with my father. That was how it started. The operation was a success and my folks and the Plumbers stayed in touch. They came out for the

Member-Guest the following year, and Gil and John have played in it ever since."

"Where's his wife now?"

"She died a year and a half ago. Something unrelated."

"So you and Gil aren't exactly strangers," Augie said.

"Hardly."

"Did you like him? Back then, I mean."

"He was very attentive, very generous, he had a thousand jokes—"

"Now you're going to marry him."

"Yes."

It wasn't said with a great deal of enthusiasm, and it didn't seem to make sense, but he didn't press on. "When's the big day?"

"December 20."

"Well, congratulations."

"Thank you," she said, quietly.

"What's this?" he asked as they came to a rustic, cabin-like structure with a screened-in porch; dark, closed up.

"It's called Halfway House," Azy said. "The ninth hole ends in the middle of nowhere; you can stop here for refreshments."

"Do you want something?"

She laughed. He liked that she laughed easily. They kept on, starting down the tenth fairway. "It's funny how things work out," he said. "When my car broke down this morning I almost bagged the whole weekend."

"I'm glad you didn't."

"Me too."

They walked along in silence. "Can I ask you something?" he said.

"Sure."

"Why are you glad?"

"I think you're very nice."

"I'm pleased to hear it. But you're engaged, it's not as if—"

"—I'm an uncommitted woman?"

"Yes."

"I still think you're very nice. Is that all right?"

"It's wonderful." Now shut up and don't look a gift horse . . .

They continued on. Azy pointed out a five-foot-tall fir tree; every hole had two, one on either side of the fairway, she said. An imaginary line drawn between the trees was exactly one hundred fifty yards from the center of the green.

"Good to know," Augie said.

"Some of these things Gordon would tell you in the morning," she said.

"I'm not too sure of that."

The dew was starting to soak through his shoes. "Ten is a very tough par-4," Azy said. "A lot of players can't reach in two. They lay up, then go for the pitch. You can't see any water on your second shot. But it's there—" she was pointing on the left. "So play *right* on your approach."

"Why don't you just caddy for me, Azy?"

"If I really had guts, I would."

"I suspect you have plenty of guts."

Suddenly Azy leaned down and reached into the grass; when she stood back up she was holding a bright red ball. "Stepped right on it," she said. "Don't you love finding a ball?"

"I do."

"I used to be a great hawker," she said.

"I still hawk."

"Did you ever find a double?"

"One time I found a *triple*—all the same color, that greenish-lime—within a two-foot circle. What are the odds on *that?*"

"High."

They skirted a fairway bunker, crossed a thick rough and emerged onto a new hole. "There's my house," Azy said.

It loomed across the fairway behind a row of large sycamores; her room was on the second floor, she told him—the two corner windows. Azy had her hand over the heads of her clubs so they wouldn't jangle as they approached the property, and he did the same. "Remember, on three, everything between you and the green is trouble, you don't want to be short," she said quietly. "On the seventh hole the distance is deceiving—use one more club than you think. On ten, remember—water on the left."

"Got it."

"Do you know how to get back?"

"I'm a little lost. I know this is the fifteenth—"

Azy pointed. "Walk toward the green. Just before you get there, a path leads to the sixteenth tee. The last three holes are links, they'll take you straight in."

"OK."

She pressed the ball in his hand. "I don't know if it's the kind you use but take it, maybe it'll bring you luck."

"Sure you won't caddy for me?"

"I'll be rooting for you."

Just easily, they kissed. Her lips were wonderfully soft, cool. She ducked through the sycamores. Augie glanced at the red ball he was holding, then turned and began walking toward the green, now and again glancing back at the upstairs corner windows of the Flannery house.

SHE TURNED A brass knob and stepped inside the garage; leaving her golf clubs in the corner, she passed in front of two automobiles and, opening a heavy door, stepped into the kitchen of her family's house on Sycamore Lane. Moonlight was coming through the window over the double stainless-steel sink and she saw the table already set for an early "tee-off" breakfast. Azy crossed the polished tile floor, walked under the crownlike chandelier in the front hallway and turned at the stairs. On the long second-floor landing, dimly lighted, she moved past her mother and father's room, past her brother Dennis's empty room, past Jack's old room, where Gil (for decorum's sake) kept his clothes and always initially retired to. Her parents, father in particular, were extremely conventional. She listened at the door; Gil was a heavy snorer, especially when he drank. Hearing nothing, she continued on, and opened the door at the end of the hall. The switch was just inside and she reached for it, lighting her room. Gil was standing at one of the windows.

"Hi," Azy said.

He was standing at one of the windows but not in front of it; to one side of it. He had on a silk robe and slippers. "Where have you been?"

"The room started swirling when I went to bed, I had to walk it off."

"By yourself?"

"Of course by myself."

"Where?"

"What is this, Gil?"

"Where did you walk?"

"Is that important?"

"I think so."

"Just out on the course," Azy said.

She was at the corner of her antique brass four-poster bed, which her parents had given her on her thirteenth birthday. It had a lovely white canopy, too girlish for her now, but she only slept here when Gil visited, and he thought it was charming. "I'm sorry if I caused you any worry," she said. "My head was spinning, I had to get some air."

"Do you know what time it is?"

"No. I imagine it's late."

"Come here."

She seemed to think he was softening. She walked across to where her fiancé was standing. Only he didn't move, step forward; then Azy realized she was fully in the window. She looked out; there, in the middle of the fifteenth fairway, a man was facing the house and waving his arms—obviously because he saw her in the window. On one side, Gil was peeking out.

"Who's that?"

"I don't know."

He stepped out and positioned himself next to Azy. Immediately the waving stopped. The man reached down, picked up his bag and quickly disappeared into the shadows.

"You're lying," Gil said.

"I'm not. Maybe somebody knows me."

"Somebody. Like Augie Wittenbecher."

"Who's Augie Wittenbecher?"

"Don't bullshit me. You know damn well!"

She made to go toward the bathroom but he grabbed her by the arm. "What's going on here, Azy?"

"You're hurting me!"

"What's going on?"

"Nothing."

He released her, not with a shove but it also wasn't a mere letting go. She went in the bathroom and took off her shirt, her jeans; some blades of grass were clinging to the back denim pocket. She brushed her teeth, then combed out her hair in the mirror. What *is* going on? she asked her reflection. Azy dipped her head, then slipped into her long terry robe and went out. Gil was already in bed, and when she got in he immediately reached for her, began kissing her breasts as if what had just happened between them was forgotten. No talk to smooth things out, no little touches. Just do it. He had a stubby, rock-hard erection.

Once in, he said nice things. He always did. He said he loved her. No man could ever love a woman like he loved her. Then he said, "Yeah!"

It always made Azy think his stock had just jumped nine points; or he had just won a big hand in poker; or Yale had just scored a winning touchdown.

He said she was beautiful, he would give her anything. What did she want?

Yeah.

Anything, Azy. Anything you want. Name it. The moon? Do you want the moon? He would give her the moon!

There was nothing for her to answer, to say; she seemed to see a man walking in the middle of the sixteenth fairway, golf bag on his shoulder, alone.

What, Azy? Tell me. Anything!

YEAH!

C H A P T E R 7

AUGIE KILLED HIS headlights just before reaching the McSweeneys' mailbox, then turned in and parked beside Gordon's bomb. The house was dark. He wondered if Rainbow slept outside on balmy summer nights.

He stepped out, pressed his door shut and walked around to the back yard; by now the cur would certainly be aware of his movements. At the guesthouse Augie tried the lift-and-push procedure on the latch—it worked! Maybe he was getting the knack.

He could see fairly well (good old moon) and made his way to the cot, where he sat down and took off his shoes, socks and trousers. Then, because he wanted to set both his travel alarm and the beeper on his watch, he turned on the lamp.

Alarms set—three and a half hours' sleep wasn't great but it would have to do—Augie finished undressing. He switched off the light and slid between the sheets, almost at once pushing the top sheet down to his waist; the guesthouse had gratefully cooled a little but it was still very hot. Almost at once he felt himself going under . . . *Then, oddly, he was playing golf again. With Azy. It didn't make sense but he loved it. She was swinging a club on the second tee, they were walking down the fairway in the moonlight, she hit her approach to the green. Then he realized—it defied explanation—that it wasn't Azy . . . It was his ex-wife. Furthermore the clubs she was using had sharp heads, resembling axes, swords, machetes—and she swung wildly. All of which was terribly scary and confusing. In the first place Abby didn't play golf. But here she was, swinging away. He kept at a safe distance—most of the time. Whizz. Why he didn't just leave her on the course and walk in, he didn't know. Because this was dangerous. Slash. They came to a water cooler. He was hot, harried, the cup dispenser was empty so he put his mouth under the spigot. Abby did the same, except she put her mouth on the spigot and began sucking on it, running her tongue up and down—then she walked over to him and unzipped his fly and started doing to him what she'd done to the spigot. He was nervous, a little frightened, but still—still it was exciting and they both sank to the ground and now she climbed on top and took him inside of her, all of him, deep inside of her, and she was crazy now, moaning, screaming . . .*

Augie's eyes opened, he came awake—startled, terrified. A woman was straddling him, naked, moving on him wildly; in the dim light her nipples looked like a pair of dancing bronze coins. Her face—contorted—was raised, and her peen-like nose kept jabbing, jabbing, jabbing. His impulse was to throw her off, to run out into the night. Except—except another force took over, stronger than fear. Obliterating conscience, loyalty, making wrong seem not so much right as an absolute necessity . . .

He reached for her jouncing breasts, taking them in his hands, and met her thrusts—and suddenly her body convulsed and she let out a long, agonized cry that had to wake every soul between there and the E.C.C. Then Augie was over the edge too, and he brought her down, drinking in her perfume, crushing her against his chest.

THEY lay on the cot and she kept telling him how she had always, always known how incredible it would be and she kept kissing him—his cheeks, his lips, his eyes. He didn't speak. He touched her hair by way of saying something, though he didn't know what. Something. Her hair felt like glazed straw. She was happy; she was so happy she was almost delirious.

Then, suddenly, she had to leave. "Good night, Augie."

"Good night."

She gave him a last kiss and put her feet on the floor. From

74

a shadow Catherine picked up a short rayon robe and slipped it on, as if it were the shadow. She said good-night again and went out and he looked at his travel clock's glinting dial: 5:27. He sat up and leaned forward, starting to shake; in the hot vault of the McSweeneys' guesthouse, he felt a deadly chill. His towel was over the steel frame at the foot of the cot and he grabbed it and wiped the sweat from his chest and arms.

He squeezed his skull with his hands, then stood and pushed through a rack of old clothes to the small window opposite the one by his cot. The panes were grimy but he could see out; the sky was an exquisite pearl. It was morning in Easthelmsford.

PART II

THE
FIRST
ROUND

AUGIE WROTE THE message on a piece of cardboard, the flap to a carton containing fifty ancient issues of *National Geographic.* Outside the guesthouse, he positioned the flap against the screen door. Logic said that Gordon would walk out when his guest didn't come in by six, and Augie wanted him to know he'd already gone to the club—he'd meet Gordon there for breakfast. He thought of adding it was "part of the package," but in the frame of mind he was in, didn't. He angled across the yard, walked past the back steps and out to the dirt driveway, wearing a pair of yellow trousers, a brown golf shirt and a tan pullover.

His station wagon's windows were covered with dew; he grabbed a small roll of paper towels from under the front seat and wiped away the moisture. The sun was just coming up and the outlook was for another beautiful day, but right now it was chilly and damp. Augie tucked the toweling back under the seat, quietly closed his door and started the engine. His eyes were half-closed, his body was stiff and crusty, he needed a shave.

He backed out and drove slowly along, preoccupied—so preoccupied and strung out he doubted his ability to play a round of competitive golf. One thing he did know: if he and Gordon lost today he'd take off inside an hour.

At the traffic light he turned right, drove a short distance and came to the club entrance; except it wasn't the same entrance they had used last night for the pari-mutuel dinner. It was a narrower driveway, a hundred yards shy of the main drive. A sign on the sidewalk, "Parking, E.C.C. Member-Guest" made Augie slow and follow the arrow in.

Even at this hour twenty-five cars were in the lot, perhaps a third the size of the main lot. He pulled into a spot next to a red BMW convertible. The car straight across was a black Porsche. Augie stepped out, yawned, feeling as if he'd just driven two hundred nonstop miles. He was looking at a fifteen-foot-high hedge. From yesterday's cocktail hour on the patio, he recognized it as the hedge that ran along the right side of the first hole.

He yawned again, vaguely watched a dozen players on the club's practice range swatting out balls; then a loudspeaker echoed across the parking lot. "Flight 14. Mr. Ohland, Mr. Rancourt; Mr. Swenson, Mr. Cleary—on the tee, please. On deck: Mr. Yourke, Mr. Gault; Mr. Kiernan, Mr. Etter."

The announcement sent a wave of anxiety through Augie, and he began walking toward the clubhouse; when he rounded the tall hedge he saw he was at the first tee. Four men were standing on it, swinging clubs, stretching and bending. Two shiny white carts were parked alongside the tee, each with two sets of clubs strapped on the back. At a small distance, positioned close to each other like newly assembled vehicles outside a factory, were sixty other carts.

The golf course itself was foggy; the first green wasn't visible from the tee. Twelve or fifteen caddies were sitting on a long bench positioned against the wall of a storage room for golf clubs. A post-and-rail fence ran behind the tee; on the top railing lay, or rested, forty golf bags. Men, all wearing sweaters or jackets, milled about on a walkway, talking, sipping cups of coffee, looking at the pairings and starting times posted on the storage-room wall. On the side of the tee opposite the hedge was a large putting green, where golfers were stroking balls at randomly placed miniature flagsticks. Augie double-checked his starting time, confirming it as 7:17—suddenly everyone in the immediate area became silent, still, including the men on the practice green. A golfer on the tee was taking his stance. Augie turned and watched.

The golfer kept shifting his feet, as if he couldn't get them both planted comfortably. He had a dark mustache and was wearing Madras slacks and a pink sweater. Augie thought his hands were shaking a little as he gripped his club. Then the man swung, got too far under the ball, and sent it straight up. For a long moment it disappeared into the fog, then landed forty yards away.

"Well, you're in play, Dick," his partner said.

The man walked off the tee, mumbling to himself as his partner went out and pegged a ball. Before he took his stance, Augie left the immediate vicinity, walking past the putting green and pro shop to the men's locker room. He took off his clothes, arranged them in front of one Martin McAllister's locker and continued on to the shower room. He stood under blasting hot water, washed his hair, then used two towels to dry, wrapping the second around his waste and shuffling into the adjoining room to a bank of gleaming porcelain basins. On a shelf above the basins were lotions and disposable razors and shaving creams and deodorants and powders and hair tonics and combs and even pump toothpaste dispensers (no toothbrushes). Augie shaved, vigorously used a tooth-pasted finger on his teeth, combed his hair and dabbed on some lotion—all in ten minutes.

Dressed again, he searched for coffee. A locker room attendant—an old man with shoe-polish-stained fingers wearing a blue apron—was inserting new laces in a pair of golf shoes; he looked up from his work station near the door and directed Augie to a doorway across the room. No mere coffee machine and donut assortment greeted him when he walked through. What greeted him were stainless steel trays of scrambled eggs, bacon, sausage, French toast and blueberry pancakes; and all kinds of juices, fruits, rolls and pastries. The tables had pink cloths and napkins and each had a vase of fresh flowers, and Augie wondered why more members and guests weren't sitting down. Only three or four of the thirty tables were taken. A

81

hostess greeted him with a pleasant smile. Good morning. How was he today?

"Fine, thank you. I'm expecting Mr. McSweeney—"

"Sit anywhere you like, dear. Orange juice? Coffee?"

"Please."

Augie chose a table by the large plate windows overlooking the first hole. Even as he observed the still-foggy scene, two carts cruised down the fairway—but not very far; both abruptly stopped and a player jumped out of each, walked to the rear of his cart and chose a club.

The hostess brought over a large glass of juice and a silver coffee pourer. "Here you are, dear," she said, filling his cup.

The woman acted like she thought of him as her son. She hoped he would help himself to anything he liked. The blueberries were fresh this morning. Just signal when he wanted a refill on coffee.

Ever so faintly he heard the loudspeaker requesting players to the tee. Augie checked his watch. Wanting to spend fifteen minutes on the range, he decided to wait for Gordon until six-twenty, then go to the food line.

He felt very distracted but it was a delightful setting, he had to admit—everything pink and bright and clean, and he was glad at least to have showered and shaved. The matron came right over when he gave her a little wave and she smiled and called him dear again and he watched golfers hitting their second shots on one. The sun's rays had just reached the first green and the course had a fairyland look. Augie glanced nervously at his wrist. He wanted Gordon to walk through the door and he didn't. He wanted to have their round start and he hoped it never would. OK, Augie, just relax now, he told himself. Try hard.

FINISHED with breakfast, Augie searched the area of the putting green and first tee, noticing that a few women were now walking and standing about. He stepped inside the pro shop; maybe Gordon was buying some balls or tees. The shop had racks of trousers and skirts, shelves filled with sweaters and short-sleeved shirts—all very handsome and, Augie imagined, expensive; and of course it had clubs. Augie had never seen so many complete sets in one place. One whole wall was devoted to putters alone, another to bags. Perhaps you needed an umbrella or a rain suit. How about a new pair of spikes? Or a specialty wood or iron? Augie felt like browsing but it was the wrong time—what he wanted was Gordon. A young man and woman were behind a glass display counter, both busy with customers. Augie was about to leave when a man about thirty-five, attired in pastels, with carrot-colored hair and a very fair complexion, came into the shop from a back room. His shirt, in blue, had an E.C.C. emblem on the pocket. Augie had a notion he was the club pro. Perhaps seeing that no one was helping the gentleman, he asked Augie if he could be of any assistance.

"I'm looking for Mr. McSweeney. I'm his guest."

"I haven't seen him, sir." He spoke with a Scottish accent. "Check down at storage with Curt Kolchak."

"Thank you. I'm Augie Wittenbecher."

"Kyle McIntyre."

They shook hands. "If there's anything I can do for you, Mr. Wittenbecher, just let me know."

Augie thanked him again and walked out. The players currently on the tee were using caddies. Augie preferred walking but he imagined that Gordon had already reserved a cart. So they would ride, if and when he got here. Maybe he should call. Only problem was his address book was in the McSweeneys' guesthouse and the McSweeneys had an unlisted number. Then he saw a man about forty-five, with a full, dark mustache and a dark-toned complexion, come out of the club-storage room.

Augie walked up; the man, in a bad mood, was instructing a strapping seventeen-year-old to reassign Mr. Reynolds's bag to a new caddy—Jeff Paxton just called in sick. Then before Augie had a chance to say anything, he turned and went back inside. Augie followed him in. It was a large room; three walls were entirely made up of rectangular slots for members' bags, and guests' bags were propped against the walls in clusters of eight or ten, each cluster designated by a flight number. The man, wearing khaki trousers and a gray sweatshirt, was preparing to rewhip someone's driver; scattered about on top of his workbench were cans of stain, rolls of tapes and threads, plastic inserts, knives, files, razor blades, steel wool, sandpaper, and a box filled with golf-club grips. He inserted the steel shaft of the driver in a rubber clamp, then put the clamp in a vise and spun the handle. For a moment Augie stood, watching, then asked the man if he was Curt Kolchak.

"What can I do for you?" He didn't look up.

"Have you seen Mr. McSweeney?"

"No, I haven't." His eyebrows collided over his nose like a couple of furry caterpillars butting heads. "His bag's been taken out, I know that."

"If you see him," Augie said, "would you tell him his guest is on the range?"

Kolchak took a razor and cut off the frayed, loose whipping; when it dropped to the floor it lay in a tight black curl. On a peg above the bench was a spool of new whipping material, which he began wrapping around the club's hosel. He was very busy, didn't waste a second. "What flight you in?"

"Twelve," Augie said.

"Where's your bag?"

"Still in my car. I thought I'd hit some balls."

"Tell Jimmy."

Augie went back out and told the boy—who had a future for himself in the NFL—that he was Mr. McSweeney's guest, Augie Wittenbecher. If he saw Mr. McSweeney, please tell him that his partner was warming up on the range.

"No problem. Take cart 76, over there. Those are his clubs."

Augie walked over, slid behind the wheel and spun out to the parking lot; at his car he fastened his bag to the back—while observing Gordon's collection of woods and irons. They certainly weren't a matched set. The irons were a mix of lower-line Wilsons and Spaldings, twenty years old. The driver, once a nice piece of persimmon, had a cracked insert; the putter looked to be from a kid's starter set, while the brown vinyl bag, dry and cracked, had a big safety pin holding shut the ball compartment. Augie laced on his spiked shoes and continued on to the range, finding an open spot at the extreme end near a big practice sand trap.

He parked and walked to the salt-box shed behind the range, a shingled enclosure resembling a fruit-and-vegetable stand. On the counter, where the tomatoes, squash and peaches would lie, were mesh-wire baskets filled with red-striped golf balls. Large size and small size. Only no one was in attendance to take his money. Just then another golfer came up, a sleepy-looking young man in knee-length shorts, and grabbed a large pail. Augie did likewise. Practice balls were like the clam bar and breakfast, he suddenly realized: part of the package.

He started with his wedge, hitting easy shots of fifty and sixty yards, then longer shots with his 8-iron. Not liking any of them. The loudspeaker kept announcing who should report to the tee. Augie kept swinging, but try as he might, couldn't concentrate. He kept looking toward the clubhouse, expecting to see Gordon ambling toward the range. No Gordon. Where in hell was he? He might remember this as the tournament that never was. *Swing.* He had told a few golfing friends at Shufferville that he was playing in the Member-Guest at Easthelmsford, and now could see himself telling them, "My host never showed up on the first tee." They would laugh, Augie would probably laugh with them. *Swing.* He didn't feel like laughing now. Maybe Gordon knew something, maybe he'd heard his wife's wild cry in the night. Good reasons not to show up, unless of course he showed up with a gun.

Swing, swing, swing.

A new announcement reached the range. "Mr. Riseley, Mr. Searles; Mr. Buckner, Mr. Godfrey—on the tee, please. On deck—Mr. Keegan, Mr. Quinn; Mr. McSweeney, Mr. Wittenbecher."

Augie took three more shots, stowed his loose clubs in his bag and drove back to the tee. He went right up to Jimmy. The high-school linebacker shook his head. "I haven't seen hide nor hair of him, sir."

The group of Riseley, Searles, Buckner and Godfrey drove reasonably well, two balls in the rough, two down the middle. The men rolled away in their respective carts—and three new players walked out to the first tee. Augie shook hands with Al Keegan, the member, and his guest, Bob Quinn; he was sorry, he couldn't explain the whereabouts of his host. Keegan scowled. If Gordon didn't show, Keegan-Quinn would automatically advance; but Keegan wanted to play golf. "I knew it —I had a feeling when I woke up something like this would happen," he said.

Bob Quinn was a man of fifty, hefty, with silvery hair and a red face. He said to Augie, "Can you reach him by phone?"

"I don't have his number—with me."

Keegan muttered something under his breath. He was in his mid-forties, with a wiry build and short, springy-black hair; he had on orange pants and was wearing a gray windbreaker over a shirt with a navy-blue collar. He had the air of a man used to making decisions and having his way.

He walked over to the starter's table and began talking to the man seated behind it; actually two men were seated behind it. Not wanting any unilateral decisions made, Augie went over to see what was going on. Just then the younger of the two officials picked up the megaphone: "Mr. McSweeney, to the tee! *Last call.*"

Keegan asked the more senior official at what point the match would be forfeited. The starter, a thick-necked man whose face had all the expression of a pan of wall-sizing, checked the clock and schedule on the table.

"If Mr. McSweeney doesn't show before his partner hits his second shot you'll win by forfeit," he said to Keegan.

"I don't believe we've met," said Augie, moving in a little closer.

"I'm the tournament chairman, Steve McMahon."

The name was familiar. "Augie Wittenbecher."

Augie gave a look around. Standing among the score of

86

golfers and observers were Gil Plumber and John Flannery; beside them stood Azy. She didn't wave but she gave him a little smile. Augie turned and walked back to the white markers. In the distance, the first green and flag were now just visible; the morning fog was burning off.

Bob Quinn was first up. He had a short, choppy swing; the ball flew out fast and low—not a pretty shot but it had good roll. Then Keegan teed up. He did a lot of fussy things as he prepared to hit—checking his alignment, his grip, stepping up with his left foot back, then bringing it even with the right before assuming his final stance. Augie figured the man had taken a lot of lessons in his life. Keegan brought the club back deliberately—and Gordon came running up to the tee.

"Augie! I thought for sure—"

Then he realized that a player was in the process of swinging. "Damn, I'm sorry," he said.

Keegan backed away, stood with his head bowed while pressing his fingers between his eyes. Then he started all over. He was using a 3-iron and, on his forward swing, hit the ball off-center; it went straight but didn't have any zip—maybe going a hundred and thirty yards. His lips were moving as he walked off the tee.

Gordon's golf spikes were untied and the wine cardigan he had on was buttoned wrong—buttons not matching their buttonholes. His left pants pocket bulged; perhaps a baloney and cheese sandwich was nestled inside. "You go, Augie," he said, dropping to one knee to tie his laces.

Augie walked out to the markers and put a ball on a tee, thinking all he wanted was to make good contact. Light grip—easy back, easy through. He brought his 3-wood away on a good path, but at the top of his swing he did what he sometimes did under pressure. Instead of swinging the club, he yanked it down. The ball started out left—and kept curving left. By any name or description it was a nasty pull-hook.

"You made the swale!" Gordon shouted, as if that were an accomplishment, like hitting a jackpot.

Augie picked up his tee and stepped back, feeling a rush of

anger and disappointment, and Gordon came out and teed a
ball he might just have swiped from someone's shag-bag, considering its grayish hue. He didn't check his alignment, his grip
—he didn't check anything. He did take a practice swing, however, digging a divot the size of a cigar packet, which he then
conscientiously replaced. The dirt stuck to the face of his club
and he commenced to wipe it back and forth along the ground
like someone trying to get dog shit off his shoe. He took a
second practice swing, continuing around with his follow-
through until his club was back on the ground again. Finally he
set up to the ball, with a stance like he was getting ready to
start a lawnmower. He looked at the ball from a variety of tilts
and angles, at last finding one he liked, then took a quick backswing and came down lustily. No little swipe. The ball took off
like a clay pigeon, spinning high and wide; it cleared the tall
hedge bordering the course and went "clunk" off the roof of
someone's Mercedes-Benz.

No one said a word. Gordon said, "I'll reload."

Only he didn't have an extra ball in his pocket. He
clumped over to the cart; he had tied his laces but *beneath* the
kilties, and the kilties flapped up and down as he walked, like
old dried fig leaves. He unpinned the compartment and came
out with a second ball, full sister to the first in its coloration. Al
Keegan's lips were now really moving. Steve McMahon gave a
quick look around; carts were backing up and other golfers—
not just Keegan—were beginning to grouse.

Gordon teed his second ball and damn if he didn't go
through the same routine. Taking a king-sized divot was evidently part of it, as was retrieving it and tamping it down.
Then he was ready again; what he was thinking of—what pre-
swing thoughts were in his head as he stood over his ball eying
it this way and that—Augie couldn't imagine. Whatever, the
swing didn't change; again his ball sliced, this time, however,
not quite so dramatically; it dropped at the base of the hedge a
hundred and seventy-five yards away.

"Better," he said.

Keegan and Quinn, making a show of their displeasure,

sped off before Gordon could pick up his tee. Augie was waiting for him in the cart but Gordon didn't immediately take a
seat beside him. Instead he reached in his bulging trouser
pocket and produced a compact camera, which he then handed
to one of the golfers in the next foursome. "For posterity,
Augie," he said, sliding behind the wheel.

The man holding the camera looked as if he might *throw* it
at them; but annoyed as he obviously was, he clicked the shut-
ter and gave the camera back. "Thanks a lot," Gordon said,
putting it in the wire basket behind his seat.

"Anytime."

"All set?" Gordon said to Augie.

"I think so."

"Great. We're off."

Veering right, Gordon directed the wagon toward the
hedge, no doubt to find and play his second drive. Augie didn't
say anything but he was thinking that Gordon was already out
of the hole. The way the tournament was set up, a team won a
hole if *either* player on that team took fewer strokes than either
player on the opposing team. Considering that Gordon's first
drive was out of bounds, a penalty of both stroke and distance,
he now lay three somewhere near the hedge. Augie, in the
swale, lay one, as did Keegan and Quinn.

"Slow down," Augie said.

"It's up further," Gordon said.

"No, it's right in here."

"I don't think so."

While the wagon was still moving, Augie jumped out and
began looking, taking a moment to watch Keegan hit his second shot, a neat lay-up short of the pond. Gordon poked
around with an iron twenty yards ahead. The hedge was thick,
impenetrable, and Augie felt that the ball was lodged somewhere deep inside it. Quinn's approach landed on the upper
right fringe of the green, and now he and Keegan sat in their
cart and waited. Back on the tee the next four players were all
standing in an identical manner: hand on hip, staring out at
Gordon McSweeney and Guest.

Augie, well aware they were holding up play, gave a final swipe in the rough. "I think it's lost," he said.

"What do I do now?"

"If you go back to the tee, you'd be shooting *five.* "

"Can't I just drop another ball?"

"That isn't the way it's done."

"Why not?"

"Because you have to go *back* for a lost ball, to the spot where you hit it from."

"Then I'll go back."

"Gordon, look. You're out of the hole."

"Here's a ball right here!"

It was right next to the hedge, against a root. What you needed to get it out was a rake. "What should I do?" Gordon asked.

"Pick up."

"No."

Gordon didn't say it crossly, he just didn't like the idea.

"Then take an unplayable," Augie said, struggling to keep his patience. "Measure it off."

"Measure it off?"

"Two club lengths, not nearer the hole. Use your driver."

"You want me to use a driver from the rough?"

"Just to measure the club lengths."

From the tee came an angry shout: "Come on! Play!"

Gordon walked to the cart, pulled out his driver and came back, flip-flopping it two times. Now clear of the hedge, he thought for a moment, went to the cart a second time and returned with a lofted iron. "Do you think a 7 is enough?" he asked, as if he had visions of his ball coming to rest next to the pin.

"It's perfect. Sure."

Gordon took his slow, awkward setup and advanced the ball twenty-five yards; at least now he was on the fairway. Augie told him to grab a club for his next shot. Gordon rattled around his irons, like a picker sorting through junk. Al Keegan and Bob Quinn had their heads lowered; they reminded Augie

of a driver and passenger resigned to the worst traffic jam of
their lives.

"OK," Gordon said. "Got it."

Augie cut straight across the fairway. The swale, it turned
out, was an abandoned sand trap—or perhaps a "grass trap"
from the start. It was deep and long and served, in part, to
separate the first from the eighteenth hole, which ran parallel
to the first but in the opposite direction. The grass in it was
wiry and dry. Augie got out of the wagon, checked his watch
and entered the swale where he thought his ball might be. He
pushed around with a 9-iron, knowing his chances of finding it
were small. Gordon rolled over in the cart, got out and came
skidding down the bank. "I hit a good shot," he said. "Cleared
the pond."

"Help me look."

They poked about, Augie mumbling to himself as he
knocked down the grass with angry swipes. Then someone was
saying angrily, "Seriously, you guys!"

Augie and Gordon glanced up; their opponents were on
the lip of the swale in their cart. "This is getting out of hand,"
Al Keegan said.

"I'm allowed five minutes to look for my ball," Augie said.

"You're holding up the whole tournament—"

"It's not intentional."

"That's beside the goddamn point!" said Keegan.

"What should we do? You tell us," Augie said.

"Concede the hole."

"No. I'm going back to the tee," Augie said.

"You're *what?*"

"We're not conceding the hole, so it's the only thing I *can*
do."

"Jesus Christ," Keegan moaned.

Augie looked at his watch; slightly over two minutes had
gone by since he'd started looking. He spoke to Gordon. "I'm
playing a Titleist 3, keep looking for it."

"OK, partner."

Augie climbed the grassy bank and got in the cart, twisting

the wheel sharply and stomping the accelerator pedal. The wind whipped his hair. As he drew closer to the tee he could see the expressions on the faces of the waiting golfers. They loved him; he was their favorite guest of all time. If he didn't come back next year they wouldn't even have the fucking tournament! You bet. Augie stopped abruptly, braked the cart, yanked his 3-wood from his bag and unzipped the ball pocket. He didn't say anything, look at anyone; there was nothing to explain. Eight carts were now lined up, ready to roll. Augie walked out between the markers; a ball was perched on a tee. He looked around and a tight little man in a lime sweater, perfectly buttoned, came out and snatched tee and ball away. Augie thanked him, took a deep breath and teed the ball he was holding. Of the two-dozen balls he'd stored in his bag Wednesday evening at home preparing for the tournament, not one was red; this one was bright red. Where . . . And then he remembered.

He took a practice swing; it was more on the order of sweeping with a broom. A quick, pointless back and forth. Then he saw he wasn't even holding his 3-wood; inadvertently he had grabbed his driver. Augie stepped up to the ball, thinking if it went, it went; if he dubbed it, he dubbed it. Stiffly, he started his club back—

"Augie!"

He stopped his backswing at about belt level.

"I found your ball!" It was Gordon, yelling from the swale.

Augie waved, then leaned down and picked up his ball and tee.

Steve McMahon's face turned crimson. *"What are you doing, Mr. Wittenbecher?"*

"My partner found my ball," Augie said.

"So?"

"I'm going out to play it."

"You committed yourself to play a *second* ball!"

"I didn't," Augie said.

A couple of men laughed. Someone said, "Who is this joker?" But mostly there was serious—if not downright bitter

92

—grumbling. "You teed a ball and took your stance," said Steve McMahon.

The tournament chairman walked out from behind his table. He'd had it up to his eyeballs. "Play your second ball or I'm disqualifying you," McMahon said.

"You can't do that," Augie said.

"Don't tell me what I can or can't do—"

"The Committee disqualifies a player," Augie said.

"As Chairman of the Easthelmsford Tournament Committee I'm *on* the Committee."

"That may be. But you can't arbitrarily disqualify me."

"Just play, for Christ's sake!" someone shouted.

"Your second ball is your ball in play," McMahon said. "You abandoned your first ball."

"My partner was looking for my first ball, I didn't abandon it."

"When you left the swale it was an admission your first ball was lost!"

"I'm sorry, you don't know the rules of golf—"

McMahon was livid. Just then Gordon called from the course, "Augie—Titleist 3, right?"

He waved his arm, then spoke to the tournament chairman. "I'll tell you what. I'll play *both* balls. Then whatever the Committee rules—my first ball or my second ball—I'll go by."

"Don't let him bamboozle you, Steve!" a golfer called out.

McMahon glared at Augie. "OK. But if you hold up play again we're penalizing your team! And believe me, Mr. Wittenbecher—we'll be watching."

He walked back to his table, announcing that Mr. Wittenbecher would be playing both balls on the hole; the Committee would make a decision. Golfers jeered, but then all was quiet as Augie reteed Azy's ball.

It looked like the sun on the horizon, sitting there; then it was a pinpoint of light at the end of a long tunnel. The silence weighed on him like twelve feet of water when he was a boy diving for balls in the bend of Willow Creek, where the tee shots that didn't carry always washed to. Augie brought the club back, holding the handle in a death-grip, then swung wildly, just letting it rip. *Smack!* The ball started out low, rose, then just took off. It landed in the middle of the fairway past the cart of Keegan and Quinn and rolled almost to the edge of the pond. Someone—it sounded like one person—clapped. Augie picked up his tee, went to put it in his pocket, missed his pocket and didn't pick it up again. He got in the cart, spun the wheel and drove off, his foot jumping on the pedal.

Al Keegan didn't at all appreciate that Augie Wittenbecher was going to play both balls. He said what McMahon had said initially, that Augie had committed himself when he'd gone back—he couldn't have it both ways. Augie only said the matter was now in the hands of the Committee, he was playing both balls.

With a fairly decent lie in the swale, his 7-iron landed on the far edge of the green. Then he and Gordon drove to his second ball. When they reached it Augie stepped out and used his favorite club for close-in play, the sand wedge, lofting the red ball nicely onto the green. They crossed the little bridge and Gordon hacked away in the trap like a kid in his sandbox. Both Keegan and Quinn had tough chips, and each was left with a difficult ten- and twelve-foot putt for par. On the ball hit from the swale, Augie putted it close—but not close enough. He had a four-footer left on the high dangerous side of the hole. Then he putted the red ball, lipped the cup and tapped in. Adding the stroke and distance penalty, it gave him a six. Two over par—double-bogey. Both Keegan and Quinn studied their putts carefully. Keegan's didn't come close, and when he missed again, he swore. That gave *him* a six. Quinn's ten-footer tailed off and he stroked in his next putt for a five.

That left Augie his putt on his first ball for a four. The roll was steeper than he had first judged and if he missed, the ball was going to run and end up off the green. He figured the line, a small right-to-left break. Just get it going, Augie. He heard Azy's voice. Just get it going.

He got it going. The ball trickled forward, began following the break, started to pick up speed—way too much speed—and fell, boom, into the hole. Gordon whistled and cheered. Augie's hand was shaking as he reached in and picked out the ball. As all four players were getting into their carts to head to the second tee, Keegan announced, "That puts us 1-up."

"Excuse me?" Augie said.

"Bob had a five."

"I had a four on my first ball."

"We're not recognizing your first ball," Quinn said.

"That's up to the Committee—"

"We're telling you right now," Keegan said with a meeting-adjourned finality to his words, "to avoid any argument."

"And I'm telling you, you have nothing to say about it," Augie said.

It was one tension-filled round of golf. Not a single word passed between teams, except to verify scores at the end of each hole. Keegan and Quinn watched Augie's every move, from tee to green, hoping to catch him on an infraction. But he gave them nothing to question. He played carefully but he didn't play well. His irons weren't working; they drifted off, falling short and to the right. Luckily Gordon got the idea that picking up on a hole, if you already had six strokes and your ball was behind a tree in someone's backyard, didn't mean you were a quitter. As a foursome, they at least sped up the pace. Going into seven, the teams were even—by one way of figuring; but if you disallowed Augie's "swale ball," Keegan and Quinn were 1-up. Augie studied the hole from the tee, remembered what Azy had said about using more club than you thought, and pulled out his 3-iron instead of his 4. It was his best shot so far; his ball struck exactly on the crest, then rolled to within seven feet and he made the birdie. That put him and Gordon 1-up by one computation and all-even by another.

Then on eight, Gordon contributed for the first time. From twenty yards off the green he topped his ball using a pitching wedge. It bounced through a bunker, over the fringe, scooted across the green, struck the flagstick—and dove. Straight in. No one said, "Good shot," because in fact it was a miserable shot. But Augie was damn happy about it. He was looking at a double-bogey, and now with Gordon's five they were sure of a tie. Gordon might've thought they'd just won the match by how he hollered and carried on.

Except for his thick-headedness on the first hole about picking up, Gordon was a wonderful partner, if a terrible player. He couldn't hit a shot that didn't slice. His drives were classic banana balls—struck hard enough, they would circle completely around and land back at his feet, like a boomerang. He was a wonderful partner because his attitude was perfect. He laughed, he didn't take himself seriously, he had no expectations about his game—and Augie, despite his preoccupations, began to relax and enjoy himself. He nailed his drive on nine, two hundred thirty-five yards straight down the middle. Gordon's ended up, as always, in the rough—but if a tee shot didn't sail into the woods, he was happy. With the sun now shining warmly, they both took off their sweaters, dropped them in the wire basket on top of the camera and drove off, Augie at the wheel.

"Great hit," Gordon said.

"Thanks."

"This is fun now. This is the way I hoped it would be."

"Plus we're holding our own," Augie said.

"I'm really sorry for all that shit back on one."

"It's over. Forget it."

"Anyway, the reason I was late"—Gordon was grinning— "this morning, of all mornings, she wants to mess around. She's half-asleep, she reaches for me—she hasn't done that for years, reach out and kind of groan a little—you know how they do."

Augie lurched; his hands clutched the wheel and the cart swerved.

"What are you doing?" Gordon yelled.

He straightened the cart out.

"More to the right, Augie. I'm over in the rough, remember? Anyway, the morning I need every minute of sleep I can get, she wants action. Can you figure a woman out?"

"No."

"It's in here. Slow down. I see it. Augie, stop!"

Gordon got out, chose a middle iron, squibbed his ball sixty-five yards and got back in. "So get this," he said, settling beside Augie. "We finish, rest a little—she wants it again! I haven't gone twice in fifteen years! It was incredible. I forgot how good that woman can fuck!"

Augie blindly pointed the cart toward his ball. When he got to it, the flag looked about nineteen miles away. "What do you think?" he asked Gordon, mostly to shut him up.

"I'd say a 7-iron."

"That's not enough."

"You're way the hell out here, Augie."

"I was going to take a wood."

"You crazy?"

"I'll go with a 6."

And pray, he thought.

HE missed the shot—dubbed it, cold-cocked it, topped it. Whatever it was, his ball plopped along for thirty yards. His next shot, an 8-iron, was fat; his divot could've resodded a suburban lawn. They lost the hole. They lost the next hole, ten, and they lost eleven and now—no matter how you figured it— they were behind. Luckily, both Keegan and Quinn three-put- ted twelve and Gordon blindly rolled in a thirty-footer for the halve. Thirteen and fourteen were also halved, but only be- cause of their opponents' missed opportunities. Augie was starting to talk to himself. On the tee at fifteen, determined to get it going again, he took extra time setting up, double- checked his alignment, grip, stance—and proceeded to yank the ball horribly; it bounded deep into the left rough, almost out of bounds.

"Son-of-a-bitch."

He smacked the ground with the head of his driver. Kee- gan and Quinn exchanged glances and zipped away in their cart. Augie grabbed a 4- and a 5-iron when he and Gordon arrived at his ball, and Gordon promptly crossed to the opposite rough. As Augie was deciding which club to use, which to toss down, he became aware of someone standing by the row of sycamores separating the course from a large white house; it was Azy.

She knew enough not to talk, even to wave, until after he'd made the shot. Augie chose the 4-iron and hit a low screamer. It had good roll, that was all you could say for it. He picked up the extra club, and Azy and he converged in the rough. She wanted to know how they stood.

"We're either 2-down or 3-down, depending on the first hole."

"That was a fantastic drive."

"I just closed my eyes and swung."

He glanced over to see if Keegan and Quinn had made their shots—he didn't want to delay play—and came back to Azy. They were standing where they had stood the night before. "You can do it," she said. Then, completely surprising him, she put her hand on his upper arm and kissed him on the lips.

Augie just looked at her, not saying anything.

Gordon came zipping across the fairway, then braked. "Hi, Azy," he said.

"Hi, Gordon."

"How's your dad doing?" he wanted to know.

"They were 6-up at the turn."

"What else is new?"

"See you," Augie said to Azy.

"See you," she said.

HE had a pitching wedge on his next shot, and he knocked it stiff and sank the putt. His game picked up; really, his *scrambling* picked up. He recovered well from bad lies, the "must" putts fell. He and Gordon won fifteen and sixteen and tied seventeen, and on the last hole they were either all even or 1-down. Gordon drove first and sent his ball into the right rough (where else would his drive end up?) and Augie, for all his new confidence, duck-hooked his tee shot. He was very close to the swale separating the eighteenth hole from the first. Quinn was straight but not very long, and Keegan hit his best drive of the day—a two-hundred-and-thirty-yarder slightly right of center.

Quinn's second shot was a honey, landing on the apron; Gordon didn't get out of the rough; Augie's 5-iron just made it to the edge of a big greenside bunker; and Keegan, hitting last, dropped a 6-iron fifteen feet from the pin. Gordon picked up after missing his third shot and they motored toward the bunker. Suddenly he was shouting, "There's Kelly!"

A woman and a girl were walking from the patio toward the edge of the green. Gordon waved and they waved back.

Fuck, thought Augie.

Quinn stubbed his chip, said something, then chipped again and hit it too far, leaving himself a thirty-foot putt coming back. Keegan, shaking his head, told him to pick up. Augie's turn. He had to clear the trap and land on the fringe of the green; if he hit too firmly he'd land on the green itself and his ball would take off. He settled over it. One's head had to stay rock-still on a sand-wedge pop. He opened the face of his club to increase the loft, brought the club back, came neatly down. The ball jumped up, landed on the last inch of fringe, slowed and rolled toward the stick, stopping six feet short. Gordon cheered like a college kid at a football game, and Catherine and Kelly applauded. Off the green, very close actually to where Catherine and her daughter were standing, Kyle McIntyre, the club pro, was observing play.

Augie marked his ball with a dime, and Al Keegan lined up his putt; it was downhill and his ball just nicked the hole and rolled seven feet past. Still farther away than Augie, he putted again. He made a nice stroke and Augie thought the ball was going in, but it died five inches away.

"That's good," Augie said.

Keegan tapped in anyway, as if saying he didn't want any favors, thank you. Augie replaced his ball and picked up the coin. His putt was similar to the one on the first hole—only longer. The break was a quick left-to-right. He didn't consciously tell himself what the odds were of making it, but they weren't good. He took his time, reading the break from both sides of the hole, then took his stance. Catherine was talking to her daughter.

Not loud, not so he could hear what she was saying, but he distinctly heard her voice. Then suddenly she was quiet. He had the feeling Gordon had turned around, indicating to his wife to *shut the fuck up.* Augie tried to get his concentration back but all he could see was Catherine squatting on top of him in the early morning grayness. Jabbing at the air with her nose. Stop, he told himself. *Concentrate.* But he couldn't, or didn't. It occurred to him, as he stared down at his ball, that God had given Catherine her long peen-tipped nose for one reason—to ream out men's assholes. What was he doing to himself? He had to make the putt. It was a total guess. Perhaps he had the line, perhaps he didn't; then, for no reason, he angled the putter blade another degree—wondering if, unconsciously, he wanted to lose so he could get the hell out of Easthelmsford—and sent the ball away, so far to the right of the hole it seemed ridiculous. The ball started to break, then tailed off sharply. It continued sliding, falling, and Augie stood there, watching it as it caught the lip of the cup, circled a full one hundred eighty degrees—and dropped.

"Whoooo-heee! Aug-ie! Fantastic!" Gordon ran across the green and hugged him.

"See you guys on the first tee," Al Keegan said; by *his* figuring, the match was all-even.

But before Keegan and Quinn could drive off, Kyle McIntyre walked over. Keegan and Quinn were in their cart. Augie and Gordon were standing on the edge of the green. "I understand you gentlemen had a little disagreement on the first hole," McIntyre said with fine old-world inflections.

"To say the least," said Keegan.

"Well, the Committee's made a ruling on it," the golf professional went on. "Mr. Wittenbecher was entitled to play his first ball."

Keegan blew a fuse, jumped out of his cart and stormed up to the pro and told him Mr. Wittenbecher had committed himself to a second ball when he left the swale. Their match was now tied. They were about to tee off for sudden death—

"The Committee sees it differently, Mr. Keegan," said McIntyre.

"He looked for his ball in the swale. When he couldn't find it he went back to play a *second ball*," Keegan yelled. "He abandoned his first ball—"

"His partner continued the search," said the pro.

"Maybe. But why did Wittenbecher take his stance? His took his goddamn *stance*. He started his *swing*."

"The backswing isn't considered a swing," Augie said.

"I'm not talking to you," Keegan snapped. Then to the pro: "I'm calling the USGA on this."

"You're entitled to do that," said McIntyre.

"This is a goddamn fucking rip!"

"Al, come on—let's go have a drink," Quinn said.

"I'm not through with this, pal," Keegan said, looking straight at Augie. He got in the cart and drove off with his guest, and Kyle McIntyre gave his head a dismal shake and walked away.

"What was that all about?" Catherine asked, coming up.

As best he could, Gordon explained; then he introduced his daughter to Augie. Kelly was a very pretty girl. She had her father's bright Irish face and her mother's legs and slender body. "Hello, Kelly," Augie said.

"Hello, Mr. Wittenbecher."

Catherine turned to Augie, giving him a small, secretive smile. "So, you won."

"*He* won—I went along for the ride," Gordon said.

"That's not true," Augie said.

"Well, I think you're both wonderful," Catherine said, first embracing her husband, then their guest. Her lips touched

Augie's ear; then she said to her husband, "Let's have lunch on the patio."

"Super idea," Gordon said. "Go ahead and grab a table."

"See you in a little bit," Catherine said to Augie.

The two men got in their cart. "Hey, we did it," Gordon said, stepping on the pedal. "We beat those bastards."

"Yeah." Augie's voice sounded flat.

Gordon cut in front of the first tee, then steered along the macadam path to the club-storage room. Jimmy came out and removed their bags. Out of old habit Augie gave his clubs a quick spot check to make sure they were all there. Then he and Gordon walked toward the locker room. Inside, men were sitting on benches changing their shoes; others had towels wrapped around their waists. Some were drinking and talking loudly; some were just drinking. Augie spotted Al Keegan sitting in front of an open locker with Quinn; they were each holding a bottle of beer. Keegan was shaking his head and swearing. Quinn saw Augie, and Keegan looked up quickly as Augie followed Gordon into the men's room. They stood at the urinals, then crossed—*clack, clack, clack*—to the row of sparkling basins.

"Are we a team?" Gordon said, hitting the soap dispenser.

"We're a team."

Augie washed, rinsed, used a towel; saw himself in the mirror; was shocked by what he saw—the lines, the incredible tension in his face.

"Christ, that was some putt!" Gordon said. "I kept saying to myself, where is he aiming? You read it absolutely fucking *perfect.*"

Gordon combed his thick gray hair; his face had a glow—he looked very handsome. "Let's go kill a couple of cold ones, partner."

"OK," Augie said.

WHEN IT CAME his turn to order, after ev-
eryone else, Gordon said, "Hamburger platter, rare, and two St.
Pauli Girls." The waitress, a round-faced young woman with
short pudgy fingers, asked him if he meant both bottles at the
same time."

"I sure do."

She went away and Catherine turned to Augie. "I'm really
thrilled you won!"

"We haven't really won. We've advanced a round."

"What really burned their ass, they thought they had us,"
Gordon said. "On the last four holes you didn't miss a shot."

"I got lucky."

"You got inspired!"

The drinks came. Catherine had a bloody mary, Kelly a
Sprite, Augie a draft beer and Gordon his St. Pauli Girls. He
poured one, picked up his glass and said, "Onward and upward, partner."

"Onward and upward."

"Who do you play tomorrow?" Catherine asked. She had
on a sleeveless green dress with black daisies on it.

"I've a hunch we'll be playing Gilliam and Hrazanek,"
Gordon said.

"Have you ever had a hole-in-one, Mr. Wittenbecher?"
Kelly asked.

"One. Three years ago."

"Did you freak?"

"Right out, it was pretty exciting."

That was enough chitchat for daughter; it was mother's turn. "Truthfully now, Augie. What inspired you?"

"Gordon said I was inspired. I didn't say it."

"Why did you say it?" she asked Gordon.

"After talking with Elizabeth Flannery he played sensational golf," Gordon said. "Call it what you want."

"Where did you see Elizabeth Flannery?" Catherine asked Augie.

"She was standing outside her house, watching play."

"Right afterward you hit that great pitching wedge," Gordon said. "That turned it."

"What did you talk about?" Catherine asked.

"She wanted to know where we stood."

Catherine's face stiffened. "Where you *stood?*"

Augie realized what he had just said; he felt forced to clarify but wasn't happy that he had to. "Where Gordon and I stood in our match."

"Oh."

A loud cheer reached their table from the eighteenth green. "Somebody else just knocked in a winner," Gordon said.

"All my friends play tennis," Kelly said to Augie.

"Tennis is a good game . . ."

"Do you play?"

"Not so I'd tell anyone."

"Golf seems so slow and boring to me," she said.

"It can get pretty tense," Augie said with a smile.

"I like to run," the girl said. "You can't run playing golf."

"You could. But you're right—it is pretty slow."

Catherine finished her bloody mary. She was beginning to wiggle her leg. From where Augie sat, beside her, he could feel the subtle rhythm. The waitress brought their lunches and she and Gordon both ordered another round. Augie said he was doing fine. Then a cart with Dr. Flannery in it rolled by; a few moments later his partner and his partner's fiancée walked in, passing between the pari-mutuel tent and patio. Plumber was talking away, flushed from the round, the victory, life, his arm around Azy's waist.

"I guess they decided to play in," Gordon said.

"What does that mean?" Kelly wanted to know.

"You explain it, Augie," Gordon said.

"It means their match ended out on the course, but instead of calling it quits they continued playing, finished the round."

"Why, if their match was over?"

"For the fun of it, the practice—with the pressure off, people relax. Sometimes it's a polite thing to do if it's a lopsided score."

"Golf is all rules and manners, Kelly," Catherine said, as if she knew.

It's also life and death, thought Augie.

Plumber and Azy continued past the patio; just then he gave a little tug on her waist, drawing her in and kissing her cheek. "He worships the ground that girl walks on," Catherine said.

"Who wouldn't worship the ground Elizabeth Flannery walked on?" Gordon said, giving her a glance.

"It's more than that, they're *right* for each other. It's a match made in heaven.

"I get the feeling she doesn't love him," Augie said.

"She reveres him, it's so completely obvious. Look!"

But he didn't want to look. Catherine took a last bite of her grilled cheese and tomato sandwich, leaving a whole half untouched, then put her napkin on the table and lighted a cigarette. Gordon was demolishing his hamburger, and Kelly had worked her tuna melt down to manageable size. "We just couldn't have a better day for the beach," Catherine said.

"That's for sure," Gordon said.

"Augie?"

"I wanted to get some practice in—"

"After playing eighteen holes you want to *practice?*" Catherine said.

"I'd like to."

"We *won*, Augie," Gordon said. "Remember?"

"We had to scramble too much."

"What does *that* mean?" Kelly asked.

"It means you're making it too tough on yourself. The odds catch up with you."

"What odds?"

"Of getting up and down."

"Up and down what?"

"You're off the green—you have to hole out in two to stay alive," Augie said. "It's not a good bet."

"Well, of course if you want to practice, Augie, you can practice," Catherine said. "But later, OK? Now's the nicest part of the day. We have a really beautiful beach here in Easthelmsford . . ."

Gordon scribbled his name on the check and they stood up. His car was in the main lot but Augie's and Catherine's were in the auxiliary lot. They both said they would see Gordon and Kelly at the house; then they all left the patio and Catherine and Augie were on the walkway that ran behind the practice green and the tee. Twenty people had gathered around the tee and Steve McMahon was tossing a coin. Watching it spin in midair were four players; one of them—Kevin Donohue —called out: "Heads."

It was tails.

"Shall we go?" said Catherine.

"Would you mind if I watched?"

"If you want to."

"I'd like to."

"Fine," she said.

She circled the hedge and disappeared. Augie moved closer. "Sudden death —Flight 4," someone was saying.

The players shook hands, wished each other luck—exactly as they'd done eighteen holes ago. Then they played away, Kevin Donohue's team second. He was the last to place a ball on a tee; while he was taking his stance he inadvertently nudged the ball and it fell off, and one of the men quipped, "No mulligans, Kev." He reteed, grinning. Augie observed him closely; he was an attractive man, and he had a quality—a sort

106

of fallible quality—that probably made him all the more appealing to some. Especially women . . . Yet Azy had broken off their engagement. Family pressure? The feud? But wasn't it more than that? In his mind he saw Jack Flannery striding across the terrace four steps ahead of Janet O'Roehrs, announcing it was time to "shoot the gap." Arrogant. Self-possessed. The opposite of Kevin Donohue. His shot was deep but drew too much and bounded into the left rough beyond the swale. The players with their caddies left the tee and the gallery followed along.

Augie walked away, rounded the end of the hedge and went out to the parking lot. At his car he gave a look at the range, at the men practicing shots, working on their swings. Perhaps if the brothers Flannery didn't give you their blessing you had to take them on and beat them at their own game. Not necessarily golf.

He slid behind the wheel. As if he had to worry. As if he had a chance with Azy. It was a fantasy. Well, dream on, he told himself, and drove away.

AFTER thirty minutes, which included ten minutes in the surf, Augie had to put his clothes on. Everything. Socks, pants, shirt, hat. From past experience he knew that a half hour, the first time, was all the sun he could take.

Catherine was lying beside him in a black nylon tank suit —on her side, back or stomach. He was sitting; sometimes she slid her hand across the blanket and touched his hand. Gordon, splashing around in the waves, looked like a big old grizzly trying to snag a salmon. Kelly was sitting with some kids three or four blankets away playing cards; the boys looked considerably older than she and her friend, a blonde girl in a light-blue bikini . . . Catherine's hand found Augie's foot. He had hoped she would want to cool it with her husband's old friend, and right about now would be saying she'd had too many rob roys last night, she'd got carried away and had made a terrible mistake. That was what he had hoped . . .

She worked her fingers down inside his sock and stripped it off. Augie looked around; if anyone was noticing, the woman in the black suit was applying a sun-block to her friend's foot. Rubbing lotions on your companion's body was commonplace on the beach. Particularly to the area between the big toe and the adjacent one. That was done all the time, for Christ's sake, using a technique of sliding the index finger in and out, working it around, probing with it—

"Catherine, we have to talk about a few things," he said, bringing up both feet.

"I know, it's not fair," she said. "Wouldn't it be wonderful if we were the only people on the beach—"

"*Listen* to me—"

"You were fabulous last night," she said.

"Catherine—"

"I've never had an orgasm like that in my whole life!"

He felt terribly hot. As if he'd had three hours of sun, not thirty minutes. "You have to understand—"

"It wasn't good for you?"

"I didn't say that."

"My ribs are black and blue, I *hope* not—"

That moment Kelly came traipsing over with her blonde friend. The McSweeneys' daughter still had something of an innocent look, but Maureen—she was introduced as Maureen Devlin—didn't, not a bit. She was Kelly's age, except the young Miss Devlin was going on twenty-three. Her bikini was really like two tiny handkerchiefs rather carelessly placed on her body. And it was a body. Kelly asked her mother if she could spend the night at her friend's house.

"You spent last night at Maureen's?" Catherine said.

"She invited me again."

"Well, it's too soon."

"Mom—"

"I don't want you away two nights in a row."

"Why not?"

"The answer is *no.*"

"That's not fair!"

"I'll decide that, Kelly."

"Are you afraid I might have some fun?"

"Don't talk back to me. Now I want you to apologize to Mr. Wittenbecher."

"That isn't necessary," Augie said quickly.

"I think it is. What do you imagine he thinks of you?"

"I'm sorry, Mr. Wittenbecher."

"Who are those boys?" Catherine asked.

"Friends."

"They're too old for you. They have one thing on their minds."

"Mother, they're very nice boys—"

"I'm sure. Get your things."

Sand squirted behind Kelly's feet as she huffed off with Maureen. "Sex, sex, sex. It's *all* they think about," Catherine said, shaking her head.

The skin on Augie's cheeks and forehead felt stiff, taut, like a pelt on a stretcher. Gordon was just coming up on the beach. He grabbed a towel, then a beer from the cooler. Augie put on his sock. Gordon, dropping onto a blanket, asked him if this didn't beat the hell out of practicing.

ABOUT four-thirty they picked up their blanket, cooler, umbrella and other paraphernalia and tromped across the hot sand to the parking lot, where they deposited it all in the trunk of the tan car. Kelly was still pouting. She and Augie got into the back and Gordon, his wife in the passenger's seat, drove away.

"Shall we drop you off at the club?" Catherine asked Augie.

"I'd like to change, I'll take my own car. Thanks."

"I was thinking, maybe I should go with you," Gordon said. "Hit a few myself. It couldn't hurt."

"No—I've things I want you to do," Catherine said. "Remember, we're having a party?"

"So I don't go with you," Gordon said to Augie. "Just tell me, why do all my shots go right?"

"You cut across the ball on your downswing," Augie said. "That puts spin on it."

"Spin, like English?"

"Same thing. The ball curves because it's spinning."

"What exactly does 'cut across the ball,' mean, Augie?"

"Attacking it from the wrong angle, from *outside.*"

"Outside *what?*"

"An imaginary line running from ball to target—say the flagstick."

"How should you attack it?"

"From slightly inside that same line. When *you* swing, you come at the ball from outside that line. That's cutting across."

"And that's my problem?"

"Basically."

"How can I stop doing it?"

"It's not easy. Remember my first drive today, in the swale?"

"That ball went to the *left.*"

"There are two forces at work," Augie said, feeling self-conscious but getting into it nonetheless. "It's physics. One force is the angle of attack, with reference to the target line. Another force is the face of the club. If it's fanned open when it meets the ball, the ball will spin clockwise—for a slice. If the club face is closed, or hooded, you get the opposite effect. The ball starts left and keeps curving left."

"So the face of my club is open when it hits the ball."

"Yes. Plus you attack from outside."

"What should I do?"

"You have to stop cutting across the ball."

"By doing what?"

"By starting the downswing with your lower body."

"My *lower body?*"

"Yes. The legs and hips. The shoulders stay back."

"The *shoulders* start the downswing!"

"No, that's wrong."

"Are you a *pro?*" Kelly asked.

He laughed. "No. Lord, no."

110

"You sound like one."

"I don't know if that's a compliment or not, Kelly."

"Why didn't you tell me any of this when we were playing today?" Gordon said, turning onto Old Forge Road.

"You didn't ask me."

"You saw me doing it. I did it one hundred and fifty-seven times!"

"Well, you didn't ask me," Augie said.

WHEN he walked into the guesthouse, all he wanted to do was take off his damn trunks; they were damp and itchy. His stomach felt hot, and looking at the skin on his thighs and upper arms he saw it had a pinkish tint. He sat down on the edge of the bed and pulled off his trousers and trunks, then reached for a pair of undershorts. The room was like a kiln and he was sweating. After hitting balls at the club he'd stop by the locker room again. Whether the men's facilities at the E.C.C. were "part of the package," he didn't know; he wasn't going to ask.

As he was pulling on his shorts he heard someone approaching the guesthouse; then that someone was at the screen door. "May I come in?"

He reached for his pants. "Catherine . . . hi. Sure."

"How are you, Augie?"

"Fine. A little burned maybe," he said nervously. "Getting myself together here."

She came toward him on the narrow path gouged through the jungle of chairs, bicycles, skis and books; barefooted, and still in her black skin-tight bathing suit, she reminded him of a panther stalking prey. "I sent him to the store," she said.

The sweat was running down his arms and chest. He said nothing.

"Would you consider . . . delaying your practice?"

"Delaying it?"

"Just for a while."

"Ha-ha."

"Is that funny?"

"No—ha-ha."

"Why are you laughing?"

"Who's laughing?"

She sat next to him on the narrow bed; his trousers were on but not zipped up. "Do I amuse you, Augie?" she said, wriggling out of her straps.

He went to stand up; she grabbed one of his hands and placed it on her left breast, squeezing his hand shut. The nipple felt like a hard raisin in the middle of his palm. For a moment her eyes closed and she let out a moan. The material of her suit was so thin—or so clinging—that it revealed a small ridge, or rise, low down on her abdomen. Her eyes opened and she smiled. "We have time," she said.

"We do? I mean, Catherine, I don't think we do."

She fell back on the cot and pulled him down on top, her thighs separating; at once she began moving her hips, her thoroughbred legs up around his ears. Augie—in spite of himself—experienced an immediate, powerful charge, but he still pulled away. Catherine seemed to think it was to get ready for what she had in mind. As if following his lead, she slid her thumbs down inside the waist of her suit. She didn't see him backing away, working as she was to slip the black nylon suit over her hips. In another second he told himself he would run out—except near the house, at that precise moment, came a girl's high shout.

"Mom!"

The suit was at Catherine's knees, rolled, exposing the white panel in the crotch. Her pubic hair was dense, tightly curled, a dull brown.

"Mom, you out there?"

"That little bitch . . ." Catherine sat up, wriggling back into her suit. Augie zipped and belted his pants.

"Mom?" Kelly was getting closer.

"What is it?"

"Betty McKeon is on the phone."

"What does she want?"

Kelly didn't answer.

"She wants to see what we're doing," Catherine said. "Everything is sex to these kids."

The woman was incredible, Augie thought.

At the screen door, Kelly looked in. Augie and Catherine were both standing awkwardly, like actors just stopped by a director. "She baked some cherry pies, should she bring them over for dessert?" Kelly said.

"Tell her yes. That would be just lovely."

Kelly stood at the door, surveying the scene inside her parents' guesthouse. Augie noticed—he felt dizzy seeing it— that one of Catherine's straps wasn't up; it formed a loop across her upper arm. At least half of her breast was showing.

"Now run along," Catherine said.

Kelly stayed a moment longer, then went off. Catherine pushed against her forehead and took several deep breaths. "We can still do it," she said.

"Catherine, no."

"Why not?" She took down her other strap.

"I'm going," he said.

"Damn you, Augie. Don't do this to me."

"I'm not *doing* anything to you."

She squeezed her long skinny fingers. "Well, *do* something then. Make love to me—"

"Come on, Catherine, we can't—"

"All *right,* all *right.* Go practice your stupid shots. At least on the course you can get it in the hole!" She brushed past him, yanked open the screen door, let it slam.

Alone in the guesthouse, it seemed to Augie the whole weekend was in shambles, one short day after it had begun.

SOME TWENTY CARS were in the auxiliary lot and seven or eight players were still hitting balls on the range. Augie got out of his station wagon and angled toward the club, trying to put his exchange with Catherine, just now, behind him. From here on he had to stay clear of her; no ifs, ands or buts—just stay *clear* of her. He rounded the tall hedge. The only evidence of first-round play was McMahon's table and two folding chairs at the rear of the tee.

Jimmy was clearing the post-and-rail fence behind the practice green, carrying golf bags into the storage room, as Augie approached. The husky young man saw him and asked if he could be of any help.

"Could I have my clubs, please?"

"Sure can. Mr. Wittenbecher, Flight 12."

The boy went in and returned in thirty seconds with the bag. Augie thanked him. "How do you do it?"

"What's that?"

"Remember guests' names."

"I don't, all of them, maybe a few." Jimmy grinned. "But anybody who tells Mr. McMahon he doesn't know the rules of golf, I remember."

"That just slipped out, I'm afraid."

"I thought it was great. We're all sick of his Ancient and Royal bullshit," Jimmy said. "You going to play or practice, Mr. Wittenbecher?"

"I'd like to play."

"It's all yours." The youth gestured to the open tee.

"But I need the practice," Augie said.

He trudged across the parking lot, bag on his shoulder; golfers were leaving the range, returning to the club. One of the men coming in was the attorney who had sat at their table last night. Davenport. Fletcher Davenport. Of the barracuda jaw. He had on snappy red-and-black golf shoes, and he walked right on by without any acknowledgment.

Par, thought Augie.

When he got to the practice area he took a large bucket from the ball shack, chose a spot in the center of the teeing area and set his clubs in the stand. A tractor with a protective wire canopy was dragging a ball-retrieving unit, sweeping back and forth across the range. Only two other men were hitting; soon just one. He was in the deep grass on the far side of the practice trap hitting lofted shots, maybe eighty or ninety yards. For a moment Augie thought it might be one of the Donohue brothers, the shots were all so consistently, so handsomely struck. Then he realized it was the storage-room man, Curt Kolchak.

He watched him swing a few more times, then toppled the bucket and the red-striped balls rolled out. It was warm and the sun was at a sharp angle and he felt glad just to be away from the McSweeney compound. He took out a 9-iron, saw one shoe was loosely tied and propped his foot on one of the several park-type benches just behind the tee, retying the lace. He did some exercises and finally hit ten or twelve shots. Each started off OK but too quickly lost distance, dropping off to the right. A well-hit ball had a staying power, regardless of the distance; these shots didn't stay. They died. It was amazing he and Gordon had won today. He had scrambled well over the last four holes and had knocked in a couple of key putts (maybe Azy *had* inspired him), but you couldn't rely on scrambling. Sooner or later you were going to miss those six- and seven-footers. OK, stop. What am I doing wrong? What would his pro in Shufferville, John Magnarella, say to him? Whenever you're in trouble, Augie, go back to the basics. "Grip. Stance. Ball position. Alignment."

He checked all four. OK. Now, slow back—easy down.

The ball tailed off—no zip.

Again.

Same.

Again. Slow back, easy down.

Same.

He kept hitting, trying to work out the problem but didn't seem able to. Everything fizzled. He sat down on the bench, thinking maybe he was trying too hard. Then he asked himself, Why does it matter? Make any difference? Why can't I have a fuck-all attitude like Gordon? Win or lose, who cares? It's for fun, right? Was he getting rich playing golf? Would his picture be on the cover of Sports Illustrated if he won his flight here at Easthelmsford?

Maybe his ex-wife was right, he *was* wasting his life trying to make a little white ball go straight. There are so many more *productive* things you can do, Augie. Like devote more time to your career. What drives you? Twice a week, OK. Do you think I'd mind if you played golf twice a week? But, for God's sake, you never miss, rain or shine! His answer was always the same, not too inspired but at least consistent . . . It was something he really enjoyed, it wasn't hurting anybody, he wasn't hanging around barrooms chasing women. How could Abby fault him for the two to three hours he spent outdoors every afternoon?

She faulted him.

Fuck.

Augie stood, stowed his club, too strung out to continue. He'd take a shower and go back to the McSweeneys' and meet Betty McKeon, who was "just right" for him, according to Catherine. Maybe get 'faced. If nothing else it might serve him later on, if Catherine should decide to make another dawn attack on his quarters. Because when he drank too much—

"How's it goin'?"

He glanced up, startled. "Oh. Not too bad."

"Beautiful day."

"Yes, it is."

Kolchak was holding his pitching wedge by its head, as if it were a cane. "Congratulations on your win."

"Thanks."

"Some rhubarb on the first tee," Kolchak said.

"You saw it?"

"Saw it, heard about it—McIntyre wanted my opinion. I told him what he already knew—a teed ball isn't 'in play.' If you accidentally knock it off, is it a stroke? The only question was, had more than five minutes gone by? I told him three and a half—max, four."

"I'm kind of embarrassed by the whole thing," Augie said.

"Don't worry about it." Kolchak seemed a lot friendlier now, far more relaxed. "How they goin' for you?"

"Terrible," Augie said.

"What's the problem?"

"Beats me."

"Hit a few."

"Really?"

"Let me have a look."

Augie grabbed a lofted club, positioned a ball and took a swing at it. Altogether he hit five shots—one fairly good one, four awful. He looked up to hear what Kolchak had to say.

"Have we met before?" Kolchak wore a frown.

The question surprised Augie. "Before today?"

"Yeah. You seem familiar to me."

"I—I don't know. Not that I remember—"

"Ever play Sea Island?"

"No—"

"Go ahead, hit."

He hit seven 8-irons, two tolerable, the others awful; he looked up expectantly. Kolchak was still scowling.

"I know where it was," he said.

Augie thought he was getting a headache. "Where?"

"Pinehurst. I was an assistant pro there—before I took the job in Sea Island."

117

"You're a pro?"

"I was."

"I've never played Pinehurst," Augie said.

"I know you from *somewhere*. Wittenbecher, right?"

"Augie Wittenbecher."

He swished the face of his club along the ground, hoping Kolchak would get the message. *My swing—I have a problem.*

"Hit a few more."

"Let me use a different club."

"Sure."

He swapped his 8 for a 6. The shots weren't any better or any worse. Which made them all pretty bad. He looked up. Kolchak had an "ah-ha" expression on his face, a light in his eye, and Augie felt *now* he was going to say something. Give him the fix he needed—

"Birmingham!"

Fuck. "Michigan?"

"Yeah. It was my first job as a pro. Did you ever play the Birmingham Country Club?"

"Yes, I did. I spent two weeks in Birmingham once, visiting my sister and brother-in-law. They were members."

"What were their names?"

"Dean and Hannah Lavalle."

"Sure! Dean and Hannah. Nice couple."

Augie was silent, thinking, going back; it was coming to him as well. "Do you know something?" His finger was raised, and he was softly pointing it at Kolchak. "I took lessons from you!"

"I never forget a swing," Kolchak said.

"You're a hell of a player," Augie said. "You won the Michigan Open that year—I remember distinctly . . ."

Kolchak grinned. "Hit a couple more."

He hit six more shots.

"You had a beautiful wife, am I right?" Kolchak said.

"I thought so." I know so.

"She'd come down to the lesson tee and kind of eavesdrop. You still together?"

"No."

"Hit your driver."

Augie hit six drives—two duck hooks, four weak fades.

"He was tall, kind of a skinny, good-looking guy—brownish hair."

"Who?"

"Your brother-in-law."

"Oh. Dean."

"Didn't play too well."

"Not too well."

"Hannah was little, she got good distance for her size. Had a nice high follow-through."

"That's Hannah."

The tractor rattled in; a thousand loose balls were bouncing around in the retrieving unit like giant-size popcorn. The rig stopped behind the shack and a kid, maybe sixteen, lifted up the protective wire canopy and jumped out.

"Hey, I got to run," Kolchak said.

They shook hands. "Good seeing you again, Curt."

"Good seeing you, Augie. Keep swinging."

The club-storage manager walked away, still holding his wedge by the head. Augie knocked out three more losers and gave up for the day, almost overlooking that Kolchak hadn't told him a damn thing about his swing. Curt Kolchak should have been a diplomat—obviously the man wasn't going to be on record as having helped any of the players, and of course he was right. Augie dumped his bag off in the back of his wagon and continued to the club, thinking to shower and get back to the McSweeneys'.

Before he went into the men's locker room he stopped on the pathway to check the results of the day's play, as indicated on the pairing sheets on the storage-room wall. First, Flight 12.

The hockey player, André Gilliam, and guest Tom Hrazanek had won decisively, 5–4. McSweeney and Wittenbecher, 1-up. It gave him a charge seeing that. Tee-off time tomorrow morning for the second-round match between the two teams: 9:05. Augie's eyes went to the top of the sheet. Flannery and Plumber had slaughtered their opponents, 8–6.

Out of curiosity, Augie checked the results of other matches. In Flight 4, Kevin Donohue and Lewis Seland had lost in a playoff on the third extra hole. In the Championship Flight, Tim Donohue and Andy Mulligan had beaten Dennis Flannery and Frank Gildersleeve, 2-up. Jack Flannery and Larry Bisell had won handily, 6–5, as had Bob Donohue and his guest from Pine Valley, Ed Sargent.

Augie continued on to the lockers and used every toilet article the E.C.C. had to offer. His clothes, unfortunately, were the ones he'd worn earlier and had just practiced in; if he'd been thinking he would have brought a change with him, but at the time he'd only wanted to get away. Fast. Just reflecting on it depressed him.

He went out, walked by the practice green. A young man in khakis and a yellow T-shirt was practicing with the aid of a dozen tees he had strategically stuck in the turf. Two men were looking at the day's results on the storage-room wall. All in all, the day's golf was coming to an end. Augie glanced down the first fairway and continued out to the lot.

When he got there, he thought at first a female officer from the Easthelmsford Police Department was writing him out a ticket. Had he inadvertently taken a spot reserved for a handicapped person or club official? But then he saw she had on white shorts and a pink blouse, no policewoman's attire—and in any case he now recognized who it was. She was putting a slip of paper under his wiper blade.

"I won't pay, I'll fight it in court," he shouted from a small distance.

She looked up. "Augie, hi! I just wrote you a note."

"How did you know it was my car?"

"With a Shufferville Landfill sticker on the windshield, whose else could it be?"

"Known by your town dump."

She reached out and squeezed his wrist. "You won. I was excited when I saw it. I still am."

"Thanks, Azy. Let's see your note."

She was closer to the wiper blade and pulled out the slip of paper. On her finger a marquise diamond, big as the Ritz, sparkled. Seeing it, Augie wondered what he was doing. Under the circumstances only a fool would let his heart run . . . Then she handed him the note, with a light in her eyes that was lovelier by far than the diamond's, and the doubt vanished. He opened it and read: "Congratulations! I like to think our practice round helped. See you."

He folded the slip of paper, feeling like a kid who'd just got the nod from the most popular girl in the class, the one everybody wanted and he never imagined even saw him . . . "I'll tell you something, on seven I wanted to use a 4-iron, then I remembered how you said use one more club than you think, so I hit my 3 and put it five feet from the hole."

"Hey, that's great! I love it."

"Some other things helped too," he said.

They were standing close and he could still feel her kiss on his lips. "What are you doing now?" she asked.

"I was just heading back to Gordon's."

"Like to go for a drive?"

He glanced at his watch, he was already late. "I'd love to. It's just that they're having a party, and—"

"It's OK."

"How about later?"

"No, it wouldn't work out tonight."

"I want to see you, Azy."

"Maybe tomorrow."

They were close, what he was feeling was overwhelming. "I feel like we're in a fish bowl out here," Augie said.

"Then let's just pretend we're kissing."

"That's impossible to pretend."

She smiled. "Good luck tomorrow."

"Thanks."

She touched his lips with her fingers, then walked to a yellow convertible, waving to him as she drove away. He stood with his hands on the front fender of his car. The range was empty, deserted. He imagined the course was too. Twenty-four hours since he'd arrived, it was the cocktail hour in Easthelms-ford again.

Augie looked forward to—and equally dreaded—the next twenty-four.

H<small>E PULLED ON</small> a pair of white trousers, grabbed a navy-blue golf shirt and, walking to the door, pulled it over his head in the relative cool outside the guesthouse; he tightened his web belt with the brass buckle, put a comb quickly through his hair and walked across the yard. Gordon was at the rusty barbecue kettle, trying to slide open the damper; a bag of charcoal and a can of lighter fluid lay in the yellowish grass, close by. Closer, on the flat arm of a conveniently placed lawn chair, perched a dry martini.

"Can I help, Gordon?"

"Get me a rock, anything."

Augie took several steps toward the McSweeney property line, found a roundish stone near some scrubby bushes and came back. Gordon promptly used it to strike the fingertip handle on the damper. Augie saw what was going to happen, and on the third strike it happened: the little handle broke off.

"Shit."

"Do you have a screwdriver?" Augie asked.

"Let's not worry about it. Get yourself a drink."

Augie glanced at the table, its pocked surface concealed by a white cloth; on it were a styrofoam ice bucket, glasses and a wide assortment of bottles: wine, liquor, soft-drink. A dented old cooler rested on the ground. Just then Catherine came out of the house carrying a tray of hors d'oeuvres. She had on smooth-fitting beige slacks and a silk, sage-colored blouse.

Augie had always thought he liked horny women—until now. But then Catherine McSweeney wasn't horny, he suddenly decided, so much as sexually insane.

"Is anyone here going to make me a cocktail?" she asked, setting the tray on the table. "I live here too, you know."

"Coming right up," Gordon said.

Catherine walked away. "You can't keep a woman happy," he went on. "Just when you think they're happy they start pulling crap on you. Make her a drink, will you, Augie?"

Oh, boy.

"Talk to her."

"Gordon, a person's problems aren't something that a friendly little chat—"

"Give it a shot. We're partners, right?"

He didn't touch that one.

Gordon yanked at the tab holding the bag of charcoal closed. "Listen, I've been thinking. Do you know what we need tomorrow?"

"When tomorrow?"

"In our match."

"No, what?"

"Strategy."

Gordon hoisted the bag of charcoal and began pouring out briquettes. "They're good but we can beat them if we have a strategy. Do you know what I'm saying?"

"I know what you're saying but I'm not sure—"

"We have to gain a psychological *edge* on André Gilliam and his partner."

"Right."

"I have an idea how to do it."

Augie waited.

"I'll talk to you later. Go ahead, see what you can do."

Augie crossed the yard. Rainbow was lying in a hole, which he had obviously dug for that purpose, to one side of the back steps. As if still harboring grave doubts about the purpose of the man's visit, he gave Augie a slow suspicious eye as he went up the steps and opened the screen door. The bathroom door was ajar and Augie glanced in. It was neater than yesterday; someone had done a good job of cleaning, straightening it up. On the cutting board by the kitchen sink lay an assortment of celery, carrot sticks and mushroom caps. He looked around. Sitting on the loveseat in the living room was Catherine. By her expression and posture he thought she was having serious abdominal cramps.

He went up to her. Would she like a rob roy? He thought he heard a yes. In the kitchen he pulled down a bottle of Scotch and dry vermouth from the pantry shelf, mixed up a cocktail, grabbed a beer for himself, and in the living room again handed Catherine the drink.

He sat beside her, not close. "Gordon started the fire."

She didn't respond and he took a swig of his beer. "It's a lovely evening for a party. The weather's been great."

She turned, her small hazel eyes on fire with passion—or totally lifeless; he thought it strange he couldn't tell until he remembered that opposites were often confusing. Sometimes hot felt cold. You could be traveling north and swear you were heading south. Then there was love and hate. He knew something about that. "I'm not in the mood for small talk," she said.

"OK."

"He sent you in, didn't he?"

"He thought—he asked me to make you a drink, yes."

"Augie, the wonder-worker," she said.

"Catherine, if you want to tell me what the problem is I'll listen—"

"I'll tell you what the problem is—I'm in *pain.*"

"Would you like some aspirin?"

"Make light of it, you son-of-a-bitch."

"I'm sorry, I didn't mean to make light of what you're feeling."

"Well, I don't need an aspirin!"

"Where are you feeling the pain?"

"Stop playing with me, Augie!"

He lifted his beer can and took a sip. His hand was shaking, just slightly. "I seem to be saying all the wrong things. Maybe I should just go."

"No."

She came closer; that smell—like kindling just before reaching the flash point—touched his nostrils. "I know what I need, Augie."

"If it's what I'm thinking I can't help you."

"You're the only one who *can* help me."

"Catherine, what happened in the guesthouse—you're misinterpreting it."

"I'm misinterpreting the bruises I have? No man's ever grabbed me that way."

"That may be . . . but it was impersonal—"

"He'd say so too, I suppose."

Augie frowned; his worst fear was materializing. "We have to forget what happened. Can we do that?" Obviously she couldn't.

"You didn't answer my question."

"I didn't know you'd asked one."

She smiled a small icy smile. "If I told him how I got these bruises, he'd kill you."

"Not if you told him the truth—"

"Like how you were in me so deep I could feel you in my throat . . . Like how when you came I tasted you. *Tasted you,* Augie. He'd accept that, right? The *truth.* That wouldn't bother him?"

He wanted to throttle her. He remembered this past May when Gordon had telephoned and invited him to Easthelmsford. They'd play golf, go to the beach in the afternoon, do a little partying at night. It had all sounded so innocent, so pleasant—just what he needed, the perfect script. Now . . . "What do you want from me, Catherine?" As if he didn't know.

"To have you again. Does that surprise you?"

"I'm sorry—"

He thought, then and there, she might lose it. Start screaming. Attack him. He didn't know. "Then I'll tell him," she said matter-of-factly.

"Will telling him accomplish that?"

"No, *if* I tell him."

He nodded quietly—and it crossed his mind to have sex with her one, maybe two more times, if that was what it would take; then when he left on Sunday he'd kiss her goodbye, shake hands with Gordon. He sensed it would work, would save the weekend. Certainly a friendship. If not his skin.

But he knew it wouldn't work. "That's blackmail," he said.

"Call it what you want. I'm telling him we made love unless—"

"Fine. Do that."

He stood up; he was the one who was losing it. "Only at least say *fucked*. Tell him you jumped my bones in my sleep. I'm leaving, Catherine. I don't know if your party's over but this weekend sure as hell is!"

She reached for his hand; he pulled away but she got up quickly and clutched at his arms. *"Don't go."*

"I'm going."

"Please, Augie."

Amazingly, she smiled. Her face, her manner, were suddenly soft, considering how on edge she was—or just was. "I'm OK. I apologize. I've been acting like a fool."

He didn't trust her but didn't want to force the issue, even if it was only a reprieve. "Catherine, all I want is to have things go smoothly for *all* of us. There's only one way that can happen—"

"I understand. I really do. Will you stay?"

"Let's not talk about it anymore," he said.

A MINUTE later she was taking her husband's arm affectionately and peering at the coals. "They're coming along beautifully."

"I'm very good at coals," Gordon said.

"Isn't this nice?" Catherine said, glancing around the yard. "Just the three of us, like this, before the guests arrive."

Gordon gave Augie a slow, curious look.

"Tomorrow let's do something just by ourselves," she said. "Dinner out, definitely. Of course, Augie, feel free to invite Betty. If that's your wish."

"Thank you."

"We can have a couple of shooters first. Either here or at the club," Gordon said. "Then we could go to Marcel's."

"They have the most succulent escargot," Catherine said to Augie. "Do you like escargot?"

"I love escargot."

"Then it's on. Right now I have some last-minute things to attend to. Oh!" She spoke to her husband. "I've changed my mind about Kelly. She's been so helpful. Would you drive her to Maureen's?"

"No problem. Whenever she's ready."

Catherine gave his ear an intimate little kiss and walked away.

"I'll tell you, Augie, you missed your calling," Gordon said.

He gave his bottle of beer a little sideways motion.

"What in hell did you *say* to her?"

"I forget."

"You forget!"

"We just, you know, talked."

"Maybe that's all it took," Gordon said. "Sometimes she feels unappreciated. I guess she's really a very complex woman."

"I guess."

"Heavy Catholic background, I don't think she's ever worked out the difference between liking sex and thinking it's evil. Do you know what I'm saying?"

"I think so. It's—it's a basic dichotomy, right?"

"OK, here's what I'm thinking," Gordon said. "André Gilliam's a professional athlete so he doesn't tend to choke but he's got an Achilles' heel—and that's where we attack him, if he and his partner get too far ahead."

"This is the strategy you were talking about."

"Yeah."

Gordon dipped his fingers into his glass. He had once told Augie that popping the gin-soaked olive into your mouth, at or near the martini's end, was one of life's great pleasures. "His wife."

"What about her?"

"She's Gilliam's Achilles' heel."

"I'm not following you," Augie said.

"Listen to me. To look at her she's a sex symbol, but she's head of the biggest Pro-Life group on the whole fucking Island. Gilliam backs her one hundred ten percent. The mere mention of abortion drives them both up a wall. So if he and this Hrazanek guy get two or three holes ahead, you drop real casual—like in an aside to me—you say, 'Gordon, I was just elected chairman of my local Planned Parenthood.' "

"What'll he do?"

"Nothing, right away," Gordon went on, "but he'll be waiting for you to say something else. So when the four of us are together again, as we're all walking off the next tee or on the green, mention how you think women have a God-given right to control their destinies. In other words, *choice.* That's the buzz word, that's the word that gets those pro-lifers crazy."

"Then what?"

"He'll start getting worked up, lose his concentration— miss putts. I've seen it happen. But really to clinch it, you'll have to hit him where he lives."

"I will?"

"Augie, I'm talking One-Upsmanship here. After mentioning your position on Planned Parenthood and coming in with 'choice,' you say, 'Gordon, I've come to the conclusion that women who are anti-abortion are *really* anti-fucking.' I guarantee his drives will go all to hell—and that's Gilliam's strength, his drives."

"Why don't you say any of this?"

"Hey, I live here. He'd know what I was up to. You— you're an outsider. Subtlety, that's the ticket. Do you know what I'm saying?"

"Well, let's see how the match goes."

"Hell, yes. But this is the ace up our sleeve."

Gordon was fairly glowing. He'd had his first drink, his wife had just kissed his ear, the night was young and he had a grand plan for undoing the opposition the next day. "Whoever would've thought we'd be playing in a golf tournament together, Augie?"

"Not me. You used to say you hated the game."

"It seemed so dumb to me back then."

"I remember."

"But it was still a hell of a lot of fun."

"What?"

"College. Jesus, they were good times."

"They were. They were great."

"Whatever happened to Audrey Foster?"

"She died."

"No!"

"Two years ago. Cancer."

"That's too bad," Gordon said. "She was a hell of a fine girl. I always thought you two would get married."

"I thought so too. Listen, Gordon, if we lose tomorrow I'll be heading on home," Augie said.

"Bullshit. We're going to Marcel's. Escargot, remember?"

"It's just a long time to leave the kids."

"They're having a ball without you—I hate to tell you that, Augie." Gordon savored the last drop of his martini. "Plus you got your neighbor's daughter coming in. Relax."

"I've pretty much made up my mind."

"Well, she won't allow it, I'll tell you right now. And I'll tell you something else—we're going to win. So it's a moot point. Christ, what happened to my shirt?"

Augie looked down; there was a dark smudge across Gordon's stomach. "Looks like grease."

"Watch the coals, partner," Gordon said.

C   H   A   P   T   E   R   12

HE STAYED AT the barbecue kettle, poking
at the briquettes with a long-handled fork—they weren't ignit-
ing evenly—but not really thinking about what he was doing.
Then he noticed loose streams of ash sifting from the bottom of
the kettle, settling to the grass like volcanic dust. Afraid that
the bottom might fall out altogether if he continued poking,
Augie rehooked the fork to the handle of the kettle.

He finished his beer. It had all started, as he thought about
it now, when the Bud's Sunoco tow truck had pulled up to his
disabled car twelve miles south of Kingston. The driver was
eighteen, probably a high-school dropout, and angry. Crash,
slam, crunch—he raised the rear end of the Peugeot as if his
intentions weren't to tow it but to tear out its differential. Then
Augie had the pleasure of riding beside this sullen young man
in the cab of his truck. The seat was cracked, repaired with
strips of duct tape, and the boy kept swearing under his breath.
Augie glanced back at his car swaying and swerving as they
careened off the Thruway exit into Newburgh. When they finally reached the garage, the youth deposited the car uncere-
moniously beside the huge dumpster on the fringe of Bud's
crowded lot and tore off down the street.

Bud was an ex-Marine, an in-charge kind of guy who inspired confidence, and he could have Augie's car back on the
road in five hours. If he wanted to continue on his way now, he

could rent Augie a wreck—a '77 Pontiac—at sixty-nine dollars a day, plus tax and insurance. Where was he going?

"Easthelmsford."

"It's nice down there—beach, everything. For how long?"

"Probably four days."

Three other people were standing close by, waiting for Bud's attention. At ten-thirty, the day was already a scorcher. "What do insurance and tax come to?" Augie asked.

"About forty per day."

"So I'm looking at four hundred and fifty dollars altogether."

"Plus gas."

"We're not talking a new Corvette here, we're talking a '77 Pontiac. Isn't that kind of steep?"

"I just wanted to give you an option."

"Thank you."

Augie took out his handkerchief, wiped his neck and headed for the soda machine, standing at the waiting-room door like the world's brawniest bouncer. It was then he heard a voice—whose, he couldn't say, but if it wasn't his, whose could it be? "Once your car's fixed," it was saying, "turn around and go home. This bodes bad. Real bad."

Maybe, he was thinking now, he should've listened . . .

AROUND the corner of the house someone suddenly appeared—a fortyish, plump woman with short brown hair, wearing a white cotton dress with a drop waist and a pleated skirt. She saw Augie and continued across the yard, a couple of pies in her hands. Her legs were heavy but not shapeless. The same could be said for her entire body. Six or eight years ago she had probably had an hour-glass figure; everything was still proportional, just bigger. So here was his date, the woman of "good values." Compared to Thelma Quick of Bud's Sunoco, Betty McKeon was a size 3. But she wasn't a size 3 or a size 10 even. She might have been considered an armful, as a first impression, if she were pretty. But she was unpretty, with a dull

round face and a thick nose. Augie watched as she stopped at
the table and put down her pies. "Betty?" he asked, feeling
depressed.

"Yes!"

"I'm Augie."

Her complexion was light, almost pasty. "How are you,
Augie?"

"Just fine." He went up to her. "Your pies look great."

"Thank you."

She offered him a smile. It brought a certain light to her
eyes, momentarily transforming her face. He also noticed she
had beautiful teeth, absolutely white and even. "I see I'm the
first one."

"Yes. Catherine and Gordon are both inside. Can I get you
something to drink?"

"A glass of wine, if you have it."

"White, red?"

"White, please."

Augie filled a glass, then reached in the cooler and scooped
out a brew. Betty thanked him for the wine and had a little sip;
she had short, stubby thumbs.

"Where do you live, Betty?"

"East of here, in Riverton."

"What do you do? I mean, do you work?"

"I'm a dental hygienist."

"In Riverton?"

"Yes. I work for a periodontist."

"They say the key to healthy teeth is healthy gums."

"That is so right," Betty said. "But there's a step you left
out. Flossing. That's the real key. Only four percent of Ameri-
cans floss on a daily basis."

"I'm one of the ninety-six then. I have trouble getting the
floss between my teeth."

"That's because you don't know your teeth. Flossing isn't
difficult if you know your teeth."

"How does one get to know one's teeth?"

"Your teeth are like a path through the woods. The more

you take it, the more familiar it becomes. I can floss in my sleep."

To sleep, perchance to floss, Augie thought.

"It takes practice and time," Betty said.

"Maybe I've never given it a chance."

"Just tell yourself you're going to start, then floss once a day religiously."

"What time do you suggest?"

"I do it just before bed. Because it's when you sleep that plaque builds up quickest."

"You mean plaque knows when a person is sleeping?"

She seemed to think it was funny. "When a person sleeps their mouth is usually closed, it's warm and dark and moist inside and the bacteria multiply. In a study that came out this spring in *Periodontics* it was proven that snorers have twenty-one percent fewer periodontal disorders than nonsnorers, for that very reason."

"That's the first good thing I've ever heard for snoring."

She gave him a faltering smile; the transformation to prettiness was only partial, but it was something. Then there was silence. Now what? But before he could think of something new to talk about—a topic that might produce a few more laughs or at least smiles—Rainbow trotted up, rear-half trailing his front-half at a five-degree angle. He ignored Augie and went directly to Betty, excitedly wagging his tail.

"Hello, Rainbow," she said.

"You know this dog?"

"Oh, yes."

She patted his head, but the flea-bitten mongrel wanted more than mere affection. He was too short to put his nose directly in Betty's crotch but he was making every effort to do it. "Rainbow!" Augie shouted.

Betty took a step back; the dog followed, then jumped her leg. Augie yelled, made a threatening arm gesture, but Rainbow pumped away, clutching at Betty's calf with his front legs, tongue stupidly lolling out of his mouth. Betty, uttering a muffled shriek, tried to brush him off; and Augie, having had it, took careful aim and caught the beast square in the brisket with a soccer-style kick. Rainbow was propelled back, then got unsteadily to his legs and began snarling at Augie, who made as if to lunge, hoping to frighten the animal away; but Rainbow didn't frighten. Finally, as if he had only wanted to make a point, Rainbow trotted off, misaligned a few extra degrees.

"Are you all right?" Augie said to her.

"My stocking will never be the same, I'm afraid."

He glanced down; there was a huge run in the nylon, up and down the shin bone. "I'm awfully sorry."

"No harm. Maybe Catherine will be able to lend me a pair."

"I'm sure she will."

"Well, I appreciate your concern." Betty smiled fully now and her face took on a madonnalike quality. "Catherine described you as someone with wonderful old-fashioned values."

"That's exactly how she described you."

She became pretty again, laughing, although it was a fleeting thing. "It's what I look for in a man more than anything else, their values," she said.

"If a person doesn't have your values, where are you?"

"Exactly."

Betty sipped her wine. "It's my opinion," she continued, "that the great majority of men today are callous and conceited. That's why men who care are so . . . exceptional."

"Caring is a good quality."

"I refuse blind dates, I haven't accepted one in five years," Betty said. "They never turn out and then the evening is always so painfully *long*. But I liked the way you sounded when Catherine called me. She gives you very high marks."

"Catherine is too kind."

"She said you were a gentleman, you wouldn't harm a flea."

"I just kicked a dog."

"That's entirely different. Most men today turn their backs on women in trouble. I hate that attitude. Where's gallantry?"

"Dead, I'm afraid."

"Not completely."

She smiled into his eyes. The back door opened and Gordon walked over in a short-sleeved Columbia-blue golf shirt. Looking at him, Augie would have thought his old friend hadn't a problem in the world. He welcomed Betty graciously, they chitchatted for a few moments, the door opened again and Catherine stepped out and waved, as if from a balcony to a crowd of hundreds; then she came down the steps and crossed to where the three of them were standing.

"Catherine," said Betty. "Hi!"

"Betty!"

"You're looking so well."

"Well, thank you. So are you." Catherine gave her a kiss, missing her cheek by three inches. "Thank you so for the pies. They look scrumptious."

"It's my pleasure."

"I see you two have met," Catherine said, giving Augie a little nod.

"Oh, yes," Betty said.

"We've been hitting it off really well," Augie said.

"Well, I knew you would!"

"I'm thinking of buying a condo," Betty said to Catherine.

"How exciting!"

"I've finally had it with rent."

"That's so understandable," Catherine said.

"What do you think of Chelsea East?"

"It isn't all that attractive from the outside, in my opinion, but the prices are excellent."

"What would you recommend?"

"You should look into Easthelmsford Arms."

"Aren't they awfully expensive?"

"You'll be pleasantly surprised. And they're elegantly appointed, in every detail."

"I'll call you."

"Wonderful!"

Then Betty was saying something to Catherine privately,

and the next moment she excused herself and went with Catherine to the house. "What do you think?" Gordon asked.

"She seems like a nice woman."

"Betty's all right. No Rose Trippico, but what the hell."

"You like Rose Trippico, don't you?"

"She has this ass, Augie. Once before I die, I want her to sit on my face."

THE women reappeared shortly, and then Kelly came down the steps carrying a small red duffel over her shoulder. Augie remembered the girl's look as she gazed into the guesthouse, seeing her mother—her swimsuit off one shoulder—standing by the cot with their weekend guest. As Gordon was about to take off to do taxi duty, new guests—a trim, athletic-looking man and a woman with highly coiffed jet-black hair—turned the corner of the house.

"Oh, it's Bill and Sally!" Catherine shouted.

Gordon stayed for the greeting and introductions. Their name was Lackaye. Bill Lackaye had on a pair of designer jeans and his wife was wearing a miniskirt and sequined blouse. Augie imagined she had probably won a beauty pageant twenty years ago in Teaneck. The man looked oddly familiar.

"How'd you guys do today, Bill?" Gordon asked.

"Whipped their tails, I had a 79 on my own ball," Lackaye said, bragging. "How about you?"

"We beat Al Keegan and his partner on the eighteenth. It turned nasty."

"I heard something about that. What happened?"

"Augie looked at a rule one way, Keegan another way."

"What was the rule?"

"You explain it, Augie," said Gordon.

Suddenly he remembered where he had seen Lackaye before, at the Flannerys' cocktail party—the man so enamored of his swing that after each shot he would pose with the club, grace itself. "On one, my first ball was in the swale some-

137

where," Augie said. "Keegan said I committed myself to playing a second ball when I went back to the tee."

"Well, didn't you?"

"We hadn't looked for five minutes, and I didn't take a swing at the new ball. So the answer is no."

"It's usually a gentleman's rule if you go back, you've committed yourself to a second ball," Lackaye said.

"I couldn't find too many gentlemen around actually," Augie said.

Gordon laughed but Lackaye didn't. He and Keegan had probably gone to Exeter together. Catherine told Gordon that Kelly was waiting and he promptly left. "Let me get you a drink!" Catherine fairly shrieked at the Lackayes.

The couple followed Catherine to the table; another couple, older, less snappily attired, and a single man with froggy eyes, arrived. Betty said she didn't know the couple but the man was one of Gordon's best friends, Frank Dugan, who had just retired as a special agent for the FBI. He was a bachelor but she didn't think a confirmed one; in her opinion he was seriously looking for the first time. Augie had nothing to say; to someone else he might have said Frank Dugan should pull his pants up, because the crack in his ass was showing. But then Augie realized it wouldn't do the former agent any good to pull up his pants, because they would slip right back down again. The man didn't *have* an ass.

Lackaye and his wife drifted over to a corner of the yard with their drinks. Augie got the impression they felt like they didn't know what they were doing here. Betty said that Bill Lackaye had the Buick-Audi-Peugeot dealership in town. He had given Catherine a very good trade on her new car.

"Maybe I should have him look at my wagon," Augie said.

"What do you have?"

"A Peugeot, getting on."

"They're a nice car. I went to the Honda agency myself. I have the Civic—I get thirty-nine miles to the gallon on it."

"Great."

Betty looked across the yard. "Aren't they an attractive couple?"

"She seems sort of brittle."

"They practically *live* in Atlantic City."

"Oh."

"Donald Trump flies them back and forth, plus picks up their entire tab—hotel, food, shows. Everything. Or at least he did before his financial troubles."

"I wonder would Donald do that for me. We have a little county airport just outside Shufferville."

"Catherine has a wonderful ability to mix people," Betty said. "It's such a gift."

"I'm noticing."

"Bill is supposed to be an excellent golfer."

"Bill?"

"Bill Lackaye."

"Oh, right. He had a 79 on his own ball," Augie said.

WHETHER it was meant to be a larger party, he didn't know, but only thirteen people showed up, and Gordon, in a chef's apron featuring a maniacal golfer wrapping his driver around a tree, cooked up spareribs and chicken, and the guests helped themselves to potato salad, corn on the cob, coleslaw and sliced tomatoes. After the main course came coffee and Betty's pies. Catherine had vanilla ice cream for those who wanted it à la mode—Gordon had his piece with two big scoops. But for all the food and drink, it wasn't a good party. Maybe Catherine had a wonderful ability to mix people, but for tonight's affair she'd messed up, bad. No one seemed to know anyone else; or everyone disliked everyone else. Whatever it was, the party never got off the ground. The Lackayes chatted with a few people but stayed mostly to themselves. When they moved about they operated as a unit. They reminded Augie of celestial bodies, their relationship forever fixed, traveling through space. Betty was talking about her first marriage. Her husband had taught fifth grade in Riverton and they couldn't have been happier; then one day he was arrested while leaving the school and charged with molesting one of his students, a nine-year-old boy. Betty was drinking wine and talking nonstop. Augie felt sorry for her (for what she was saying) but she really went on and on. The upshot of it all was that the discovery of her husband's aberration had forever changed her life. How would she ever be able to have faith in any relationship again? Because you never knew. You never *knew*.

"A man seems loving and thoughtful, but underneath what is he? *What is he?* A pervert!" She emptied her wine glass. "Trust. That's the key. Is someone really *there* for you, or is it surface? Surface!"

"Hold still," Augie said, setting down his beer. "Mosquito."

He gently removed Betty's glass from her hand and gave her elbow a tap. When a little trickle of blood appeared, he went to the table for a napkin and came back, using it to dab at the blood.

"You have such a nice way of doing things," she said.

"How many ways are there to kill a mosquito?"

"You thought of my wine. Most men are such klutzes."

"I wasn't into ruining your dress."

"That's what I'm *talking* about."

She gave his wrist a little touch, accompanied by a smile. If he wasn't careful, he'd find himself in Betty McKeon's warm round arms before the evening was over. He felt certain she had a fabulous king-size bed and he could use a good night's sleep! But was it what he wanted? With Catherine, he should have made it absolutely clear from the start—clearer than he had—that he wasn't interested. In some unintentional way, had he led her on? Invited her to the guesthouse? Had her racy legs weakened his resolve sufficiently, so that, in spite of his outward rejection of her, he had given out subliminal signals to the contrary? He didn't know, he would never really know. But, early as the evening was, he felt the same thing happening with Betty. Because here he was making points on top of points! What in hell was he doing? Maybe he should start into some heavy drinking—

"Augie, your daughter's on the phone."

He looked over. Catherine was on the steps. Augie excused himself and crossed the yard to the house. Feeling anxious, he took the phone at the little table in the kitchen. Actually it was his neighbor's daughter, Maria, who was on the line. She and Heather were just cleaning up the kitchen and the dishwasher started smoking and Heather thought she'd better call.

"Is it still smoking?"

"Some. We turned it off."

"OK, Heather will show you where the circuit breakers are. The dishwasher is the sixth or seventh switch on the right —it's labeled. Just throw it."

"Throw it?"

"Grab it with your fingers and snap it, like an ordinary light switch."

"All right."

His son picked up. Today he had parred the sixth hole for the first time. Augie was worried about the smoking dishwasher (really about the house), but he was glad for Brian, who then told him exactly how he had played every shot for the par. "Isn't that all of them now?" Augie asked.

"No. I still have the second hole."

"Two's tough. I'm always happy with a bogie there. How's the dishwasher, Brian?"

"Still smoking. How you hittin' 'em?"

"Not great. It's a different kind of golf down here."

"Why is that? A ball's a ball."

"It's a little difficult to explain."

"Dad, look—just pretend you're home."

"I'll try."

His daughter came on. They had flipped the circuit breaker. Now what should they do? Augie said if it continued smoking, call the fire department. Explain the situation so the dispatcher doesn't send out the new hook and ladder. But don't hesitate.

"OK."

"I'll call you tomorrow, right after the match," Augie said. "Have you met anyone?"

"I've met a beautiful woman—I like her. I think she likes me."

"Hey, great. What's her name?"

"Azy . . . She's engaged."

"Bummer!"

"I know."

"Go for it anyway, Dad."

"We'll see. Good night, angel. Keep your eye on the dishwasher."

"Good night, Daddy."

He hung up, stayed by the phone for a moment, thinking, then went past the bathroom door, ajar, and back outside.

Catherine broke away from one of her guests, a fifty-year-old man with a devilish laugh, and walked over to Augie as he came down the steps. "Is everything all right?"

"My dishwasher was smoking."

"Is it serious?"

"It could've been. I don't think so now."

"Well, that's good."

She smiled intimately. She was getting that look. "Did you have enough to eat?"

"Oh, yes. Gordon did a great job."

"One thing he can do is barbecue." She sipped her rob roy. "How do you like Betty?"

Augie looked across the yard. At the moment she was talking with Frank Dugan. Augie hoped she was falling madly in love with the ex-fed and in another forty minutes would run off with him into the Easthelmsford night. "She's a really nice woman," he said.

"She favors you," Catherine said.

"Excuse me?"

"She favors you."

"You mean, over Frank Dugan?"

142

Catherine laughed. "Silly, they've known each other for years. They're like brother and sister."

"Oh."

"Augie, you're not jealous, are you?"

He was about to answer no, then thought if he answered yes it might help build a barrier between him and Catherine. A shield. Betty McKeon would be his own private "strategic defense initiative" for the rest of the weekend. "She seems interested in him, that's all I meant," he said. "And I was just wondering if I should step aside—"

"Step aside!" Catherine was charmed. "Augie, you are such a boy—so innocent! For the third time, she *favors you.*"

"I favor her."

"There you go!"

She leaned in to give him a congratulatory kiss, as it were. Her face was turned slightly, so anyone would see that Catherine was merely bestowing a harmless affection on her guest. But son-of-a-bitch if she didn't glide her hips in and flick his bic. She was a goddamn bic-flicking pro. And Betty McKeon didn't worry her a bit. Then Betty was there, all warm and aglow. Showing a certain proprietary right, she put her hand on Augie's shoulder and asked if everything was all right at home.

"At home? Oh—everything's fine—house might burn down."

BY TEN-THIRTY everyone had said goodnight and Catherine suggested they move the party; it was a glorious evening but she wanted to sit down for a change. Rainbow was sleeping in the dirt by the steps as she, Gordon, Betty and Augie went inside.

Gordon suggested stingers and Catherine seconded the idea. Betty's hand was between Augie's shoulder blades, just kind of making little circles as they sat together on the loveseat. He had the weird sensation that something was crawling on his back. Gordon immediately started for the kitchen to perform the high office of mixologist when Catherine spoke up. This was silly, she said. It was one of the big weekends of the summer season. They should all go out!

Gordon appeared receptive. "Where did you have in mind? The club?"

"I was thinking of the Inn at Quidnock."

"Oh, I love the Inn at Quidnock!" Betty said.

"Partner?"

Even with the insufferable heat and monster mosquitoes, the guesthouse had a sudden, wonderful appeal. Just to go there and barricade the door and be alone. "Sure," Augie said.

R IVERTON, WHERE BETTY lived, was on the far side of Quidnock. Therefore she'd take her own car. Augie —well, what was he going to do, drive with Gordon and Catherine? Trail along in his station wagon? No. He slid beside Betty in the passenger seat of her new Honda.

Gordon, maneuvering his wife's "Lackaye" Buick, followed Betty out of the driveway. She made a left where Old Forge crossed Beach Boulevard. Augie said her new Honda drove nicely. As if waiting for the cue, she then gave him a rundown on all its features: four-wheel disc brakes, rack-and-pinion steering, climate-control, McPherson struts, five-speed synchromesh stick; but the thing she loved most was the "hunt-and-lock" capability on her am-fm stereo. The only "extra" was the moon roof. Would he like it open?

"Great."

"It's a perfect night for it," she said.

She operated a handle above her head and a panel popped up; if they didn't actually see the moon they saw a whole lot of stars. The radio was on, though at the moment it was locked on a station Betty didn't like, so she touched a button and it began "hunting." When it stopped, Augie had the sensation of a cat pouncing on a sparrow. It was a Neil Diamond song and Betty loved Neil Diamond; his lyrics spoke to her. Behind them headlights flashed up and down; up and down. She raised her hand through the opening in the roof and made a waving motion.

"They're such fun, aren't they?" she said to Augie.

"They're a barrel of monkeys."

"Catherine always has such good ideas."

THEY drove for seven minutes, crossed a bridge spanning an ocean inlet. A mile farther along Betty turned off the main highway and went down a street that for the first fifty yards had an exquisitely landscaped median separating the flow of traffic. There was no traffic. It was a quiet area. No gas stations, no fast food, no night spots. Looming in the shadows, behind beautiful shrubbery and trees, were houses even grander than the ones in Easthelmsford. "This is Quidnock," Betty said.

He imagined the zoning laws were carved in granite. They passed a quaint business district, little turn-of-the-century stores and shops, long closed for the evening. Then Betty was saying, "Here we are. Good, a spot!"

She pulled over and parked diagonally on a sandy shoulder. Just ahead stood a large frame building, all-white, all-lighted, with a neatly trimmed hedge in front and a wide flagstone path leading to a red door. Catherine and Gordon didn't find a parking place and had to make a U-turn. Betty kept the radio on; the stars were glimmering through the open roof. She filled up the driver's seat, but her hips were round and her breasts heavy and her dress fell sensuously through her thick thighs and she was kind of smiling at him, looking quite pretty actually—her smile worked miracles—and he told himself to go with the flow. Catherine was a maniac, and what was the worst that could happen to him here? Was it such a hardship to sleep in a woman's bed? If Betty McKeon wanted a roll, he could handle it. He wasn't attracted to her but what the hell. Ease off, Wittenbecher, he told himself.

"Quidnock seems a charming little town," he said.

"It's *the* place."

"Why don't you buy a condo here?"

Her head went back in a laugh. "To start with, there are no condominiums in Quidnock. If there were I wouldn't be able to afford the *kitchen* of one."

He smiled at her, liking to think he was loosening up. "Do you come here often, I mean to the Inn?"

"I was here with a girlfriend earlier in the season."

"Is it a singles spot?"

"Kind of, kind of not. It's just a fun place—a lot of awfully nice people. How long will you be staying?"

"The McSweeneys want me to stay through Sunday."

"Is that a problem?"

"If Gordon and I lose tomorrow, I'll probably head back tomorrow."

"Then don't lose . . . I'd like to see you again."

"That would be nice."

"Are you good?"

"It depends. At what?"

She liked that he was showing interest, was flirting with her. "I meant golf."

"At golf I'm so-so."

They were looking at each other and he seemed to think they were coming closer and would kiss. "Oh," Betty said, glancing over his shoulder, "here they are now."

COMPARED to last night's crowd at the E.C.C., the people at the Inn at Quidnock seemed considerably younger, Augie thought, as he and Gordon followed Catherine and Betty (themselves following a very slender hostess) to a table in the lounge. He spotted several affluent-looking men and women seated at tables and at the bar, probably in their fifties, but mostly it was a late-twenties, mid-thirties crowd. If he could recognize a yuppy, these were yuppies. This was a yuppy fucking haven. A black piano player, wearing a red ascot and a white shirt with frills, was singing, and couples were dancing in a small area just off the lounge.

Their waitress, a big blond woman—not unattractive but

hard—appeared at their table. Catherine ordered a stinger, Gordon seconded the motion, Betty went for a Baileys on the rocks and Augie asked for a bottle of domestic beer. Everyone in the lounge was laughing and talking and the piano player was crooning, "Gibral-tar may crum-ble, the Rockies may tum-ble," and people were dancing; and Augie told himself, again, to make the effort. Deep down he felt lousy—he saw himself sitting on the Easthelmsford beach, alone, just staring out at the dark ocean. But he wouldn't give in to his mood. He was here, make the most of it.

Their waitress returned. Augie reached for his wallet, wanting to pay, but Gordon said no, run a tab. Then he lifted his glass and made a little toast, celebrating friendships, new and old. It was nicely said, and Betty seemed particularly touched. Before she sipped her drink she made intimate eye contact with Augie.

"Ummm! Love a stinger," Gordon said. "How's your Baileys?" he asked Betty.

"Wonderful."

"I like Baileys. It's a nice drink," he said.

"The periodontist I work for buys Emmets."

"It's half the price," Gordon said.

"Whenever he has a barbecue he puts out his briquettes with a sprinkler can, then lets them dry and uses them again. The other day he was telling us he got three cookouts from one shake."

"This vice-president I do a lot of work for at Shore," Gordon said. "He's got a nine hundred thousand dollar home and he tells you not to flush the toilet if you just do a tinkle."

"I can't stand it when somebody doesn't flush the toilet," Betty said.

"It's so disrespectful of the next person," Catherine said.

"Then another thing he won't do," Gordon said. "He's got this dishwasher with enough buttons on it to get you to the moon, but he'll never let it run through the dry cycle."

"What does his wife say?"

"They're two of a kind."

"That's what leaves spots on the glasses," Betty said.

"Most rich people are cheap," Catherine said.

"That's how they got rich," Betty said.

BETTY and Catherine were talking mortgages and Gordon was telling Augie on the q.t. that his brother Brendan had got fucked out of this bar every weekend from Memorial Day to Labor Day for three years running. "Then he went and tied the knot."

"To someone he met here?"

"Right at that bar. He had these black cowboy boots on. That was what she saw when she first walked in—and she had this feeling, she knew."

"Knew what?"

"That this was the man she was going to marry."

"By his *boots?*"

"That's what she always says."

Their waitress came up, inquiring if they wanted a second round, and Gordon said yes. The new drinks arrived and Augie asked Betty if she would like to dance. She said she would love to. They walked out to the floor and began. She was surprisingly light on her feet and she followed him easily; her face was nuzzled into his shoulder and chin. His hand was on her back; her dress had a damp feel. She didn't seem interested in talking, just dancing. The next song was faster and they did a mild jitterbug. She again followed his leads, smiling a couple of times as she came in from a twirl. Walking back to the table, they held hands.

Seated again, Augie picked up his glass, almost emptying it, and Betty used a napkin to dab under her chin. "You two cut a mean rug," Catherine said.

"Augie's a very good dancer," Betty said.

They talked, drank; then Catherine announced, quietly, "The Flannerys just walked in."

Augie kept his eyes on his beer glass but Gordon and Betty looked over. Dr. Flannery and his wife and Gil Plumber and

Azy were following the hostess into the lounge. "Always like to see the competition out partying," Gordon said.

"So that's Elizabeth Flannery's current," Betty said.

"Slightly more than current, they're engaged," Catherine said.

"Oh, really. What does he do?"

"He owns the Chicago Blackhawks," Augie said.

"And he's the nicest man," Catherine said. "So funny!"

"Well, she held out—she must be thirty-five," Betty said.

"Elizabeth Flannery has always known exactly what she wants," Catherine said in a definitive tone.

"I knew Kevin Donohue's father, he was having periodontal work done at our office when—when Kevin tried to, you know," Betty said. "Mr. Donohue had no love for her, you can bet on that. He called her a user."

"I'm not defending her," said Catherine.

"Then she lands a man that's rich and charming. Where's any justice?"

"She hasn't paid a price? Where are her best years?"

"That's true," Betty said. "I can't stand anyone who thinks love is a card game—you deal, you discard, you draw. Where are people's values?"

"Exactly—where are they?" Catherine said.

"Well, I guess you took care of *her*," Gordon said.

"I hate being catty, but she deserves it," Betty said.

"Augie, dance with me," Catherine said.

"Excuse me," Augie said to Betty.

"Of course."

They got up and he followed Catherine to the floor. It was a slow number and she came in close. Her face was pressed against his and he tried to pull slightly back but her sinewy right arm held him snug, like a goddamn bungy cord. Over her shoulder, as they continued dancing, Augie saw the Flannery table. Dr. and Mrs. Flannery were seated facing the dance floor, while Gil Plumber and Azy were seated at forty-five degree angles to it. He could see them both in partial profile. Plumber was talking away; he had on a tan blazer and a red silk shirt. A waitress was just putting drinks on their table. Azy was wearing a cotton dress, a cool melon, arms and shoulders bare. Catherine looked at Augie and smiled, her body flat against his.

"Tell me you'll still be staying," she said, "even if you lose tomorrow."

"I'll probably stay."

"Oh, wonderful. We could all drive to Brewster Point. It would depend when you finish but we could have a late lunch —the town has some terrific restaurants. And the lighthouse is beautiful."

"Fine."

"Then I was thinking for later—we could have a cookout on the beach right in Easthelmsford instead of going to Marcel's. Get some big blankets and do steamers, corn and lobsters."

"Terrific." The tone didn't match the word.

"Unless you and Betty would just prefer being by yourselves."

"There's always time for that."

"You like her, don't you?"

"She's nice."

Her hand slid up his back and her fingers touched his hair. "I know she likes you."

"If you say so—"

"I used to think you understood women, Augie. She's *crazy* about you."

He didn't respond and Catherine smiled. "I'd love to see this work. She's such a wonderful girl, she has such great values—and what a mother she'd make for your children."

"It's important that I remember that," Augie said.

THEIR waitress took their order for a third round. On the floor Plumber was slow-dancing with Azy. Unless Augie turned his chair he more or less had to look. Catherine and Betty were both watching. "I like a man who dips," Betty said.

"Nobody dips anymore," Catherine said.

"Hell, I can dip," Gordon said. "Come on, Betty."

They went to the floor and squeezed their way in. Gordon immediately maneuvered Betty into a dip-sequence but lost his balance while actually dipping and they almost fell down. Augie had to laugh but Catherine didn't laugh at all. Gil Plumber glared at the left-footed jerk who had just jarred him and his fiancée, and Gordon said something. Azy recognized who it was and smiled, but Plumber didn't feel inclined to dance any longer and they left the floor. Gordon and Betty continued dancing. He had the knack now and they were dipping well together. The noise in Augie's chest was beginning to drown out all other sounds. Catherine was talking to him but he wasn't sure what she was saying. He kept saying yes and no to her; she didn't say anything to indicate he was saying one when he should be saying the other. The new drinks arrived and Catherine picked up her stinger as if it were her first of the night. Then Gordon and Betty were back, and he was laughing and held her chair and they were all together again.

"I did OK. Right, Betty?"

"You easily outdid Fred Astaire."

"What did Gil Plumber say to you?" Catherine asked.

"Who cares?"

"I hate when you make a fool of yourself."

"When you come right down to it, he's a horse's ass."

"He has a lot of influence at the club," Catherine said. "More than many members do. I just hope you didn't say anything rude."

"It was all really pretty funny," Betty said. She picked up her fresh drink and smiled at Augie over the top of the glass.

"Anyway," Catherine said to her, "I was just telling Augie that tomorrow we might all drive to Brewster Point. Then later do a seafood cookout on the beach. We were thinking of going to Marcel's because they have just the greatest escargot but really in this kind of weather nothing beats a real old-fashioned beach cookout. Steamers, lobsters, garlic bread. How does that sound?"

"It sounds wonderful to me. Augie, how does it sound to you?"

He wasn't paying attention; he didn't know what they were saying. He was looking across at the Flannery table.

"I already know how it sounds to Augie," Catherine said. "Terrific. So we're all set."

They were all kind of staring at him. Then he said, "Excuse me," and proceeded to walk across the main lounge of the Inn at Quidnock. Mrs. Flannery was the first to see him. She didn't smile but something in her eyes told Augie she didn't hate him—maybe she even liked him a little. Then Plumber looked up. There was no misinterpreting *his* look, and finally Dr. Flannery and Azy. No one greeted him, said his name.

"Good evening, Mrs. Flannery," Augie said.

"Good evening, Mr. Wittenbecher," Margaret Flannery said.

There was a small pause; it seemed, to Augie, an extremely long pause. Then he said, "Azy, will you dance with me?"

She didn't say anything immediately but her movements —as she prepared to get up from the table—told him she would. "Yes, I'd like to," she said.

Plumber brought his vodka and tonic to his lips and took a long, slow swallow, and Augie followed Azy to the floor. They began dancing. The song was "Pennies from Heaven," and she came in closer than he might have thought, though not so close as to have their bodies touching, except casually. What he particularly liked was that their faces *were* touching. She was shorter than Augie by some four inches, and his lips were near her eye and her lips were just under his ear at the corner of his jaw. In no way was he nuzzling her, nor she him; it was just very pleasant. Dancing was such a remarkable custom. If someone came up to you in a public place and said he would like to borrow your wife or girlfriend for the purpose of holding her, you'd punch him in the nose or at least tell him to get lost. And here he was holding Azy.

"How was your party?" she said.

"Not so good. No one liked each other."

"That's too bad."

"I kept thinking about the drive with you, the one I didn't take."

"We still have time."

He liked hearing her say it, and they danced quietly again; perhaps she came in closer but he didn't know, didn't care. It was all wonderful. Then the music stopped and she smiled at him.

"Thank you, Augie."

"Could I call you, meet you somewhere tomorrow?" he asked.

"It's better if we don't plan."

"OK."

They walked off the floor. At her table Augie made to hold her chair but Plumber stood abruptly, blocking him out. The Mid-West Businessman of the Year was stewing. "Good luck tomorrow, gentlemen," Augie said. "Good night, Mrs. Flannery. Thank you, Azy."

He turned and walked back across the room. Betty wasn't at the table and he sat down, not saying anything. "You're piece o' work, Wim'besher," Gordon said, grinning.

"I don't think it's at all funny!" Catherine said to her husband.

"I din't say wuz funny, called Wim'besher piece o' work."

"That was the most *insensitive* thing I've ever witnessed," Catherine said, her eyes burning into Augie.

He scratched his head above his ear.

"Such a terrible slap in the face!"

"Catherine, I'm not a teenager—so cool it," he said.

"She was humiliated! You humiliated her! And me—you humiliated me!"

"I think you're overreacting. I danced with a woman—"

"I'd like to go," Catherine said.

"Whassa rush?" Gordon said.

"Shut up, you're drunk—you fool!"

Catherine stood up imperiously and Gordon rose and followed her, weaving through the tables. Augie looked about for their waitress, finally catching her eye, and she came over. He had budgeted fifty dollars for an evening out with the Mc-Sweeneys, and by rough calculation that was what the rounds would cost. Hopefully the fifty would also take care of the tip. The big blonde totaled the tab, scribbled in the tax and handed him the check. Augie had a ten and two twenties in his hand ready to give to her—when he saw the bottom line.

"I think there's a mistake here," he said.

The waitress refigured the bill. "Six stingers, three Baileys, three Buds. Sub-total. Tax. No, it's correct. $102.68."

"That's an average of eight dollars a drink," Augie said.

"I don't set the prices, sir. But you *are* paying for the entertainment."

He opened his wallet and took out all his money, another fifty-three dollars. "Keep the change."

She was indignant. "A tip is usually fifteen percent."

"A beer's usually two bucks. That's all I have."

He walked out, wanting to kick a chair. Gordon and Catherine were at the foot of the path. No one spoke on the short walk to the car. When they reached it she made a unilateral decision to drive, slapping the shift into reverse and backing out without looking. Augie thought it best to buckle his seatbelt as she took off down the quiet, dark road. In the back Gordon was struggling to stay awake. "Strajee. On'y way we're gonna win 'mor'ow. Right, par'ner?"

"Right."

She raced by the flowered median, didn't brake for the stop sign—

"Catherine, slow down before we get in an accident," Augie said.

"There's *been* an accident, all right!"

"Strajee, par'ner—"

"Shut up!" Catherine told him.

Augie covered his eyes. They were on the main drag to Easthelmsford and Catherine seemed to think it was her due to straddle the white line. Traffic, approaching on the two-lane road, appeared to be coming right at them. Headlights flashed up and down; then the cars would shoot past while the drivers lay on their horns. Catherine seemed oblivious. She didn't care. Fuck 'em all! She tore on, Augie held on, Gordon snored on. Finally they were on Old Forge. Did she slow down? She only slowed down when she saw her rusty old mailbox. Then she stabbed at her brakes, pulled into the packed-dirt driveway and killed the ignition.

Augie offered a quick silent prayer to someone and Catherine stormed immediately ahead to the house and Augie opened the back door of the car and helped his old friend out. Rainbow came streaking down the steps, made for Augie's left ankle, veered off at the last moment and pissed on the front tire of his station wagon. "Whip their ass 'morrow," Gordon said.

"You bet."

"I thought Plumber was gonna swing agjah, I woul'bin there—you bet yer fuckin' ass I woul'bin there. Som'bitch!"

"Easy now."

They finally made it up the steps and into the kitchen. Catherine came out of the bathroom and Gordon went in, then said g'night to his ol' par'ner and continued to his room. Catherine thought she and Augie should have a nightcap, they had to talk things over.

"I thought I'd go back into town," Augie said.

"What's in town?"

"Catherine," he said, "we have to understand something here—"

"Are you going to meet Elizabeth Flannery?"

"Suppose I said yes. Suppose I said we had plans to meet on the beach, with a blanket and a pitcher of sombreros and watch the sun come up, then what? What would you do? Call up Gil Plumber? Notify the local police and have me arrested?"

"I'd be totally disillusioned in you."

"Why?"

"Because I've always thought of you as a man of character and integrity!"

"Fuck, Catherine—leave me alone."

"You are basically a crude and vulgar person, Augie."

156

"True. Now excuse me."

But she wouldn't let him go. "How do you think it reflects on us?" she said, throwing her head toward the bedroom. "Did you ever think of that? The McSweeneys' house guest prancing across the floor to dance with Elizabeth Flannery. By now everyone in Easthelmsford is talking about it!"

"I seriously doubt that's true."

"You don't live here, that's easy for you to say. It wasn't good judgment."

"Then I made a mistake in judgment."

"Gil Plumber wanted to kill you!"

"I'm flattered."

"Augie, Augie—what is it? What's happening to you?"

"Is something happening to me?"

"This isn't you!"

"How would you know, Catherine? Do you know me?"

"I remember how you always used to be with Abby. Understanding and kind and sensitive—"

"Abby's gone," he said. "God bless her."

"Have a drink with me."

"No."

"You ungrateful fucking bastard."

She lunged at him furiously, pummeling him with her fists, screaming obscenities. Augie raised his arms to protect himself, then turned and pushed open the door; Rainbow was waiting for him on the tiny front deck, teeth bared. Augie ignored the animal and Rainbow went for his ankle and he gave the dog a sideways swipe with his foot, sending it off the deck. He continued down the steps. The screen door opened and Catherine came out and next thing he knew a bottle was whizzing past his head and smashing against the front bumper of Gordon's old Chevy. Augie got in his car, slammed the door, started the engine. Backed out and was gone.

H E HAD EIGHTY cents in his pocket, which at home would buy him a draft beer, but it was silly to think it would buy him one here. Still, he parked on a side street, got out and began walking toward the center of the village. Guys, gals, couples—tourists all—crowded the sidewalks and a few shops were still open and certainly all the bars were. He walked along and looked in the store windows, watched the people and took in the snappy cars. Mixed in with the BMW's and Mercedes-Benzes and Jags were the locals' souped-up Chevys and Fords. Seeing them prowl up and down the streets, Augie recognized a similarity between Shufferville and Easthelmsford after all.

He continued along, nerves still jumping, thinking what he'd really like was a shot, but he'd settle for a beer. Maybe eighty cents was enough. He pushed open the door of a restaurant and bar called The Terrace and walked in, immediately recognizing, by the people standing and sitting at the bar and by the general feel, that he might get a glass of water for his money; but at least it wasn't another Inn at Quidnock. The crowd here seemed more down to earth. You didn't get the impression that the men had made themselves cool millions doing sleight of hand for the late Drexel Burnham Lambert. Though, by the activity in the place, mergers were still distinctly in. If you could swing one. Augie walked halfway down the bar, stopped, didn't know what he was doing, looking for, and decided to leave.

"Can I help you?"

One of the bartenders had singled him out and was trying to talk to him, though the bartender's view was obscured by a thirty-year-old woman with auburn hair, seated at the bar, and a man about forty standing next to her, in a black rayon shirt, trying to pick her up. "That depends," Augie said. "How much is a draft?"

"Two-fifty." He was tall—crew cut, thick neck; had probably started as a bouncer.

Augie gave his head a shake. "Could you cash a check for me?"

"It's against house policy, sorry."

The bartender moved away and Augie was about to; he would walk a little more, then crash in the back of his wagon. Then someone close by was calling his name. Surprised, he looked over. Seated at the bar was Curt Kolchak.

Augie stepped by the rayon-shirted and auburn-haired twosome, happy to see someone he knew. He shook Kolchak's hand warmly. "How you doing, Curt?"

"I thought that was you," Kolchak said. "What's the matter? Run out of cash?"

"I picked up a tab at the Inn at Quidnock—a small gesture. It wiped me out."

"What did you go there for?"

"Curt, I'm new around here—I just went."

Kolchak laughed. He had on a solid green golf shirt and a pair of brown slacks. "Let me get you a drink."

"I won't be able to buy you one back—"

"Don't worry about it. What are you drinking?"

"Bourbon. On the rocks."

Kolchak signaled to the bouncer turned bartender. "Another for me." He then glanced at Augie. "Any special brand?"

"No."

"Make it a Wild Turkey," Kolchak said. "The one hundred

proof. Anyway," coming back to Augie, "that was something this afternoon, wasn't it? Small damn world."

"It was, it is."

"It got me thinking for the rest of the day," Kolchak said. "Boy, time flies. A lot of golf balls in the old water hole."

"That's for damn sure," Augie said. "Were you originally from the Birmingham area, Curt?"

"Detroit. Father worked on the Ford assembly line, twenty-one years. Helped put together the first Edsel."

"Had one now, it would be worth something."

"People knocked that car, it was a good car. My father loved that car."

Their drinks came and Augie picked up his rocks glass, Kolchak his bottle of beer; he wasn't using a glass. "To you, Augie—hit 'em good tomorrow."

"Thanks."

"Who you playing?"

"André Gilliam and Tom *Hrazanek.* However you say it."

"Hrazanek." He pronounced the name without the *R.*

"How do they play?" Augie asked.

"They're tough competitors. Gilliam hits it a ton."

"I'm hearing."

"You'll do fine, Augie," Kolchak said.

Augie took a sip of his Wild Turkey; it was smooth stuff, smooth and strong. "Do you still play, Curt?"

"I'll knock out a bucket almost every day."

"That's it?"

"No time. They keep me running—between storage, club repair, managing the carts and caddies. Then McIntyre always wants something extra out of me, like do a clinic somewhere."

Augie scowled. "OK, a clinic. But what happened—I mean, you won the Michigan Open."

"I had my card," Kolchak said.

"You were on the tour?"

"Seventh in the Crosby one year, third in the Quad-City; my best finish was a play-off at Greensboro."

Augie was excited. "I had no idea. That's something!"

"I was making a name for myself. Footjoy signed me, Wilson gave me a contract, I was going from one event to the other in a big Olds 98, compliments of GM. Hell, I could've *won* Greensboro."

He had a pull on his bottle, grinned, gave his head a little shake. "Halfway through the front nine on Sunday's round, the head flew off my driver. Flew right the hell off. I had to drive with my 3-wood—hit it good but couldn't reach any of the rest of the par-5s in two—and I'd had an eagle on Friday and on Saturday. So figure one shot lost on Sunday because I didn't have the big lumber. You only have to win by one."

Augie had another taste of his bourbon. "Then what happened? After Greensboro?"

"Ninth in the B.C. Open, made the cut in the P.G.A. That was my goal, just to make the cut in a major. Finished ahead of Hale Irwin, Lee Trevino, a lot of big names. The pro at Sea Island retired, I got the job over sixty-five applicants. We bought a house, everything was great. Next year I started off with a couple of successive top tens, then I went and did something awfully fucking stupid." He stopped, looked down, scarred the label on his beer bottle with his thumb.

Augie wondered if he would continue. Kolchak was silent for several long seconds. Finally he said, "I was qualifying for the U.S. Open, thirty-six holes in the national competition. A hundred and twenty-eight guys fighting for three spots. In the regionals I'd played good, a 71 and a 68 at Bermuda Run; we were at Pinehurst and I was only playing mediocre, every hole was a scramble. I knew exactly what I needed to gain a spot, a 143—on my first round I'd had a so-so 74. So I had to shoot a 69, and I had to make two birdies on the back nine to do it. Right off I birdied ten. Then I played along even and on the final par-5 I crushed a drive and was thinking eagle. Problem was I pushed a 3-wood trying to get there, all day I'd been playing right-to-left and this one stayed out on me. I was in the high grass maybe eighty yards from the green. The two other guys I was playing with were both sweating bullets to make it, they'd both went left—so I was by myself with my caddy, and he's looking in one area and I'm looking in another. Kicking around in the rough. It wasn't that thick and if I could just find the goddamn ball I'd have a shot. Then I see it—up against a clump of dirt in a goddamn hole! I couldn't believe it, Augie. What I needed was a hoe! So now I was looking at a hard par and probably a bogey and then I thought, Who's lookin'? The other guys are across the fairway, my caddy's looking down frantic to find the ball, we got no gallery—at least in my group there wasn't none. So I give the ball a flick with my club, perfect—shout to my caddy, 'Got it!' Make a great pitch, sink a ten-footer, par all the last holes—and I'm in the U.S. Open."

One of his elbows was on the bar and he was half-facing Augie. "I *thought*. As it turned out, another player—not one of the guys in my group—saw me move the ball. The head scorekeeper questioned me about it, the guy was right there with us—a pro from Raleigh named Kenny Pettit who wasn't in the running. He described what he'd seen—out on the course after shooting an 81, depressed, just sitting among some pines—and I thought, Lie, deny it. Say Pettit was drunk. I didn't deny it, Augie. He had me, but the thing was, *I* had me, do you know what I'm saying? The Committee got together and disqualified me. Word got back to Sea Island—I was fired. And I never got another job worth a hill of beans. Started hittin' the sauce, chasing skirt, my wife split on me. I was in sad shape, owed a lot of money. Anyway, to make a long story short, Kyle McIntyre knew me from the mini-tour years before. He'd tried a couple of times for his card, he never come close. The year I made it through the qualifying school he had a pair of 79s —that's about what he shoots today. Anyway, winters I was waiting tables in Florida and who's in the restaurant but him and his wife and he offered me a job, May through October, doing what I'm doing. For twelve grand plus room and board."

Augie had both hands on his glass. "People make mistakes, Curt—you've sure paid for yours."

"I'd say so," he said with a quick grin. "But golf's the only game where you don't get a second chance. Cheat in other sports, you *boost* your reputation. Like the pitcher who loads up a ball. In golf, move a ball one time, you're dead. People who know me say, Oh, sure, Curt Kolchak—he cheats. Not, he *cheated.*"

"But everybody doesn't know Curt Kolchak," Augie said. "Go to San Diego, New Orleans—start over."

"The PGA knows me," he said.

"Change your name. You're a golfer, Curt."

He finished his beer. "I was. I could play with the best. Once I was passing through Sulfur Springs and gave Sam Snead a call—took a hundred bucks off him. Oh, was he pissed!"

Augie smiled at the image of Slammin' Sam getting beat and hating it. "If you weren't still a golfer, Curt, why would you go to the range everyday?"

"When I figure that one out I'll know something."

They were silent. Augie gave the ice cubes in his glass a small swirl. Then Kolchak said, "Sometimes when I'm on the range, I'll hit a 9-iron that just hangs there and you see your whole life in the ball. Maybe that's why I go out there. Still trying to understand why in God's name I moved that ball, that day at Pinehurst."

He looked at Augie with honest anguish in his eyes. "If I ever find out, then maybe I'll play again."

Augie finished his Wild Turkey.

"How about another?"

"One more I wouldn't make it to the first tee."

"We wouldn't want that," said Kolchak.

OUTSIDE The Terrace, Augie walked toward the corner. He had parked his car in front of Easthelmsford Stationers, about a hundred yards down Grove Street; where Grove met Main he turned and continued along. It was another beautiful night, and his mood was improved—bumping into Kolchak had helped. Had put things in perspective for him, somehow. Had taken him out of himself. That was it. He had heard another man's story.

His car was just ahead. Before he reached it, however, his attention was drawn to the opposite side of the street. A black coupe—red flames painted fancifully on the sleek hood—was parked at the curb. Two guys, local toughs, were talking to a couple of girls, a blonde and brunette. The girls were maybe seventeen, very pretty, both smoking cigarettes and wearing miniskirts; of the two, it was the blonde that caught Augie's eye—if not his imagination. She was just about the sexiest thing—then he realized he knew her, or recognized her. She was Kelly's friend Maureen from the beach. Augie took a closer look at the other girl—and stopped dead in his tracks.

Son-of-a-bitch!

A voice told him to keep going. He wasn't Kelly Mc-Sweeney's guardian, and he certainly wasn't Maureen's. If they wanted to mess around with a couple of creeps, who was he to butt in? Only he didn't convince himself; the voice in his head had a hollow ring. Just then Maureen tossed away her cigarette and moved closer to the car and Kelly did the same. "That's not a good idea," Augie shouted across the street.

All four looked over.

"Hooz 'at?" the shorter of the guys asked Kelly. He had dark hair and his trousers had a silvery shine under the street light.

"My parents' guest for the weekend."

"C'mon."

"Don't do it, Kelly." Augie started across.

"What's it to you?" she came back at him.

"Just don't get in that car—"

"Hey, Mac, fuck *off!*" said the kid with the silvery pants, acting like he had eight hundred dollars in his pocket and you shouldn't mess with him if you valued your life.

"I want you girls to come with me," Augie said.

"I said *fuck off*, asshole."

"That means *now,*" said the second kid. He was tall and lean and had strong down-sloping shoulders; he wore jeans and a powder blue T-shirt with "Life's A Bitch, Then You Die" printed across the chest.

"Kelly, did you hear me?" Augie said on the sidewalk ten feet away.

"I'm not doin' what you say, Mr. Wittenbecher! Who are you? Making out with my mother! *Who are you?*"

"We'll talk about that later, Kelly. Just don't-get-in-that-car."

"Scumbag, maybe you're not gettin' the message," said the shorter guy.

"Do you want the message? These girls are underage, you mess with them you're in big trouble—"

"You're gonna be sorry you ever fuckin' breathed, man, in about three seconds." He looked at the girls. "Get in."

"Kelly, don't—"

"Drop dead, *Mister* Wittenbecher."

She went to get in the car and Augie came forward quickly —and that was it. Both kids jumped him, swinging, kicking. He fought back, enraged, landing a punch on the tall kid's chin. But the two easily overpowered him. The girls watched, horrified. Then the shorter one hit Augie with a vicious shot to his cheek while Augie was defending himself from the taller kid, and he went down, just managing to break his fall. He lay there, half on the curb, in terrible pain.

"Come on," Silver Pants yelled at the girls.

He moved closer to hustle them into the car and Augie reached out and grabbed one of his legs, tripping him, and he spun and kicked Augie savagely, catching him in the thigh. It wasn't where he had aimed. Kelly screamed. She and Maureen backed away. "Let's get outta here, Richie!" said the kid wearing the T-shirt.

"Fuck yez all."

They both got in, T-shirt behind the wheel. The black coupe burned rubber to the corner, hooked a left and tore down the street, fishtailing. Augie lay for several seconds until his brain cleared, then managed to sit up, resting his head on his knees. Both girls were crying. Augie groaned, feeling sick, then got unsteadily to his feet and stood at the curb, staring down at a crushed pack of Marlboro cigarettes. He spit. He wiped his mouth with his handkerchief. Red.

"You OK, Mr. Wittenbecher?" Kelly asked.

"I'm OK."

"You sure? Oh, God."

Augie got unsteadily to his feet. "Come on, I'll drive you home."

HE watched until the girls were inside—it was Maureen's mother's place two miles out of town, a raised ranch house in a development with an r.v. in the driveway—then drove back to the village. He needed attention, but there were no parking spaces near The Terrace and he kept on, at last pulling into the auxiliary lot of the club and stopping at the tall hedge. His eye was swollen, his head was pounding and his left leg ached brutally.

He limped around the end of the hedge to the area of the first tee, storage room and practice green. Here and there a light was on in the sprawling complex, but the grounds were deserted. He saw no reason why the locker room door should be open; he tried it and it wasn't. He felt dizzy, nauseous, and sat down on the steps, clasping his head—

"Hey, you!"

He looked up. A man about fifty holding a flashlight was walking toward him from around the corner of the patio. Augie didn't stir and the man came closer. He was wearing a long-sleeved shirt with an emblem on the pocket and a matching pair of light gray trousers; attached to his belt was a time clock. He seemed to have a scar, as from a partially healed cut, on his upper lip. "What are you doing here?"

Augie told him he needed a towel and some ice, a couple of guys had just beaten him up on Grove Street in Easthelmsford.

"What's your name?"

"Wittenbecher. Augie Wittenbecher. I'm Mr. Mc-
Sweeney's guest . . ."

"Sure, I know Mr. McSweeney. I'm the night security, Ray
Brasovic."

He stared at Augie's face, eye. "Come on. Let's see what
we can do for you."

Augie got slowly to his feet and Brasovic went several
steps in the direction of the patio, stopped, examined a key ring
and opened the door to the men's lounge. Inside he turned on a
light. "Sit right here," he said.

Augie sat at one of the tables. The security guard went
behind the bar and soon came back with a white towel filled
with ice, a glass of water and a small bottle of aspirin. "Here
you go, Mr. Wittenbecher."

"Thanks." Augie swallowed two aspirin, finished the water and pressed the icepack against his eye.

"Did you notify the police?"

The man was closer to sixty, Augie decided. He had a
small chin with a cleft, and the cut in his upper lip was a birth
defect.

"No."

"Do you want me to give them a call right now?"

"I'll call first thing in the morning. You've been really
helpful," Augie said.

"It's no fun getting mugged. Where you from, sir?"

"Shufferville."

"I know Shufferville. It's a nice little place."

"Where are you from?"

"Originally, Gouveneur."

"That's *way* the hell up there," Augie said.

Brasovic said Augie could take the towel with him, and
five minutes later they were outside again. "Any problem if I
spend the night in my car?" Augie asked.

"Whereabouts?"

"In the auxiliary lot."

"We have a regulation on that. I'm glad you told me."

"Thanks, Ray."

167

Brasovic continued on his rounds. Augie limped past the pro shop, practice green, first tee, stopped and looked down the moonlit fairway, then continued around the hedge to his car.

He started the engine, made a big circle and parked in the extreme corner of the lot near the range. He locked the doors, then dragged his sore body over the seat to the back, where he took off his shoes and trousers. Moonlight shone in his car. The bruise on his inner thigh was the size of a saucer, no more than three inches from his groin.

He pressed the ice pack to the bruise, then to his head, then back to his thigh. After some forty minutes the ice was melted and he lay down on his sleeping bag and just held the wet towel to his face, wondering what the hell next.

PART III

THE
SECOND
ROUND

C H A P T E R 15

"—TO THE FIRST tee, please. On deck: Mr. Kiernan, Mr. Etter—"

Augie woke with a start, immediately squinting at his watch, afraid he had overslept. No, just 8:03. He relaxed, only to realize he felt horrible. His head was throbbing, his eye was swollen, his left leg ached like hell.

He sat up, glanced out the window. Golfers were already on the practice range. If he could get himself together he should knock out a bucket to loosen up. Otherwise he'd whiff his first shot; he might anyway. He stretched once, wriggled free of his sleeping bag and pulled on his trousers, then crawled —groaning—over the seat. Twisting the rearview mirror he saw his reflection, wished he hadn't and twisted the mirror back. He opened the front door and stepped out. A heavy morning mist was hugging the ground. He went through a mock swing. If his life depended on it, he couldn't hit a ball ten yards.

Moving to the back, he opened the tailgate, worked his feet into his spikes, leaving them untied, then stood and brushed his pants with his hands, trying to get the wrinkles out. Clubs on his shoulder, he hobbled across the lot, reminding himself of a wounded soldier carrying home his buddy. On the first tee Steve McMahon and his assistant were seated at the table with two mugs of steaming coffee and a battery-powered megaphone. Carts were parked on the path, ready to roll, and players were stretching, getting ready to hit. Fog concealed the first green but the sun was coming on. Jimmy, the husky all-county, was suddenly at Augie's side.

" 'Morning, Mr. Wittenbecher."

" 'Morning, Jimmy."

The boy took his bag. "What happened to *you?*"

He gave Jimmy the oldest line in the book, trying to make light of it. "You should see the other guy."

"Well, all right!"

"I'll be in having breakfast, if you see Mr. McSweeney."

Augie continued along, not without glances from some of the eight or ten players on the putting green; other men were studying yesterday's results and today's tee-off times on the storage-room wall. Everyone had on a sweater or a jacket. The pro shop was open and men were drifting in and out. Augie had no reason to go in but did glance in. Just coming out the door, smoothing a new chip-red golf glove on his left hand, was Bill Lackaye.

They said good morning but Augie had the feeling Lackaye was saying to himself, I know that guy from somewhere. *Where?* Augie figured after the tournament he'd drop by Lackaye's dealership and pick up a new Peugeot: modest trade-in, the balance in cold cash. On the barrel head. Then Lackaye would remember him. He pushed open the locker room door.

He passed between two rows of lockers; just before going into the showers he slipped off his spikes, then his clothes, laying them on a bench. Compared to the McSweeneys' shower it was dull, boring; no buttons to push, bathtubs to negotiate, hoses to attach. All you did was position an enamel-handled pointer between warm and hot and step in. The water pounded his body and he stood there, head dipped, letting it work its cure. Afterward he grabbed a big white towel from the double stack and at the basins shaved (carefully because of bruises), then used the toiletries, "part of the package."

His clothes hadn't suddenly become clean and crisp but he put them back on, no alternative coming to mind; then, all combed and lotioned, he limped in for breakfast. The hostess recognized him and made a concerned face; he told her he'd had a tough night in town. The dining room was again almost empty and he sat at the same table near the windows. The woman brought coffee over immediately. The special this morning was waffles with one-hundred-percent pure maple syrup.

"Sounds good."

"You sure you're all right, dear?"

Augie made to smile; what he did was grimace. "I'm fine, no problem."

"Let me bring you your breakfast this morning. Did you want the waffles?"

"Really, it's OK. Not necessary."

"And how about a nice side-order of scrambled eggs and sausage?"

He surrendered. "Sure. Thank you."

He looked out the window and through the fog that was rapidly burning off saw players on the fairway. Faintly, the loudspeaker drifted into the dining room. "Mr. Yourke, Mr. Gault; Mr. Thompson, Mr. Fay. On the tee, please."

It was the breakfast of all time. When he finished he thanked the hostess for her thoughtfulness and went out. Jimmy pointed out his cart among the twenty-five waiting: 51. His and Gordon's bags were strapped on the back and he drove across the lot, parked and pulled out a couple of clubs. Only one hitting spot was open on the range; a large bucket of balls three-quarters full awaited the next golfer. There was only one drawback, as Augie saw; the player hitting shots next to the open spot was Gil Plumber.

Augie walked out, wondering what was so different between now and last night at the Inn. He had been nervous walking across the lounge, thinking Plumber might say something, stand up and tell him to leave; but now he was much more nervous, self-conscious. It didn't make sense. He kicked over the bucket and topped his first three shots, perhaps because of the pain in his leg; perhaps for other reasons. Augie didn't have eyes in the back of his head but he saw Plumber anyway, standing there, sizing up his swing. If not the man himself. He tried again; not wanting to top another shot he over-compensated and knocked a divot farther than the ball. It was time to regroup, try a different club. Augie dropped his 9-iron and picked up a 7. New club in hand, he gave Plumber a glance; suddenly Gil was totally absorbed in his own practice. He took a powerful if abbreviated swipe with a 3-iron. The ball tore straight out and landed in front of the two-hundred-yard sign, hitting it on the first bounce with a resounding "whack!" Plumber knew the player on his left; he turned and said something and the man laughed. Then he smashed out another long iron.

Augie tried to concentrate but couldn't get into it. He hated that Plumber was on the tee; more, that he was allowing Plumber to throw him off. He stared down at the red-striped balls scattered on the ground, again thinking how lousy a piece of luck it was that Gil was here, playing in the tournament—in the same flight. If he and Gordon, and Dr. Flannery and Plumber, won their respective matches today, then—but Augie didn't want to think about it. He swung again, and again, at last hitting with a semblance of authority; but he wasn't comfortable. He picked up his loose clubs, dropped them in his bag and left the range.

WHEN he stepped onto the green next to the first tee the three men already practicing glanced at him suspiciously. Augie stroked his ball toward a hole ten feet away; it rolled ten feet by. On the come-backer he was two feet short. Then Dr. Flannery appeared with his putter; he took a shiny new ball from his pocket—and their eyes met. Augie quickly looked down, made to tap in the two-footer. Missed.

I'm in a bad way here, he thought.

Then somebody was calling his name; standing on the path was his playing partner and old friend, looking pretty rusty.

"Let's get some coffee."

174

"We got time?"

"Two more foursomes," Gordon said. "Who clobbered you?"

"I went in town last night and got messed up."

"I guess you did! Jesus Christ, Wittenbecher! You OK?"

"Don't know yet."

"Can you play? You up to this?"

"Don't know yet."

They went through the lockers and pushed open the door leading to the dining room. Augie didn't want anything; he sat with Gordon while he slurped a coffee, ate a cherry Danish and talked about Betty McKeon. "I've seen women go pale," he was saying "but never like that. She had the look of a stiff! Then up and out. No goodbye, nothing. Just up and out."

"I didn't want to hurt her feelings, I only—"

"That woman was going to fuck your ears off."

"What can I say? I blew it."

"I'm not going to say you did the wrong thing," Gordon said, "I'm just filling you in on the details."

"Right."

He signaled for more coffee, started on a second Danish. Lemon. "You wanted to dance with Azy, you danced with her. Big deal. Why do women get so fucking hyper?"

"I don't know."

"Did you and she have a fight?"

"Me and Azy?"

"No!"

"Betty?"

Gordon was speaking plain goddamn English, why wasn't he getting across? "Will you listen? Someone threw a bottle last night; hit my car, smashed it all to hell. I thought maybe she got pissed at you after I went to bed, because of what happened at the Inn."

"No. I mean, I don't remember. Maybe she did, I—I was pretty drunk."

"Who can understand a woman? One morning they'll go like gangbusters, the next morning they're a total bitch. Maybe

175

around seven-thirty I make a little move on her, just easy. I don't know about you, but whenever I wake up with a hangover I'm hornier than a wart hog. 'What the fuck you trying to do?' 'Leave me alone!' 'You got some rotten nerve!' Hey, pardon me—yesterday morning you were hot to trot. I don't say it but I'm thinking it. So I leave, go play golf with Augie. That's when I see the bottle of Beefeater smashed in the driveway, only two drinks out of it. I almost cried."

Augie pressed his fingers against his forehead.

"Anyway, here we are, partner. Round two."

"Round two," Augie said.

"When did you leave?" Gordon asked.

"Last night for town?"

"I meant this morning for the club."

"Oh. Six—it was just six."

"That early?"

"I didn't sleep that well—jitters."

"Easthelmsford's got a really bad element."

"I found out."

"I'm sorry," Gordon said. "You go out for a quiet drink, you get worked over by some creep—you know what I'm saying?"

"There were two of them."

"Two creeps. Did you report it?"

"What was I going to say?"

"Tell them what happened! We can't have visitors coming here and gettin' beat up."

"It's over," Augie said.

"Why was she so pissed? I mean, *she* threw the bottle, right?"

They sat at the pink-covered table with fresh flowers in the dining room of the Easthelmsford Country Club and Augie wanted to lay it all out, knew he had to. Why not now? Bad timing as it was, how about now? It would mean the end of the tournament; it would mean a lot more than that but it would certainly mean the end of the tournament. I have to do it, Augie thought.

"Gordon, I have to tell you something," he said.

"What's that?"

"This isn't easy."

"I'm listening."

He hesitated, needing a moment or two to phrase what he wanted to say—

"You did it," Gordon said with a grin.

"Did what?"

"Threw the bottle. And I know why. Rainbow was making an asshole out of himself and you chucked the bottle at him when he wouldn't stop. I was drunk but you must've been out of your fucking mind!"

Augie stared at his old friend.

"No big deal. Tonight we'll just have to use the Gilbey's," Gordon said.

"Mr. McSweeney, Mr. Wittenbecher *on the tee, please.*"

"Shit, Augie, what the hell we doing, jawing away here? We're up!"

They stood and walked quickly out.

When he saw André Gilliam on the first tee, chatting with his partner, Augie had a distinct feeling that the match would end quickly. Gilliam and Hrazanek would win, 8–7. The man had a professional bearing; he was calm, at ease. What was a second-round match in Flight 12 of the Easthelmsford Member-Guest to a player in the NHL—except a pleasant Saturday outing?

Gordon and Gilliam knew each other; they introduced their respective guests. First Gilliam and Hrazanek inquired about Augie's condition, but it was Gordon who answered. His partner liked to party and it sometimes got him in trouble. Last night was no exception. "I think they're asking us for strokes," Gilliam said to his partner.

It was pretty funny. "Where you from, Augie?" Tom Hrazanek asked.

"Shufferville."

"I'm from Kingston."

"That's right, Wiltwyck. It's a terrific course."

"I hate it," said Gilliam. "I can never score on it. Tom, in all the times we've played Wiltwyck, have I ever parred the ninth hole?"

"You had a double-bogey on it once."

Augie had to laugh. "OK, gentlemen," said McMahon from his table. "Play away. André, your team is up."

"Good luck to you guys," said Gilliam.

"Same to you."

Augie stood beside Gordon while Gilliam teed a ball. The hockey player was wearing white pants and a baby-blue shirt and he had thick curly hair and a tremendous physique and he whaled on his ball with a 2-iron, sending it almost to the edge of pond. He smiled modestly. Gordon stared and Augie stared—

"Beautiful drive," Augie managed to say finally.

"Thanks."

Tom Hrazanek walked out. He was using a metal wood and took two or three warm-up swings. He was thirty-seven or so, a tall rail of a man with kinky light-brown hair. His drive was a medium-low two-hundred-yard draw that ended up shy of the swale. Hrazanek picked up his tee and stepped to the side.

"Go ahead, partner," Gordon said.

Augie hobbled out to the markers, then, from behind his ball, lined up the shot. As always he had first-tee jitters. He was also preoccupied and didn't have any faith in his ability to hit a decent shot. But—ball waiting and people looking—what could he do? He was on. He inhaled, took his stance, didn't like how the swing felt—to his great surprise the drive was straight and far. Pure fucking luck.

"Good ball," said André Gilliam.

"Thanks."

Now it was Gordon's turn. Same old set-up, same old swing. His ball sailed away to the right and ended up in the rough, short of the hedge. The players rode off in their carts as a blaring announcement requesting four new golfers to the first tee followed them down the fairway.

Gordon was steering. "It's nice playing with friendly guys for a change."

"I was just thinking the same thing."

Gordon drove into the rough, located his ball, swung at it and knocked it into the pond. They rode to Augie's ball. Hrazanek, shooting first, landed on the fringe. Augie's turn. 8-iron. He still felt jittery and again the swing he put on the ball didn't feel smooth. But it flew crisply away, landed five feet from the pin, and stuck.

He couldn't believe it.

"Great shot," shouted Tom Hrazanek.

"Thanks."

Gilliam only had a half-pitch but it was slightly off line and he had fifteen feet to the hole. Gordon, learning, said he was picking up. They crossed the small bridge. Hrazanek's chip was a honey and Augie conceded the putt for a par. Gilliam's putt skimmed the hole and rolled five feet by; because his partner already had a par, he picked up. If Augie could sink his putt, he'd have a three, and he and Gordon would take an early lead. He read the break, took his time getting the line, and tapped the ball. It rolled true, and fell.

"Nice hole, Augie," said Hrazanek.

"Thanks." Getting repetitious, but he'd say it all day with pleasure.

They followed Gilliam and Hrazanek along the narrow path to the second tee. "Starting out with a birdie always scares me," Augie said.

"Why is that?"

"It just does. I can't explain it."

Gordon eased up on the peddle as they went over a bump. *"Don't* explain it, just make another one."

GILLIAM hit super-long tee shots but his wedge and chipping game weren't that accurate; his partner was erratic off the tee but he chipped and putted well. They complemented each other beautifully, but nothing they did as a team could better Augie, who played as well as he'd ever played in his life. On the strength of a par on two and another birdie on three, after the first three holes he and Gordon were 3-up. On the fourth tee there was a delay—a golfer had taken off his shoes to play from the water—and Gilliam, Hrazanek and Augie talked while waiting. Gordon stood to one side, practicing his swing.

Hrazanek worked for IBM, and Gilliam was married to his sister. Gilliam said he had tried using a computer once. Tom had lent him his PC when Sports Illustrated had asked him to do a story on the Stanley Cup. He'd lost the whole damn thing trying to follow his brother-in-law's advice "to always make a back-up."

"It was user-error," Hrazanek said.

"I should've never listened to you."

Hrazanek grinned. "What do you do, Augie?"

"I'm a lawyer."

"Do you use a computer?"

"No, but I've been thinking of getting one."

"Save your money," Gilliam said.

Tom Hrazanek shook his head and Augie walked up to the markers, took a couple of practice swipes, and smacked a beauty.

"Good ball."

"Thanks."

Gordon curved one into the pond, but at least it wasn't the big banana ball of old. More of a long, lazy fade. He was getting better. Gilliam hit a shot that landed where Augie's had stopped; then the ball bounced and ran for another sixty yards. Hrazanek pulled his drive into a bunker.

Augie and Gilliam both had fives for the halve. Mc-Sweeney and Wittenbecher still 3-up. Which is the way it remained until the eleventh hole, when Hrazanek chipped in for a birdie. 2-up. But Augie came right back and won the next hole. Going into fifteen he and Gordon had a three-hole lead. If they won fifteen, they would win the match, 4–3, and advance to the finals.

There was another delay, this one somewhat longer. Lost ball, players looking for it taking up the full five minutes; then one of the players returned to the tee. Augie thought back to the first hole of the opening round, seeing *himself* returning. The player, a stout man wearing a Panama hat, took his time setting up but dubbed the shot; he swore, yelled to his partner that he was picking up and floored the pedal on his cart. Soon the teams were out of reach, and Augie teed up a ball.

Just easy, he told himself. He determined his line, took his stance and swung. When the ball sailed two hundred thirty-five yards straight down the middle, he breathed a sigh. Whatever the magic going for him was, it was still going.

"Nice drive, Augie."

"Thanks."

Gordon curved his ball into the right rough. Gilliam then hit a huge towering draw that almost went out-of-bounds, stopping at the line of sycamore trees. Hrazanek was safe, not too deep, on the left side of the fairway. The teams boarded their wagons. "I haven't contributed shit today," Gordon said.

"You're playing a lot better."

"I'd like to figure in *one* hole, for Christ's sake."

Gordon steered for the rough, stopped the cart and they both got out and began searching for his ball. The rough was deep and thick and they couldn't spot it. As Augie was kicking around in tall grass, a ball popped up. "What are you playing?"

"Who the hell knows?"

"Then I just found your ball."

Gordon got out of the cart, looked at his lie. "6-iron," he said.

"Hit a good one."

It was a terrible one. Gordon sat down in the cart, dejectedly.

Tom Hrazanek swung and put his ball on the left fringe. Now it was Augie's turn. He studied his ball, the distance. 5-iron. He took his stance. Easy grip; arms loose, comfortable.

Backswing smooth, unhurried. This was going so close he'd be able to tap in with his eyes closed. He came forward with the club—great rhythm and tempo—and the ball squirted sharply away to the right and bounced into a clump of evergreens.

Gordon looked at him with an expression of complete bewilderment. Augie stayed in his spot wondering how—when he was playing so well—he could hit a goddamn *shank*. He walked over to his ball and chipped it out of the trees, then hit a tentative 8-iron to the green, fearing another shank. The ball, poorly struck, landed on the green but thirty-five feet from the hole. Gilliam was in a trap. Blasted out, lying three. Tom Hrazanek used a putter from the fringe and his ball stopped ten inches from the cup. Augie, looking at a bogie at best, conceded Hrazanek the tap-in for his par.

McSweeney and Wittenbecher, 2-up.

"Maybe we should hit 'em with our strategy," Gordon said as they motored to the sixteenth tee.

"I don't think so."

Gilliam's team took the honors, and both he and Hrazanek hit good shots, clearing a pond one hundred sixty yards out. Augie teed a ball, his mind free, clear. One bad hole didn't mean a thing. He then duck-hooked his drive into the pond's bank. Gordon, thinking this was his opportunity to contribute, lashed into a drive. But if he was getting better, this wasn't one of his better shots. His ball hit a roadway running along the right side of the hole, took a gigantic bounce and landed in someone's swimming pool. Augie tried to play from the bank and hit the ball deeper into the mud.

McSweeney and Wittenbecher, 1-up.

"This is the time to do it," Gordon said when they were in the wagon. "On the next tee make like you're telling me a little news. You were just elected to the board of your local Planned Parenthood."

"Gordon, fuck your strategy. We're splaying like *shit.*"

Number seventeen. Long par-3. Boom. Gilliam's ball sailed over the pin, drew back and stopped four feet away. Hrazanek hit a high, straight shot that landed just short of the green.

Augie told himself to relax. Swing *through* the ball, not *at* it. But something was taking over his game. It was eerie. Did he want to get the hell out of Easthelmsford? Was that it? He swung poorly and pulled his shot into a greenside bunker. Gordon's ball landed in the right rough. As if his ball ever landed in the left rough. When he located it he hacked around with a pitching wedge and finally made the green, lying five. Augie got out of the trap leaving himself a seven-footer for par; then Hrazanek chipped in for a birdie.

Match: all-even.

To eighteen.

"Augie, I'm telling you. Do you want to win? I want you to say, '*Roe v. Wade* is the greatest decision ever handed down by the U.S. Supreme Court.' That'll do it."

"Gordon, don't bug me. You're bugging me!"

"For a lawyer you don't know shit, Wittenbecher!"

Gilliam unleashed a 280-yard monster tee shot and Hrazanek, pumped up from the birdie, tried to put too much on his drive and dubbed it into a marsh in front of the tee. Amazingly he did the same thing when he drove a second time and said he was picking up; his partner, after all, was in perfect position. Gordon and Augie were sitting in the cart, not talking. They got out and Augie walked onto the tee with his driver and teed a ball. He stepped behind his ball and got a good line on the flag, three hundred seventy-seven yards away; straight down the fairway, just beyond the flag, was the clubhouse. He took his setup. No big deal. He was on the ninth tee at Shufferville with his son, playing at dusk. He swung back, felt a hitch in his initial move down; his shot was strong but off line to the left, ending up in the swale between the first and eighteenth holes. Hrazanek gave Gilliam a look and Gilliam returned the look with a minute nod. The NHL star didn't smile; perhaps in his mind he smiled. Augie walked off the tee and sat heavily in the cart. Gordon teed a ball and Augie thought, Hit it straight for once, you Irish son-of-a-bitch! For once in your goddamn life hit the ball *straight.* Gordon hit a beast of a slice.

Gilliam said that the ball could be out-of-bounds. Did Gordon want to shoot a provisional?

"No."

The pair of carts moved down eighteen—Gilliam and Hrazanek, talking brightly away; McSweeney and Wittenbecher, ready to choke each other. Gordon braked at the swale. Augie grabbed four clubs and Gordon cut across the fairway to the opposite rough. Augie began knocking aside the tall grass. Gilliam and Hrazanek entered the swale and also started looking, but not with any great purpose. If their opponent's ball was found, fine; if it wasn't, Wittenbecher would have to go back to the tee and take a stroke-and-distance penalty—

"Here it is," said Augie. He leaned down, identifying the ball.

"Good," said Gilliam. He and Hrazanek climbed out of the swale and watched from the cart.

A fir, maybe fifteen feet high, was directly in Augie's line; but if he cleared it he could reach the green. His lie wasn't that bad. He was approximately a hundred and forty yards away and he thought, big 7-iron. He dropped his other three clubs and took his stance, thinking, Career shot. Keep your head still, it'll go. He took a vicious rip and the ball came out hot—it was on its way, straight in line with the pin. Augie's heart surged—and the ball hit the top limb of the tree—*crack!*—and dropped like a stone.

He climbed out of the swale, dizzy with disappointment. His ball was so close to the trunk he didn't have a normal shot and had to swing left-handed. The ball just made the fairway. He was lying three and Gilliam was sixty yards ahead lying one. Augie hit another 7-iron to the back edge of the green. Unless he chipped in from sixty feet he was looking at a double-bogey. Really what he was looking at was defeat. They had lost; the match was over. But then, so were his problems. Gordon would want him to stay but he would say no, he really had to get going. Thanks. Thanks for everything but he really had to get going . . .

Gordon, still looking for his ball, told Gilliam to go ahead and shoot; which André did, lofting a pitching wedge nicely to the green.

He and his partner were beside themselves; it was hard for them to conceal their joy. A come-from-behind win was always far more exciting. They rode over to the rough to help Gordon look and Augie followed on foot. Gordon was poking about with a club near the out-of-bounds stakes. Augie was thinking of looking for another minute or two, then making the gesture and conceding the match; it would be the sporting thing to do.

"Got it!"

Everybody walked over to where Gordon was standing. His ball lay in heavy grass between two white stakes—inbounds by all of a foot. Augie looked at the ball, though really all he could see was the top of it; then he glanced up at the green—one hundred seventy yards away. If Gordon wanted his opinion, he would say take an 8-iron, try and make the fairway —then go for it. Gordon didn't want his opinion. Fine. Augie went over and sat in the cart; Gordon selected a club and went back to his ball.

He set up for the shot, giving his head a tilt this way and that, looking for an angle he liked. He fiddled and adjusted and shuffled, and Augie watched, waiting for the inevitable. A feeling of emptiness came over him, really of despair, even as he continued rationalizing that it was better this way—better for them to lose—so he could split. The shank on fifteen had said all, told all. He had had the win in his pocket . . .

Gordon swung. Not expecting the ball to clear the rough, Augie kept his eyes low. Didn't see it. Had Gordon even hit it? Then a whizzing dot, black against the blue sky, caught Augie's attention. The ball was sailing high, drifting left to right in an easy fade—and Augie and Gordon and André Gilliam and Tom Hrazanek stood in the tall grass by the out-of-bounds markers on the eighteenth hole and watched it curve and fall and land on the green, near the flag; it bounced once and stopped.

No one said a word. Then Gilliam mumbled, "Holy fuck-ing Christ."

"Great shot," Hrazanek said flatly.

"Thanks," said Gordon.

He walked over, slid behind the wheel and drove toward the green. Augie was still speechless when Gordon stopped the cart and grabbed his putter. Augie managed to get out a few words—he was picking up. Gordon padded to his ball, marked it and shoved it into his back pocket. Gilliam was away. The hockey player lined up his putt from both sides of the hole. From where Augie was standing it looked to be straight in, twelve feet; because it was slightly uphill, Gilliam would be able to give the ball a good firm rap. He gave it a good firm rap. The ball rolled well, staying on line, and stopped one rotation short. Gordon told André it was good. Gilliam snatched up his ball and stepped away.

Gordon walked to his coin, shoe kilties flopping, and ex-changed the penny for a ball. There were two or three in his pocket and he pulled one out at random. Augie thought it might be a different ball; it had a lighter color, but Gilliam and Hrazanek didn't object—if they noticed. The distance to the hole was seven or eight feet: closer than Gilliam's putt but on the uphill side of the hole. If Gordon hit the ball too hard it would roll fifteen feet past and he could miss coming back. He read the break; whether he read it correctly they would all find out in a few short seconds. He went into his crouch, waggling his putter like an old man with a metal detector hoping to find a dime, then brought it back and made a jerky stab forward; the ball rolled, curved, and disappeared.

Gordon gave a triumphant yell and threw his putter in the air. When it landed it almost hit Gilliam, who repaired the dent in the green, picked up the club and walked over to Gordon. Tom Hrazanek also came up. Like his partner, he was in minor shock.

"Nice playing, Gordon."

"Thanks."

"Augie, good round. Good luck tomorrow."

"Thanks."

"How about a beer?"

"Sure."

"See you in the bar."

Gilliam and Hrazanek walked to their cart—stiffly, as if they had forgotten how—and drove off. Gordon dropped his putter in his bag and slid behind the wheel. "That was something else," Augie said.

"It was then or never."

"I'm glad it was then."

Gordon, grinning, stepped on the pedal. "It was a good shot, wasn't it?"

"It was a fabulous shot. What did you hit?"

"4-iron."

"How the hell did you get it up?"

"I thought of Rose Trippico's nice round ass!"

Augie had to laugh. Gordon motored past the patio, cut in front of the first tee and braked at the bag-storage room. Jimmy came up, offered his congratulations and unstrapped their bags. "How'd Dr. Flannery's team make out?" Gordon asked.

"They won, 7 and 6."

Augie was checking his clubs; his fingers stumbled over the 9-iron.

"Partner, why is it *we* always have to win on the eighteenth goddamn green?" Gordon said.

"Hey, you're in the finals, Mr. McSweeney!" the boy said.

EVEN WHILE HE and Gordon rapped with Gilliam and Hrazanek in the men's grill, Augie's eyes kept going to the large Member-Guest plaque on the wall. The names meant something now—or at least they were more than mere names. *Tim Donohue* and *Andy Mulligan,* last year's winners of the Championship Flight. *Dennis Flannery* and *Frank Gildersleeve,* winners the year before. *Kevin Donohue* and *Bob O'Meara,* winners the year before that. And still going back, *Kevin Donohue* and *Bob O'Meara* again.

Kevin Donohue.

Used to be the hottest golfer at the club. Engaged to Azy Flannery but she ended it. They found him in his garage, drunk, engine running—

Plays with men's emotions, strings them along.

User.

It was Gordon's turn to buy a round. Four new beers appeared on the table. Tom Hrazanek likened Gordon's iron on eighteen to Bobby Thompson's ninth-inning homer at the Polo Grounds. Snatching victory from the jaws of defeat.

Gordon was beaming. It was his moment. Gilliam said, "I'm going to suggest at the next directors' meeting that we erect a monument out there. 'From this unearthly spot Gordon McSweeney hit a 4-iron to within eight feet of the hole.' "

"Hey, come on—my partner hit a couple of good shots too," Gordon said.

"He sure did," said André Gilliam.

"Especially that nice little shank on fifteen," Augie said.

HANDSHAKES, once again, were offered, congratulations given. "Good luck tomorrow," Gilliam said.

"We'd like to see you guys take home all the marbles," Hrazanek said.

The two men walked out. By themselves at the table, Gordon suggested they have a bite. "What would you like, Augie?"

"I'm not hungry, thanks."

"Jesus, I'm starving."

"Go ahead."

"No, no. Second thought, I don't want to keep her waiting. Let's go."

"I was thinking of getting in some practice," Augie said.

"Practice?"

"I'd like to hit some balls."

"You crazy?"

"My swing started leaving me."

"Your swing was a thing of beauty all day, Wittenbecher."

"Look, you go with Catherine," Augie said. "Maybe I'll catch up with you later."

" 'Maybe you'll catch up with us later.' What is this shit?"

"I have to ease off a little."

"What are you talking about?" Gordon said.

"I get drinking, I seem to—you know—find trouble," Augie said, "like last night. I, ah, want to keep a low profile today—stay in training."

"So you'll play better tomorrow?"

"Basically."

"Wittenbecher, today you played the first fifteen holes in even *par*. Tonight you should get *really* fucked up. Now, let's go."

Gordon stood and they walked out, went past the pro shop, rounded the hedge and moved into the auxiliary parking lot. "And another thing, she won't go with me, alone. Not with this world-class snit she's in."

"I don't think—I don't know if I could be of any help," Augie said.

"After that performance yesterday? Give me a break."

They were at Gordon's rattletrap. "Personally, I think this has to do with last night. She doesn't own you but you *are* her guest for the weekend, so why the fuck are you dancing with someone she can't stand? Do you know what I'm saying?"

"I think so."

"All she needs is a few strokes, Augie—to bring her back."

"Well, I'd like to help. I just—"

"Look, hit your bucket. Who am I to say don't practice? When you're finished, come on back and we'll hang out, just the three of us. Like we were talking about. We can soak up some rays out at Brewster Point—"

Just then Kelly and Maureen, wearing shorts and halters, came riding into the auxiliary lot on bicycles. They saw Gordon and Augie and pedaled over quickly. Augie read Kelly's expression; it dominated her face. Had he told her dad about last night or hadn't he?

Gordon greeted the girls with the good news. "We won! We're in the finals."

"That's terrific."

But Kelly didn't smile; she looked worried. "Dad, something funny is going on at the house."

"What do you mean?"

"Mom's still in bed. She's just laying there with the shade pulled—it's weird."

"Is she all right?"

"She's not talking, I don't know."

"Is she breathing? I mean, didn't you go in?"

"She's breathing. It's just—"

"I'm going home right now."

The door to his Chevy creaked; he started it and chugged off. The girls didn't ride away. Kelly had shorter legs than Maureen and had to straddle her bike at a sharper angle. Augie wasn't going to start any conversation. Finally Maureen said, "We're really really sorry about last night, Mr. Wittenbecher."

"It was awful how we acted," said Kelly.

"You didn't get in their car, give yourself credit," he said.

"Because of you we didn't!" said Maureen.

All this while Augie had been standing with his golf bag on his shoulder; now he set it down and held it in front of him. "I'm just glad it worked out, that I happened to come along."

"Mr. Wittenbecher—" Kelly started to say something, then stopped.

"Go ahead."

"No, it's OK."

"Am I having an affair with your mother, is that what you want to know?"

"It's none of my business," she said.

"But you didn't think that yesterday, did you?"

"I was very confused yesterday . . ."

He felt he could say the next in good conscience. "The answer is no, Kelly—I'm not."

She was biting her lips. "I didn't know what to think, Mr. Wittenbecher. When we met those boys—"

"I understand," he said. "I didn't say anything about it, and I won't."

THE sun was high and very warm and you had to be crazy to bang out balls, which meant that the ten or twelve men on the range, besides Augie, were crazy. He started with a 9-iron, hit a dozen shots, exchanged it for a 7, then a 5. The shots were adequate—by no means crisp. When you hit a ball well, you almost couldn't tell you'd hit it, and the way he was hitting now, he could tell. Instead of a sharp *click* he was getting closer to a heavy-sounding *thunk*.

Sweaty to the point of griminess, Augie took out his 3-wood and stroked a half-dozen balls, thinking each time he set up that he had to reach the green two hundred twenty yards away to beat Gil Plumber in tomorrow's match; but the shots tailed right or curved left. He stopped, head lowered, knowing he was pushing himself. Then, again, he thought of tomorrow's round and hit a dozen more shots.

He would finish with his driver; but before taking it out he decided to sit down on the bench for a breather. As soon as he sat down, however, he realized what he wanted wasn't rest but honest to God *sleep*. He was dead tired. Beat. Maybe that was the whole problem. If you were exhausted how could you hit a goddamn ball crisply? Augie pulled off his sweat-soaked glove, shouldered his bag and left the range. He would drive somewhere until he found a quiet, shady spot—

Suddenly he was distracted by a horn tap. Looking over, he saw Azy sitting in her convertible; the roof was down.

"Hi," he said, going up to the car.

She was frowning. "What happened?"

"A couple of guys decided they didn't like me."

"Where *were* you?

"On Grove Street," he said.

"Grove Street, in Easthelmsford?"

"Last night. I'm OK, really."

"Augie—"

"Seriously, I'm fine."

"That's awful."

"How you doing, Azy?"

She was wearing tan shorts and a yellow halter top. "All right, I guess."

His hands were on the top of the passenger door. "Where's Gil?"

"He has business in the City."

"On a Saturday in July?"

"That's Gil—he plans ahead. Now he can write off the trip."

"What can I do to write off my trip, Azy?"

"Come for a drive with me."

"Would the IRS buy that?"

"Probably not. But I would."

Augie smiled. "Listen, give me a chance to shower and change. I'll meet you here in, say, thirty minutes?"

"Wonderful."

She drove off. Augie started toward his wagon but he hadn't taken two steps when Jimmy came rolling by in a golf cart. Curt Kolchak's assistant braked and stopped. Could he relieve Mr. Wittenbecher of his bag?

He had planned on stowing it in his car but this was preferable; his clubs would be here in the morning, all cleaned and wiped down and strapped on the back of a cart. Part of the package. "Sure. Thanks, Jimmy."

Jimmy took the bag, and Augie continued across the lot to his car, free of his bag, and suddenly free of his weariness . . .

A T THE McSWEENEYS' mailbox he turned off Old Forge Road and parked behind the tan sedan, got out and walked around to the back, expecting an ambush from Rainbow ever on the alert for infidels. But the animal's dusty lair beneath the steps was vacant. Continuing on, Augie glanced at the rear window; the blind was completely pulled. The house had a deserted, a forsaken, an eerie feel. He passed the picnic table; on it lay a box of plastic utensils, two un-opened bottles of tonic water and a thin, oval-shaped kitchen sponge that at first glance Augie took for a sea shell. Then he was at the entrance of the ramshackle little structure equipped with a state-of-the-art security system, guaranteed to keep out all prowlers, burglars and estranged upstate visitors.

However, if you understood the system, it presented no problem. Augie tripped the latch, heaved up and gave the door a hard kick at its base, and he was in his hideaway. Where the golfer, after a long, trying match, could come and relax with a tall drink. Nap in the cool breeze always blowing through. Augie grabbed his next-to-last pair of socks, a pair of navy blue pants and white golf shirt, shorts and handkerchief. It was then he noticed the new arrangement of wild flowers in the vase.

He stayed for a moment longer, then, clutching his clothes, went out and crossed the yard. At first he thought of going inside to tell Gordon he'd made other plans but then decided against it. Gordon would want to know what they were and, unless he lied, that could lead to the pros and cons of spending the afternoon with Azy Flannery. And he still had to shower and get dressed and he didn't want to keep her waiting. As he was about to round the corner of the house, however, the back door opened and Gordon stepped out. By his expression, he didn't have it in mind to chat about his match-winning 4-iron on eighteen.

"I want to talk with you," he said.

"Listen, can it wait? I'm in kind of a rush—"

"No, it can't."

He wasn't weaving but he'd probably had a drink or two since they'd finished lunch. Augie tried to stay cool. "What's up?"

"That's what I want to know."

"Can you ease off a little?" he asked, walking toward the stairs.

"That depends."

"On what?"

"On what kind of answers I get."

Gordon padded back inside and Augie went up the steps, though part of him was saying, Why are you doing this? Get out of here. But another part of him wanted to face it, finish it one way or the other. In the kitchen a stainless-steel cocktail mixer was on the cluttered counter, and Gordon was topping off a long-stemmed martini glass. His bulky shoulders, usually straight across, sloped ominously downward.

"I should punch your nose in, you son-of-a-bitch."

Augie stood by the cluttered sink, looking at his friend. "That's a statement, Gordon. You want an answer, you have to ask a question."

"Don't fuck with me. Is it the truth?"

"What?"

"That you fucked her Thursday night in the guesthouse."

"It was Friday morning, but there's more to it—"

He cut down cocktail mixer, olive jar and ice bucket with a swipe of his arm, sending them crashing to the floor with a box of Triscuits and a plastic container of Cheese Whiz. From the master bedroom—as if that were the cue—came the ranting of a woman and a dog's raucous bark.

Gordon's chest was heaving, his head slightly lowered. He reminded Augie of a wounded water buffalo about to charge. Augie put his bundle of clothes on the counter to prepare to defend himself. "You only know one side of the story, Gordon—"

"Is there a second side? You fuck a man's wife, is there a second side?"

"Yes. In this instance—"

"What, you were drunk? You going to pull that drunk shit on me?"

Catherine was still raving in the bedroom, Rainbow barking away. Augie was beginning to have an eerie feeling that the world was coming to an end. "She came out to the guesthouse while I was sleeping and when I woke up she was on top of me—"

"Just on top of you?"

"We were having sex."

"Augie Wittenbecher always sleeps with a hard-on."

"I sleep with a hard-on if someone gives me a blow job while I'm sleeping. You have to believe me, Gordon. Then suddenly I woke up—"

"Did you have to go through with it?"

"Speaking now, no—I didn't have to. I should've stopped and I'm sorry I didn't. But at the time—"

Gordon lurched toward him and swung his fist in a big looping arc that would have dropped an ox. Augie managed to parry the blow, though the force of catching it on his shoulder made him stagger; and Gordon's throwing it—abetted by alcohol—caused *him* to stagger. As much to keep himself from falling as to prevent Gordon from swinging again, Augie wrapped him up with his arms. Gordon swore and sputtered—

The bedroom opened and Catherine emerged, barefooted, wearing a wrinkled gray nightgown, her hair all over frizzy; her eyes had a red psychotic glare. She was dishevelment itself, a living horror. Gordon and Augie, as if by common agreement, ceased in their struggle. Catherine began a slow advance to the kitchen. Just then Rainbow streaked past her legs.

"Go back to the bedroom!"

Whether Gordon was commanding the dog or his wife was unclear. Whichever, neither paid any heed. Rainbow swooped in low, as if to avoid detection, and made for Augie's ankle. Catherine was screaming, the dog yelped as Augie's foot caught its ribcage, and Gordon's voice boomed out as a kind of contrapuntal bass to the whole cacophonous composition. "I said go back to bed!"

"Get him out of my house!"

"Shut up!"

"Bastard fucked me!"

The animal was snarling, preparing for a new attack. Augie picked up a kitchen chair. "Keep the dog back, Gordon."

"Sick, Rainbow," Catherine screamed. "Tear his balls off!"

The dog, exhorted, made another ferocious effort to sink his teeth into some part of Augie's anatomy, if not the specific place his mistress had mentioned. Augie stepped aside and brought the chair down on the animal's head. Rainbow howled, retreated on wobbly legs to Catherine, where he collapsed. She shrieked in outrage. Gordon, at that precise moment, thought it best to polish off his martini. Gulp. Olive and all. He told Augie he'd caused enough trouble and should get the hell out.

"I'm going."

"Sex sex sex sex sex sex—all he thinks about!"

"Will you shut up."

"You shut up," Catherine hurled back. "He fucked me, took me to the guesthouse and fucked me . . ."

She was screaming and weeping, squatting on the floor out-of-her-mind drunk stroking Rainbow's head.

"Fucked me! *Your best friend fucked me!"*

"Shut up."

Augie made for the door, ran down the steps and out to his car.

Inside, the lunacy continued. "Fucked me! Sex sex sex! Fucked me in the guesthouse! *Sex sex sex sex sex!*"

"Shut up! *Shut the fuck up!*"

His hand was shaking as he twisted the key in the ignition.

SHE was fumbling with the Scotch, spilling most of it as she poured, leaving the bottle uncapped. "Do you need that?" Gordon asked.

" 'Do you need that? Do you need that?' " she said, mimicking him. "What's it to you, anyway? Took me to the guesthouse and fucked me—and you just *stand* there." She was yelling, screeching. "Don't even speak to me! Look at you, drunk—fucking alcoholics, all of you! Goddamn McSweeneys!" She took a kick at the mixer on the floor, missed it, slipped and fell, lay there in a heap.

"You OK?"

"Fuck you."

"Will you please just try—"

"Bastard fucked me—understand that? Best friend fucked me! He fucked me, your best friend fucked me, took me to the guesthouse and fucked me!"

She tried to get up but her feet skidded in a small pool of melted ice and she went back down. She made a second attempt. On her feet again she commenced to add vermouth to her glass, swirled the concoction with her finger and had a quick swallow. "I think," Gordon said, in a tone meant to pacify, "you should go back to bed, darling."

"Don't 'darling' me," Catherine yelled. "Best friend fucked me! Took me to guesthouse—"

"You had nothing to do with it."

"Are you siding with him now? Is that what you're doing? Because you went to college together? 'Roar, lion, roar!' Fuck you!"

"He says he was sleeping. You went down on him, then when he woke up—"

Catherine grabbed for a bottle of booze and hurled it

across the kitchen; it missed its mark, because its mark made a nice move—that is, Gordon dropped to his hands and knees. But it didn't miss everything. Like a missile, the bottle crashed into the pyramid of dishes and utensils on the drain board. Glasses, plates, mugs, knives, spoons flew up, dropping with a huge clatter to the floor, into the sink. A second bottle flew, and he scurried around on all fours, like a St. Bernard seeking cover. Rainbow started barking again. Then Gordon, still on the floor, met the dog face-to-face. The hair went up on Rainbow's neck and he snarled. Gordon snarled back. Catherine continued raving and screaming. Another bottle whizzed through the air, breaking against the leg of the table. His Johnny Walker Black. Shit.

He stayed low, expecting a new attack. Calm. Silence. He glanced over. Catherine was grasping the countertop but her fingers were slipping. Then her legs just seemed to give way and she fell to the floor, her head narrowly missing a ragged edge of broken glass. Gordon crawled over to her. Rainbow was sitting on his haunches, tongue hanging out, drooling, the tip of his penis sticking out like a bright red lipstick.

GORDON half-carried, half-dragged her into the bedroom and managed, with a great deal of heaving and tugging, to get her on the bed, then went outside and sat in one of the lawn chairs, wondering if he could believe Augie: the part about sleeping. Then he thought, What difference does it make? Did they do it or didn't they? Did he have sex with her or didn't he? That was the bottom line. Like the number on the score card. Who cared how it got there?

Gordon thought he heard noises. He walked past the mower and looked in the bedroom window. She was out cold but wasn't quite in the position, on her back, he'd left her in; she sputtered and groaned and heaved—and was still. Gordon returned to his chair, thinking the tournament was over. Maybe in a year or two he'd be able to forget—to forgive Augie —but he just didn't want to ride around with him tomorrow in a cart, shooting golf balls, pretending like everything was OK. Because it wasn't. It wasn't OK. He wished he'd caught him with one good one, decking him—that would've helped. Wife fucker!

I need a drink, Gordon thought.

He stomped across the yard, feeling terribly injured and angry. Not just at Augie but at her too. It took two. And here he'd thought Friday morning she was coming around again; it was only because she was already turned on and wanted more. Played him for a fool, was what she'd done. Gordon kicked open the screen door and walked through the little hall to the kitchen.

He looked around, stunned, as if seeing the debris and rubble for the first time. Like a soldier who lives through a battle and goes back the next morning. Except for a variety of liqueurs his booze was gone, so he took a beer from the refrigerator and went back out, still pissed and hurt but kind of worried too. Confused by how something so pleasant, so happy as having an old friend visit for a weekend of golf could turn so sour, so fucking rotten. Anyway, it was over now. He would give McMahon a ring first thing in the morning and tell him that the team of McSweeney and Wittenbecher, Flight 12, was defaulting.

He picked up his beer bottle, took a swig, wondering what he should do with himself for the rest of the day. He had some copy to write for his job, due Monday; maybe he'd crash for an hour in Kelly's room, then have a go at it. The idea didn't appeal to him but everything was anticlimactic now. What was left for him? He couldn't even see himself going to the club anymore, playing golf . . .

He sat in the sun in his back yard, looking at the tall grass, the overgrown vegetable garden, wondering if he could find it within himself to start over in an entirely different part of the country. It wasn't the first time he'd had the idea but it had never had the force behind it, the impetus, it had now. He really hated his life, hated himself for letting his days slip away, one after the other like ineffectual slices into the rough.

His 4-iron to the green was a freak shot, the last gasp of an old pilot—one last grasp at glory. The only bright spot was Kelly. She was all that mattered to him and he wouldn't want to lose her, lose the last three or four years he had with her before she went off and made her own way—

Then, even as the thoughts were in Gordon's mind—even as he pictured his daughter so clearly—she was standing in the back doorway of the house, looking out at him. Unless he was hallucinating. Kelly came down the steps, barefoot, in her light green shorts and yellow top.

"Daddy, what happened?"

"I—I wasn't expecting you back so early."

"The kitchen is a disaster area!"

"Sit down, angel."

"Are you going to tell me?"

"I'll tell you. It isn't the easiest thing to do, Kelly."

She sat down next to him. He had never seen her look so frightened. "Your mother and I had a fight," Gordon said. "She got real angry, she was drunk, she really didn't know what she was doing. One thing led to another and she threw a bottle at me and it hit the piled-up dishes. From there on everything just went downhill, she was throwing bottles left and right."

"Where is she now?"

"Back in bed."

"What was it over?"

"These things just happen, Kelly. You know your mother—"

"Was it over Mr. Wittenbecher?"

"Why would you say that?"

"I wasn't born yesterday, Daddy."

"What are you saying?"

Kelly picked up the oval sand-colored sponge on the table and pressed it with her thumbs. "I saw how Mom was behaving with him at the beach, I saw them together in the guesthouse when you went for groceries Friday afternoon—"

"Friday afternoon?"

Gordon grabbed the box of utensils as if wanting to throw it. "What were they doing?"

"They weren't doing anything."

"If they weren't doing anything what in hell were they doing in the guesthouse?"

"Maybe thinking about doing something."

"Fuck!"

Gordon stood up, pressed his head. "I'm sorry, honey. I don't mean to use words like that, I'm really sorry."

"That's OK."

"I'll kill that son-of-a-bitch!"

"Nothing happened. Mom came back inside the house two minutes later, then he drove off."

"You just spoiled it for them."

"I don't think so."

Kelly laid the sponge down. Her eyes were lowered. "I have to tell you something," she said, as if talking in a confessional. "I mean, I thought the worst—I really thought something was going on. More on her part, maybe, like how she was acting. I was so angry, Daddy, so worried by it—I was thinking of running away. Anyway, last night—"

She looked into her father's eyes, very upset, almost crying. "Last night, me and Maureen were in the village and these two guys started talking to us and they said they had some grass and did we want to party with them? I wouldn't tell you this and I'm ashamed of myself but it was because of Mom and Mr. Wittenbecher, like how it looked between them, that I said sure. Maureen was all for it. These weren't very nice boys but it didn't matter, I didn't have any sense—I just wanted to do something. Do you know what I'm talking about, Daddy? And we're just about to get in their car and who shouts across the street to us *not to* but Mr. Wittenbecher. I was a little bitch to him and told him what I thought and the guys told him to get lost and much worse but Mr. Wittenbecher wouldn't listen. He didn't want us getting in the car. So finally there was a fight, that was how Mr. Wittenbecher got those awful marks and bruises—they beat the hell out of him, Daddy. He was in the gutter and they kicked him and then Maureen and I changed our mind, we didn't go—we saw what dirtbags they were. Mr. Wittenbecher sat up and after a while got himself together enough to drive us home, and then we didn't see him again until this afternoon in the parking lot. Daddy, when I think what would've happened if he hadn't stopped us—"

She was crying. Gordon reached out his arms, holding his daughter as she sobbed. "It's all right, angel," he said. "It's OK."

HE COULD'VE STAYED under the hot blasting water in the men's showers for an hour, but after several minutes he stepped out, dried himself and shuffled into the adjoining washroom. As he shaved he recalled the expression on Azy's face when he'd come back and walked over to her car; instead of showered and changed, he'd looked more disheveled than before. He'd told her about the fight, but not the reasons for it, saying he'd left his clothes in the McSweeneys' kitchen in his hurry to get out. He was really upset by the whole thing, he said. He had it in his mind to leave.

"Augie, I'm really sorry. But don't leave."

"I think it's best, Azy."

"We'll talk. Come on, get in."

"Look at me. I'm a mess."

"Do you know Jerry, in the locker room?"

"I don't think so."

"He takes care of members' shoes."

"Oh. Sure."

"I'll leave clothes with him," she said. "Go take your shower."

"Azy—"

But she drove off.

Augie rinsed his face, put on lotion, applied a squirt of tonic to his hair and worked it in; then, towel around his middle, he walked out of the baths to the lockers. The low-handicap players were just finishing their rounds, sitting on the long benches with bottles of beer, shooting the breeze. Augie went up to the friendly old attendant at the shoe counter and introduced himself. Immediately Jerry produced a blue nylon gym bag with a green-and-red stripe.

"Thank you. How would I go about getting a beer while I'm dressing?"

"I'll get you one. Whose name shall I sign?"

"Mr. McSweeney's. Put my initials underneath, A.W."

"Any special brand, Mr. Wittenbecher?"

"No. Just cold."

Augie returned to the bench, where earlier he had dragged off his sweat-soaked clothes, and sat down—across the aisle, as it turned out, from a foursome of Jack Flannery, Larry Bisell and two other men. They were talking golf. Oh, were they talking golf. Eagle putts and rifled 1-irons. The chip on fourteen that dove into the hole like a scared rabbit. The driver off the fairway on ten that never got eight feet off the ground—and carried the water. The wedge on sixteen that bit so hard Bisell had called the dog catcher. Laugher. Lots of laughter. Augie picked up his bottle of beer, just that moment delivered, and had a pull on it, then unzipped the nylon bag and looked in.

She had brought everything—socks, underwear, a blue-and-white Perry Ellis golf shirt, a pair of light-blue cotton slacks, even a crisp white handkerchief. The clothes weren't new; she hadn't visited the nearest men's shop. But they were pressed, immaculately clean, and he could tell they would fit. He put on the crew socks; the runner-style shorts had navy piping on the seams; he slipped into the shirt. The trousers were a little loose but they were comfortable and the length was right. He stashed his dirty clothes in the bag, finished his beer. At the end of the row of lockers was a full-length mirror. Standing in front of it he gave himself a look while combing his hair—

"You."

He didn't turn, not liking the "you," especially when Jack Flannery knew damn well who he was.

"At the mirror there!"

"Are you talking to me?"

Flannery's eyes dropped to the distinctively striped bag resting on the bench. "Where did you get those clothes?"

"Excuse me?"

"I said where'd you get those clothes."

Augie's heart kicked over. Not again, not another one. "I think it was Jordan Marsh."

"You're a lying sack of shit."

"Maybe Bloomingdale's."

"Take them off."

"What's the problem, Jack?"

"The problem is, they're my clothes."

"I don't think so."

"That's my shirt and those are my pants!"

"You're mistaken—"

"Look, *dick head,* if I have to tell you one more time—"

"Jack, we've been introduced, that's not my name."

"Sorry. I forgot. *Asshole.* Now take them off."

Augie put his comb in his pocket. "You want them so bad, come and get them then. That's the best I can do."

Flannery jumped to his feet but Larry Bisell grabbed him by the belt. "Jack, let him go. It's not worth it."

"I don't like that bastard," Jack said, in a kind of general announcement. "He ripped Al Keegan and Bob Quinn in Friday's match. He has no business playing in this tournament."

"Amen," echoed from a different aisle; from elsewhere in the men's locker room someone applauded.

Flannery wasn't finished. "Furthermore, Wittenbecker, you're going to find yourself in a bunker, face down, with a rake sticking out of your ass if you don't stop messing with Azy."

"You've got a real way with words, Jack."

He picked up the nylon bag and walked away. The old man was wrenching new spikes into the heel of a black shoe.

Augie put his last three quarters on the counter and continued on.

He walked past the pro shop and practice green and out to the auxiliary lot. Azy circled closer and stopped her car. He tossed the gym bag in the back and got in.

"Lookin' good," she said with a big smile.

She took her foot off the brake and they began moving. "What would you like to do?"

"It doesn't matter."

"Is something wrong?"

He rested his head against the restraint. "Something very weird is happening, Azy."

"What do you mean?"

"I haven't had a fight in twenty years." Augie pushed his fingers upward across his forehead. "Now every time I turn around, I'm having one."

"What happened, what was it over? Can you tell me?"

He saw how she was thinking. "Not that fight—that fight is already an *old* fight. Just now, in the locker room."

"Who was it with?"

"Your brother, Jack. I was sitting across from him and Larry. He recognized the clothes."

"Damn."

Augie felt he had just compounded the problem by telling her. Why had he done it? He was beginning to think he couldn't handle situations anymore—deal with people, life. He had lived too long in the goddamn provinces. They came to a traffic light and Azy braked.

She turned slightly, facing him. "What did you say?"

"I told him he was mistaken. The clothes were mine."

"Did he believe you?"

Augie scratched the side of his jaw. "No. He called me a liar—or words to that effect."

"I can't tell you how sorry I am, Augie. I just went into the house and grabbed. I never thought—"

"Azy, it's not *your* fault. My God. It was damn nice of you."

The light changed and she moved onto a boulevard.
"Where're we going?"

"I know a little place—very quiet," she said.

"Great. But I have to tell you something."

"What now?"

"Last night at the Inn I picked up the tab, it wiped me out
—a hundred bucks. I'm out of cash. Unless they'll take a per-
sonal check—"

"This place is also free."

"Now you're putting me on, Azy." ·

She gave him a smile, zipped along; just shy of the bridge
spanning the ocean inlet, she turned off the highway onto a
small street. The houses here weren't the biggest he'd seen
since arriving in Easthelmsford but they were still impressive—
just not mansions. He felt a sense of neighborhood in the area.
As he was looking at a handsome Cape Cod with brown shingles and a tennis court on one side Azy made a sharp turn off
the street between two hedges, pulling up to a cottage also
sided in brown shingles. It had wooden boxes beneath the windows filled with geraniums, and ivy-covered lattice separated
the front yard from the back of the property. "Here we are,"
she said.

"What is it?"

"It's my house."

"Your *house?*"

"A friend and I rent it from the family across the street."

"But you live at your parents'—"

"No. Only because Gil's visiting."

There was a front door, painted red, but they didn't use it.
Instead Azy led him through an archway in the lattice to an
open, grassy area that abutted on a small canal—at least a canal
was the way Augie thought of it. Its sides were buttressed with
heavy timbers, and a small boy was fishing for crabs at the far
end, a hundred or so feet from the cottage. White wooden lawn
furniture was set up on the grass. The boy waved.

"Hi, Azy."

"Hi, Jeff." To Augie: "That's our landlord's son."

He nodded, continued looking around.

"I'll show you inside."

They crossed a tiny terrace that had a glass-topped table and four matching chairs; under a geranium pot next to the door was a key. She led him inside. A stone fireplace was in the main room, its walls and ceiling random widths of knotty pine. A straw rug covered the floor. It was an unpretentious place; everything about it was natural-looking. She showed him the kitchen, her bedroom and a second bedroom, Nora's.

"What does she do?"

"She's a school teacher. Right now she's in Europe. Would you like a drink?"

"Great."

In the kitchen—no appliances except for a toaster—Azy mixed up a couple of gin and tonics and they went back outside and sat in the wooden chairs near the canal. The sun was high but thick clouds were rolling in from the west.

"Cheers," she said.

"To you, Azy."

They drank. The chairs had broad arms, especially good for holding a glass. "I'm surprised you and Gil don't stay here . . ."

"He calls this 'Azy's camp.' "

"So that's it for this place, then, once you're married?"

"Yes."

"What are your plans? I mean, will you be coming back to Easthelmsford?"

"We're looking at houses out on Ocean Drive."

"Houses, plural. Like one for you and one for him?"

She smiled. "The house I like doesn't have enough land, he says. The house he likes has ample space for a tent."

"A tent like for camping?"

"No, for a party. Gil likes big parties. He has this recurring dream where he gives a great bash—guest list of thousands. Just as it's ending everyone circles around him and sings, 'For he's a jolly good fellow.' "

"What about you? Do you have a recurring dream?"

"I have a terrible one," Azy said. "It's about golf."

"Tell me."

"I'm playing—it's a tournament, a competition of some kind—and my ball won't stay on the tee. My brothers are watching and keep yelling at me to hit but I can't—the ball keeps falling off the tee. It's total frustration."

"Here's one I have," Augie said. "My ball stays on the tee but when I go to take the club back it's obstructed. Like by a water cooler. So I retee and I'm blocked again—by a bench. The thing is, no matter where I stand I can't get a free swing at the ball."

"Are we hopeless cases, Augie?"

"I think so," he said.

THE little boy at the end of the canal was hoisting up a crab that he proceeded to unhook and drop into a green pail. He was dressed in a pair of cut-off jeans and a red polo shirt and his arms, legs and face were very brown. The boy rebaited his hook and flipped his line back in.

"There's a nice feeling here," Augie said, beginning to unwind. They were finishing their first drink. "I really like it."

"It's available for next year. I'd be only too happy to talk to the Tomlinsons."

He laughed.

"Is that funny?"

"Azy, I can't make it through four days at Easthelmsford. How could I get through a whole summer?"

"Living here would be different. You'd have your own . . . you know . . . circle. I'd be part of it, I hope."

"If you were part of it, Azy, I wouldn't need a circle."

"I could visit you. Stop by with croissants, early."

"I love croissants—early."

A small cool breeze blew her hair. She brushed it away from her face, her rock glittering on her finger. "Fantasy is wonderful," she said.

"Then you *wouldn't* visit me?"

"Augie, if you rent my place I'll visit you. How's that?"

"Fair enough."

A solitary gull flew over the canal, head tilted down. "But you really wouldn't," he said, "even if I did."

"Why do you say that?"

"I just think once you're actually married—well, it's different when you're married."

"Well, it's a nice thought, stopping by to see you with croissants."

"Oh, it's a wonderful thought."

Augie finished his drink. "Tell me about yourself when you were a kid, Azy."

"How old a kid?"

"OK, jump to eighteen."

Holding her glass loosely in her hands, she began to tell him . . . She had just started Wake Forest on a golf scholarship. Her brothers were very ambitious for her and it was their hope, if not their conviction, that she'd win the National Collegiate Championship. Her last year at Mt. Saint Agnes fifteen colleges were after her—schools with the best golf programs in the country. But an odd thing happened. Instead of her game improving through college it got worse, and her last year she didn't even make the team.

"Can you explain it? I mean, looking back," he said.

"No. It just happened."

"Who chose Wake Forest?"

"My brothers. I didn't object. It was the best all-around deal."

"What about your parents? Did they have any say?"

"Dad was always busy at the hospital, but it was never like Dennis and Jack were planning Azy's future behind his back. My mother—well, she's the go-along-to-get-along lady of all time."

"How did you feel about it, back then—to have your brothers taking such an . . . interest in your life?"

"They were great golfers, they cared about me and wanted the best for me—it was wonderful," Azy said.

211

"How about now?"

"They're my brothers, they still have my interests at heart—"

"Is it still wonderful?"

"No. Actually, I hate it."

She frowned, swirled her ice cubes. "It was awful—fighting with them all the time when Kevin and I were engaged. Finally they just broke me down, I gave in, just like when I was a kid—and I really loved Kevin. Then I just stopped fighting. I wanted to break away but, well, old habits . . . and Gil entered the picture. Generous, wealthy—we'd travel, have a good life. I was thirty-three years old. I said yes." She paused. Was it his imagination, wishful thinking, or were her eyes really misting?

They were silent for several minutes. Another seagull flew over the canal, scoping the water. Then it swooped down and landed on the top timber on the opposite side. Jeff left the canal with his pail and rod and ducked around the far end of the lattice. The clouds were getting thicker, breeze picking up. He looked at her. "Azy?"

"Yes."

"Why didn't you and Kevin just take off? I don't understand—"

"I wanted to."

"What stopped you?"

"At the last moment I'd hear my brothers' voices. Or their open disapproval. I've been a phony in a way . . . liberated career woman on the outside, little girl scared of displeasing her big brothers on the inside. I guess it would have helped if Kevin had been more aggressive, but he had his family problems too. He's the black sheep in the Donohue family. No one could understand how he could be such a great golfer with so little killer instinct. He was *patient.* Patient with his game, patient with *me.* Then what did I do? He was giving me time, waiting for me—and I ended it. No more excuses, I did it."

A drop of rain hit her cheek. Another, his.

"And now you've given up, right?" Augie knew he was

pushing it, but he was no Kevin Donohue; let her be sure of that, at least.

"Well, I'm not in love with Gil . . ."

"You're not married to him yet either."

"No." They were quiet for a while, then she said, "I'd better go put up the roof on my car."

"I'll do it," Augie said.

"Are you hungry?"

"I am, yes."

"Me too. I'll make us something," Azy said.

When he came back she was at the small kitchen counter preparing a crabmeat salad. She said she had some Chablis in the refrigerator, would he pour it? They sat on the sofa in the living room, their plates and wine on a coffee table made from an old walnut headboard—taken from the bed her parents had conceived her in. The salad was delicious and he drank his wine and somehow drifted into talking about his children. Brian got good grades without working, Heather had to work for her grades, and even then they weren't all that good. Brian loved (what else?) golf; Heather loved ballet and painting—and was her father's confidante and social adviser. He'd told her, he said, about a beautiful woman he'd met in Easthelmsford on Thursday night who, unfortunately, was engaged. Now every time he spoke to Heather on the phone she wanted an "update."

"You'll be able to report we had lunch together."

"She'll be happy to hear it. Yesterday I told her we'd met in the parking lot."

"What did she say to that?"

"She thought I could do better."

THE dishes were cleared away—what few there were—and outside it was raining. She was resting against him in the sofa, feeling amazingly happy. He kissed her then. It was a sweet kiss, she was glad he wasn't fast. They kissed again, his hand rose to the edge of her breast, and she began to have that

213

honey feeling come over her. She loved having it again—she thought she might have lost the ability to have it. And she knew it was only starting. They went into her bedroom and the rain was striking the roof as they undressed and got beneath the sheets. He was a slow and gentle lover, bringing her to a point where she couldn't wait to have him. Then he was entering her, gliding in so easy, and she was filled, completely filled, more than filled. She loved it, and she reached up and kissed him, her eyes wide with pleasure—and almost at once she had an orgasm, then another—she couldn't stop—and then she said, "Augie, you. You, Augie!" and he let loose the reins—that was how she felt it, experienced it. He was running free and then he was there and then—oh God—she was there again, and then she couldn't think anymore, she was in a different place, a different world and time and place . . .

"WHERE will you be later?"

They were in Azy's car, parked beside his station wagon in the auxiliary parking lot. "The schedule calls for dinner at Dennis and Kate's."

"Then I'm not likely to accidentally run into you again," Augie said.

"You could drop by, knock on the door."

" 'Oh, hi, Dennis. How you doin'? Azy around? Ha-ha.' "

She laughed. She was pushing it, for time, but she didn't seem to care. "How about you?"

"No plans," he said.

"Won't you be with the McSweeneys?"

"No, I'm staying away."

"Where will you sleep?"

"In my car."

"Augie, that's crazy!"

"I'll be fine. I've got a sleeping bag and—"

"Go back to my place. You know where the key is."

"I'll be OK here, really."

"Why sleep in the back of a car when you can sleep in a bed?"

"Will you come over?"

She laughed. "Augie, you know I'd love to. I don't see how I can . . ."

"Once Gil goes to sleep—"

"I'll come over in the morning," she said.

"With croissants?"

She touched his lips with her fingers, tracing their shape. "With croissants. What time are you teeing off?"

"Not till nine-thirty or so."

"How's seven?"

"Six would be better."

She laughed again. "It was a beautiful afternoon, Augie. I want to tell you, you're one fantastic member guest."

His face grew very warm.

"I've made you blush," Azy said.

"You have."

"Go over right now, if you want," she said. "If you get hungry later on, raid the refrigerator. Make yourself at home . . . Just one thing—"

"If a man knocks don't let him in."

"No—don't worry about that. I'll call you in the morning if I can't make it. I'll let the phone ring once. That'll be the signal."

"I wish you hadn't said that."

"Gil gets up early, I might not be able to get away. I'll try. I want to see you again before you go, Augie."

"Why don't you come back to Shufferville with me?"

She didn't answer and he was immediately sorry he'd asked. It put her on the spot. "Forget I said that."

"I'm glad you said it. I have to go."

"I'll see you in the morning."

She started to speak and he said, "Just say OK. I'll sleep better."

"OK."

He held her and they kissed for a long time—it was torture for him to leave her. To let her go. In more ways than one.

"Good night."

"Good night."

Augie got out, ducked into his car, shut the door against the rain. Azy flashed her lights twice and was gone.

Azy swung off Sycamore Lane at the circular driveway to her parents' house; parked directly at the front door was her brother's fire-engine-red Ferrari.

There was only one reason he was here.

She turned off her wipers and ignition, then stayed behind the wheel for an extra minute trying to steel herself for the meeting. She stepped out and ran the six steps to the door, tripped the heavy brass latch and went in. The house had a quiet feel despite the faint sound of the TV in the den. Her parents were probably upstairs taking a nap. It had become their custom before an evening out. The door leading into the den was open and her brother was inside watching a golf tournament.

He was too proud, of course, to turn, and if she just kept walking he would yell at her. And she would come back anyway. Azy detested the feeling. She went to the den doorway and—well-bred young woman and respectful sister that she was—announced herself.

"Hi."

Wherever the tournament was being played, it was a sunny afternoon. Craig Stadler had a fairway wood in his hands and would need every bit of it, the announcer was saying. The touring pro swung; no sooner was contact made than Jack blurted out, "You pulled it, asshole." How he could make out the trajectory so immediately, Azy didn't know, but sure enough, the ball landed in the left rough, bounced twice and dove into a greenside bunker.

"Did you see the swing he put on that ball?"

The question was rhetorical. Twisting about in the burgundy leather chair with brass fittings, he decided to recognize his sister. He had on a mauve short-sleeved shirt, tan slacks and tasseled loafers (no socks). "Gil called. Because of the storm all chopper flights were cancelled. He left on a 5:23 train."

"Thank you."

"Where've you been?"

"Out."

"That's what kids say, Azy. If I asked you what you did, I suppose you'd say nothing."

"I might."

She came in another step but didn't sit. Some water was running down her hair and she ran her hand over her face.

"What's going on, Azy?"

She remembered the time at Mt. Saint Agnes when Sister Caroline had caught her necking with Patrick McLewis in the chapel during a joint glee-club rehearsal. When she and Patrick had stood, a muscle behind Azy's left knee had started jumping —it was jumping now. "With regard to what?"

"Don't give me that *shit*. You know damn well *with regard to what.*"

The old feelings of nervousness, of even being frightened were back, but at least she wasn't going to volunteer information. "I'm sorry, Jack, I don't—"

"My goddamn clothes! You gave that Wittenbecker idiot my clothes."

"Oh. That."

Jack looked at her as if she were a witness for the other side. *"That,* yes. Why?"

"He didn't have anything to wear."

"How in hell would you know? Unless you're—"

"Is everything all right down there?" came their mother's

218

voice from the top of the stairs. Mild, quietly inquisitive, concerned.

"No problem," Jack called out. He stood and kicked the door shut. "I want an answer, Azy. What's going on with you and this *Wittenbecker?*"

"That's not how you say his name."

"Pardonnez-fucking-moi. Understand something—I've enough on my mind with Janet, I don't need any additional grief from you." He was talking into her face. "Now I'll ask you again—"

"Nothing's going on. I lent him one of your shirts and pair of pants. Is that a crime?"

"You just don't see it, do you?"

"Why are you getting so excited?"

He shook his head. "So what we have here is Azy to the rescue of indigent golfers. Azy, the Florence Nightingale of the links!"

Craig Stadler had reached the bunker, and Jack broke off his cross-examination to watch. Stadler sized up his lie, squiggled his feet and swung. Sand flew up, evidently too much—the ball landed way short; when it stopped rolling it was twenty feet from the hole. Jack reached for the clicker. "What was he trying to do, top-dress the green? And they call themselves pros."

He jabbed at the power button, came back to his sister. "I worry about you," he said in a quieter tone. "We all thought when you finally dumped Kevin you were finally getting it together. Now I'm thinking we thought too soon. Because if you're messing with this Wittenbecker you're a damn fool. And you're making a fool out of me and Dennis and Dad." His voice was rising again. "Not to mention Gil! The man is crazy about you, he's building a goddamn empire for you—and what are *you* doing? What the fuck are you *doing,* Azy?"

She sat down in the matching sofa, leather cool to her thighs and back: so cool she felt a chill. "I don't have to answer that."

"Anyone who pleads the Fifth is guilty."

219

"Then I should've said it's none of your business!" Had she actually managed to say that?

"It is my business—that's just it."

His piercing blue eyes seemed to pin her to the sofa. "When I see a member of this family doing something hurtful or self-destructive it affects us all. If Gil found out you were thick with Wittenbecker, what do you think he'd do? I mean, it's all pretty embarrassing when you stop to think of it. So don't say it isn't my business, because what happened today cuts right across the family—it hurts us all."

She was trying, like never before, to hold her own, but she also knew she was no match. So many years of conditioning . . . as a kid she'd never even argued with her brothers.

Jack Flannery glanced at his gold watch, thin as a coin. "Why are you fooling around with him, Azy?"

"I'm not fooling around with him."

He laughed. "You still think it's a big game, don't you, playing with guys' affections like you're a high-school junior? Another notch on Azy's belt."

"I can have friends—"

"Tell that to Gil, tell him you spent all afternoon with this *friend.*"

"You don't know what I did."

Jack Flannery gave his head a slow sad shake. "We had big hopes for you . . . Dennis, Dad and I. I never thought I'd say this, but I'm saying it now. You're a loser. My sister Azy is a loser!"

He walked out, leaving the den door open but slamming the front door. His Ferrari fired. Then silence.

She sat alone for several minutes, furious, and scared too. Maybe he was right. It was hard to see yourself, to make a judgment on yourself. Finally she stood, went out to the front hall with its royal chandelier, fine antique furniture and polished oak floor—scarred by spikes. Her mother had never said a word, had allowed it—these were her men, they made the money and paid the bills and if they chose to stomp in wearing their golfing shoes, who was she to object? Azy took the stairs up to the second-floor landing, walked slowly along to her room. Inside, she crossed to the north window and looked out at the fifteenth hole. But she saw nothing; the course was totally obscured by mist and rain. Closer in, the sycamores leaned, swayed in the wind . . .

She showered, put on a white terrycloth robe and combed out her hair. As she was looking in her closet, trying to decide what she'd wear, she heard the sound of footsteps in the hall: heavy, solid. A rap on her door, and Gil walked in—suitjacket wet, hair wet. He walked across to her.

"How are you, Azy?" He took her in his arms. "God, you feel good."

"How did it go?"

"We signed LaRue!"

"That's great."

He kept holding her, began nuzzling her neck. She felt pressure, a stiffening low against her abdomen. Making love to him was the last thing she felt like doing. "You're wet, you'd better change. Dennis and Kate want us by seven—"

"So we're late. We'll be seeing them all evening."

"Did you give LaRue what he was asking?" she stalled, pulling away.

"I'm not worried, we'll make it up at the gate in two seasons. The Stanley Cup's coming to Chicago, Azy."

He took off his rain-darkened cord jacket, draped it over her vanity chair while removing, from the inside pocket, an oblong blue velvet box. "Sit down here," he said, patting the bed.

She sat beside him, suddenly feeling nauseous.

"I was walking along Fifth Avenue thinking what a great day it was, mostly because you were in my life and I couldn't wait to see you, and there I was right outside Cartier. Anyway, here."

He handed her the box. She held it, looking down, her hands motionless.

"Open it, Azy."

She lifted the top; lying on pale blue satin was a small, exquisite bracelet of diamonds and rubies.

"Do you like it?"

She could hardly answer. "It's beautiful, Gil." Her voice was small. "I've wanted a tennis bracelet—"

"This is a golf bracelet."

"What's the difference?"

"There isn't one. But why should it be a tennis bracelet?"

She forced a smile. "I love it. Thank you, Gil."

"Put it on."

She did; it sparkled on her wrist and Gil kissed her neck, her ear, lifting his hands to the floppy white collar of her robe, parting it, kissing her breasts. He kicked off his shoes, stripped off his trousers, pulled her down, smiling happily, taking what was his. In her mind Azy saw the sycamores outside her window—

"Yeah."

—bending, bending.

ON the side of the glass-enclosed deck overlooking the ocean Azy and Janet O'Roehrs were talking intimately. On the house side of the deck, at a black-leather bar with big brass wheels, their fiancés—and all the other men at the party—were talking about golf.

More specifically, they were talking about the tournament. Dennis Flannery and Frank Gildersleeve had lost the day's match to Bob Donohue and Ed Sargent, who would be facing Jack and Larry in the final round of the Championship Flight in the morning. So Dennis and Frank had plenty to say about Bob and Ed's strengths and weaknesses as a team and as individual players.

Bob Donohue had unveiled a new driver, Dennis was saying; he had put aside the classic Tommy Armour oil-hardened persimmon he'd used for the past ten years and replaced it with a steel-headed Mizuno with a "gold graphite" shaft. It was adding fifteen to twenty yards to his distance, but at a price,

Dennis believed. Bob just wasn't hitting the fairways with any consistency.

"Is he going left or right with it?" Jack asked.

"Both. He's spraying the ball."

"I thought he hit the club pretty good," Frank commented. "On four he went o.b., then on ten he had to play from the fifteenth fairway. But on the thirteenth hole he almost drove the green. How often do you see that? Then on sixteen he had a half-wedge going in. I hit a full 8."

"What about on eighteen?" Dennis asked. "Where did he go? I'm trying to make a point, that's all. Bob was steadier with the old club. I think that's good for Jack and Larry to know."

"How's Sargent playing?" Larry asked.

"He putted great," Frank said.

"That's because he gets the ball close from forty to ninety yards out," Dennis said. "If you can get the ball close, who isn't a good putter?"

"The man carries three wedges and he has a touch with each one," Frank Gildersleeve said.

"A lot of players are going to a third wedge," Jack said.

Then: Where would pin placements be for tomorrow's round? Jack said on certain holes there was no telling, it would all depend on how devilish the course superintendent felt in the morning. But he could guarantee the placements on one, seven, ten and sixteen.

"Go ahead," said Bisell.

"On one—upper left, that little plateau."

"That's where it was last year," said Frank Gildersleeve.

"On final rounds, that's where it always is," Dr. Flannery said.

"Two years ago, final round, I knocked an 8-iron stiff," Gil said. "Then four-putted. Remember, John?"

"I'm trying not to."

"Tomorrow," Dennis said to his brother and Larry, "the word on the first green is *lag,* if you're on or near that plateau."

"Unless you're going for a halve," Dr. Flannery said.

"Then you have to go for it, no question there. But for a

win, I wouldn't do it," Dennis said. "You don't want to lose the first hole. Settle for a split and head for two . . ." And so it went.

LIGHTNING brightened the sky. Everywhere on the vast ocean whitecaps flickered. For Azy it was all extraordinarily dramatic, almost scary, as she stood at the huge plate windows—not that watching the storm was all she was doing. She was listening to Janet talk about Jack and trying to respond with some interest. But her own head was so mixed up—so clouded with her own problems—she wasn't sure what Janet was saying, let alone if she was helping.

"If I ask for his attention he makes me feel demanding, childish," Janet was saying in a low voice. "If I don't ask for it, I feel isolated and miserable."

She picked up her glass resting on the sill and finished off her gin and tonic; it was her third since they had started talking. She had a lovely, near-angelic face, but tension was eroding the softness, almost making it hard, Azy was thinking. She was reed-thin too. Since the start of summer Janet had probably lost seven pounds, and she didn't have seven pounds to lose. She was wearing a little cloud-washed denim dress with a low neckline.

"Personally, I think my brother's just about impossible to please," Azy said. "I'm an expert there."

"It's so ironic," Janet said. "We walk around our new house, talking about all the hundreds of details—the fixtures, the appliances, where we want the bar, what kind of exercise equipment we should buy, where to put our bed for the best view of the ocean, what kind of wallpaper to have in the children's rooms—and we never share any real, intimate moments. On Thursday, after the party at the club, he rolled over on me half-asleep. And that was the first time in two weeks!"

Azy sipped her glass of wine.

"What am I asking for?" Janet said. "I can understand being second to his career. But *third*, after golf? I used to be proud that he played well, won tournaments. Now I hate the damn game."

"I know the feeling," Azy said.

"All I want from Jack is what Gil gives you, making you feel important to him, special. Maybe it's a cliché, but isn't that what every woman wants? If I didn't love you so much, Azy, I'd be envious of you. I only want a little of that with Jack. Look at him now, look at him. I'm sick of it."

Jack was demonstrating the swing—without a club—as Azy had seen him do so many times through the years. Hands flat, palms facing each other with the right slightly higher, both elevated over his right shoulder, then making a neat little motion down with his hands. "Right here," Azy could hear him saying to the group; they were all looking, nodding. It was very serious stuff. "This is the golf swing, *right here.*"

"Why do I love him?" Janet's eyes were taking on a strange glaze. "What does he give me to love?"

"He gives nobody anything to love, Janet. I don't know why you love him—but at least you do."

"I wish I didn't."

Azy was turning the diamond-and-ruby bracelet on her wrist. "Suppose you didn't love him, and he loved you?"

"I wouldn't care. It's so much *worse* not to be loved."

KATE Flannery was moving about the spacious dining room, making last-minute touches to the linen-and-lace-covered table. She was wearing draped pants and a deep-purple silk tunic top: tall, slender, with shoulder-length hair and a handsome tan. Azy had always thought of her sister-in-law as a very together woman—attractive, incredibly efficient, completely supportive of Dennis. If she had any problems Azy didn't know what they were.

The table—set with Kate's finest china and silver—was situated on the oceanside of the house overlooking the beach. Her husband sat at one end, she at the end nearer the kitchen; then came Dr. and Mrs. Flannery, Azy and Gil, Jack and Janet, and finally the brothers' golfing guests—all across from each other. Larry and Frank poured the wine. Candles were glittering softly. Dr. John Flannery stood, lifting his glass for a toast.

"To this wonderful tradition of our Member-Guest Saturday dinner," he said. "I want to thank Kate and Dennis for having us. Gil and Azy are on for next year, Jack and Janet the following—at this rate, Margaret and I are going to get out of practice."

"It's breaking your heart," Dennis said.

People laughed. John Flannery was still holding up his glass. "I love what it says about our kids, all of you out here on the Drive. We're very proud of you. But to the business at hand. Dennis and Frank played extremely well today but lost. Jack and Larry are still in it, Gil and me as well. So the Flannerys will be well represented out there tomorrow. This is the eleventh year in a row that one Flannery has reached the final round. I—"

"Dad," interrupted Jack, "we're going to have to penalize you for slow play. Could you wrap this up?"

"Right, right. Good luck, Jack and Larry. Gil, good luck—the way I'm playing, we're going to need it. To everyone, we love you!"

People clinked glasses, sipped their wine. Kate had prepared sirloin tips in a rich wine sauce with mushrooms, asparagus with a cream sauce and roast potatoes. She started the food around. People began eating, praising Kate on how delicious everything was. Then the topic turned—or came back to—golf. Dennis said there was serious talk of not renewing Kyle McIntyre's contract at the end of the year.

"I like Kyle. What's the problem?" Azy asked.

"His game's gone to hell, for one. He's too busy giving lessons," Dennis said. "We need a professional who competes now and then. Not on the PGA tour necessarily but in substantial regional tournaments. Personally, I don't play with Kyle anymore—it's embarrassing to beat your pro by five or six strokes."

"There's more to it than that," said Dr. Flannery, slicing off a morsel of beef and making sure a mushroom got on his fork. "Al Keegan expressed it pretty well in the men's grill yesterday. McIntyre is employed by the club but he doesn't represent the members. He doesn't back the members. Like in Al's first-round match with McSweeney and Wittenbecher. There was obviously a breach of the rules there, and Kyle supported Wittenbecher. Al doesn't take that kind of treatment lightly. He talks and other members with their complaints talk. So it's not looking good for McIntyre for a couple of reasons. What Dennis said is certainly true. On a good day he'll break eighty. On a good day *Azy* breaks eighty."

"On a very good day," Azy said.

"When Kyle supported that jerk Wittenbecker over Keegan, that did it for me. I'd vote to dump him," Jack said.

"That goes back to what we were talking about earlier," Gil Plumber said. "I don't have any vote, but if and when I become a member at Easthelmsford—when Azy and I become members, hopefully next year—I'm going to suggest a stricter policy of screening guests. And I don't mean just calling up to verify handicaps. Because some people coming here and using the club's facilities are pretty questionable characters, if you want my opinion."

"I don't disagree," Dennis said. "But I think a lot of it, this year, has to do with McSweeney's guest. Steve McMahon mentioned it at an emergency meeting of the Golf Committee. Does the Committee have the authority to disqualify a team on grounds of poor sportsmanship on the part of a guest?"

"Without a question," said Dr. Flannery.

"Golf is still a gentleman's game, or should be. That's the number-one rule," Gil said.

"Wittenbecker has done nothing but cause trouble," Jack said.

"I thought you were going to kill him today in the locker room," Larry Bisell said.

"Oh, what happened?" Dennis asked.

Everyone was silent, waiting. Azy's hands rose, then

dropped quickly to her lap. She looked at Larry, coughed, picked up her napkin and coughed again—

"You OK, Azy?" Gil asked.

"Fine—just something in my throat. Sorry."

"Go ahead, Larry," Dennis said.

"Well—ah—he was having a beer with another guest, just criticizing hell out of the course and the club generally," Bisell said. "I couldn't stand it but I wasn't going to say anything. Jack told him if he didn't like it here, he should pack up and get out."

Dennis said, "What did he say to that?"

"He was abusive, really abusive," Jack said. "Then he picked up his stuff and left."

"The nerve of that creep, it's unbelievable," Dennis said.

"I've been playing in our Member-Guest for over twenty-three years," Dr. Flannery said, "and I'll tell you something. I've never seen anyone cause this kind of disruption before."

"He seemed like a perfect gentleman at our cocktail party," Mrs. Flannery said.

"Mom, I love you, but you'd give Jack-the-Ripper the benefit of the doubt," Jack said.

Azy wanted to kill him but bit her tongue.

"Dennis, this is terrific wine," Frank Gildersleeve said.

"Saint-Emilion is one of our favorites; the '78 is a particularly good year," Dennis said. "We bought four cases—it worked out to a forty percent saving."

"Let's open another bottle then," Jack said.

Another bottle was opened. Gil started talking about a golfer he knew in Winnetka. One day he hit a wild tee shot— landed in the woods behind the mower shed. Caddy told him the best way to get his ball back into play was to shoot it through the open door and out the back window of the shed. "So he said he'd try to. *Smack*. Ball sailed through the door and window, flew across the fairway, shot through an upstairs window in his condo and killed his wife. Four years later this same player found himself in the same spot after a bad drive and a different caddy told him his best bet was to hit through the shed. 'No way,' the golfer said, 'the last time I tried that shot I had a triple-bogey.' "

Laughter. More golf talk. Larry Bisell said if he were a member at the E.C.C. he'd recommend a change in the rules; in his opinion a ball in a cart path should be a free drop. His second shot on fifteen landed right in the path: hard, packed-down earth. Pan. A chip from pan was one of the hardest shots in golf, and he'd hit it thin. Jack had a par on the hole for a halve so it didn't make any difference, but it could have made a big difference. Dr. Flannery said the question of a free drop came up every spring when the Rules Committee initially met but it was always defeated; the majority of members felt they would rather have dirt cart paths and no free drop than macadam paths *and* a free drop.

"Golf's hard enough," Bisell said. "To play from pan when otherwise you could play from grass is unnecessarily punitive."

"I'll tell you one thing," Jack said, "the pan chip's not as hard as you're making it. You have to nip that ball. What club did you use?"

"Sand wedge."

"Jesus Christ," Jack said. "We have to win tomorrow, and my partner uses a sand wedge from pan." He looked at Bisell. "Larry, now listen . . . the sand wedge has a rounded sole, it's called bounce, in case you didn't know. It's great in loose sand and thick grass. Use it off pan, you're *asking* to thin the ball."

"Thanks, Jack. Check's in the mail."

People were laughing, drinking the Saint-Emilion; still another bottle was opened. The sirloin tips went around a second and third time. "I see no reason why there should be out-of-bounds markers on five," Frank Gildersleeve said, "on the right side."

Dr. Flannery said, "You're talking about Judge William B. Callahan's lawn, that's why."

"But Frank makes a point," Jack said. "You push a tee shot on five, you're looking at stroke and distance. I'm not talking slice. Just leaving it out there a little."

Even for Azy, who had grown up with it, the golf talk was

becoming too much. And it wasn't letting up. Across the table Janet filled her glass, for at least the fourth time. The peculiar shine in her eyes seemed more intense. As she drank, her lips were moving in a strange manner—twitching, oddly contorting. A drop of wine was running down her chin. Azy turned to Jack on her left. He was having a deep discussion with Gildersleeve about whether a player could stand *out*-of-bounds to hit a ball that was *in*-bounds. Frank said no, you couldn't stand out of the batter's box when hitting a baseball. The same concept applied to golf.

"The rules of golf are enigmatic and arcane, but there's a certain logic to them," Jack said. "That logic *isn't* governed by the fundamentals of baseball."

"Jack . . ." his sister was saying.

"Wait a minute, Azy . . . The batter's box has a distinct and special purpose—"

"Jack!"

Then everyone was staring at Janet. Drinking her wine, she had decided to eat the long-stemmed vessel containing it. She had broken off several hunks of glass with her teeth, and blood and wine were dripping down her lips and chin as she chewed. Kate Flannery screamed and Mrs. Flannery cried, "Oh, my God," and Jack, leaping up, yelled, "Jesus Christ, Janet!"

Dr. Flannery was on his feet, rushing to Janet's side, giving instructions to Dennis to call the Easthelmsford Rescue Squad. "Janet"—she was still jawing fiercely away—*"don't swallow.* Relax. Just relax, Janet. Jack, get my bag."

Jack ran out. Everyone was standing now. Dr. Flannery took a linen napkin and inserted it in Janet's mouth and worked his fingers inside.

"Janet—it's going to be all right, let me help you," he said in his calm professional way. "Just don't swallow. Please, *don't swallow.*"

Jack came running back in clutching a black grip. His father opened it and pulled out a syringe and a small vial, and then Azy couldn't look anymore. Gil came over and stood next to her and held her, and for the first time in a long time his arms felt good. Janet was a very confused girl, he said. Too young for all Jack was giving her, she wasn't ready for it. Azy was crying now. She seemed to see herself going to the side of the tee at her parents' cocktail party and standing next to a stranger—because she liked his look and heard a voice saying to her, "Why not?" One last chance at it, Azy. In five months you'll be married."

But how romantic could a person be? How young! She really wasn't so different from Janet. Maybe just a little luckier. So far.

Azy put her arms around Gil and held on. Kids dreamed. It was time she acted her age. If that meant settle, well, women settled. She had to get on with her life.

Her mother was weeping and Jack's mouth was open, his fingers pressing against his lips and teeth. The surf pounded the beach and far out a flash of lightning brightened the horizon, like gunfire at sea.

PART IV

THE FINALS

WHEN HE WOKE UP sunshine was streaming
through the window by Azy's bed. Augie looked at his watch,
then sat up and peered out. Two gulls were swimming in the
little canal. When he had turned in at ten-fifteen he had fore-
seen the possibility that the final round might be canceled because of the unrelenting rain; but sometime in the night the
storm had passed. It was a beautiful morning. Glistening and
clear.

He put his feet out, sat on the edge of the bed. So, golf as
usual at the E.C.C. All flights teeing it up—with the possible
exception of 12; member Gordon McSweeney might not show,
harboring great animosity toward guest Augustus T. Wittenbecher for having had sex with his wife. Augie headed for
the bathroom. The shower didn't pound at him like the showers at the club; it was plenty strong, just more needlelike.
When he finished, he dried himself in the bathroom doorway.
It was getting to be that time when the phone could ring and he
wanted to make sure he heard it if or when it did.

But it's not going to ring, he thought.

He put on Jack's clothes, having nothing else to wear, then
went into the kitchen, took off the plastic top to a coffee can,
ran water and set the glass percolator on the range, turning the
burner on high. A window in the kitchen faced the driveway
and he crossed and stood in front of it, looking past his car to
the opening in the hedge, where Azy, coming along the street,

would turn; at this hour Sunday morning no cars were coming along the street. The coffee pot started perking; he went over and lowered the setting—and the phone rang.

He gave the knob a brusque flip all the way to off.

But then it rang again. And again.

It was a wall telephone near the refrigerator, and Augie guessed and double-guessed. Should he answer? It could be Gil, or brother Jack, having suspicions, checking out a hunch. But then again it *could* be Azy. To say Gil was on his way over with a shotgun. Finally, on the fifth ring, Augie picked up. "Hello."

"Carl, I'm gonna be twenty minutes late. I'm tied up here—"

"This isn't Carl."

"Oh? He there?"

"You have the wrong number."

Click.

Augie kept his hand on the receiver after hanging up, then returned to the stove and turned the burner back on. He walked to the window and looked out, staying there until the coffee was ready. He poured himself a mug and drank it at the same window. Just because the caller had asked for Carl didn't mean it was a wrong number. The caller could have been Larry Bisell, doing a turn for Jack, seeing if a man answered. Or Frank Gildersleeve, doing one for Gil for the same reason. And any minute now two cars were going to pull into the driveway—

A car went slowly by. Augie's heart thundered but it didn't stop. The hour wore on. Another possibility was that Azy was simply late. He would finish his coffee and leave . . .

No brothers, no Azy. Augie emptied the pot, rinsed it and washed and put away his mug. The key was on the mantel and he went out, sliding it under the flowerpot. For a few seconds he stayed by the door looking at the two chairs by the little canal. She probably hadn't been able to shake free to even pick up the phone. Simple as that. Not to worry, Augie told himself, walking out to his car, but he worried nonetheless.

"MORNING, Mr. Wittenbecher."

"Good morning, Jimmy. Have you seen Mr. McSweeney?"

"No, I haven't."

They were standing outside club-storage, by the steps. A few golfers in cardigans and jackets were practicing on the green. Some twenty bags lay against the low fence, and Steve McMahon and his assistant were setting up their table at the back of the first tee. "I'm going to have a bite to eat," Augie said. "If you see him—"

"I'll tell him. Good luck today."

"Thanks, Jimmy."

Augie continued along the path, then through the locker room and into the dining room. The kindly matron greeted him with her warm smile. He was looking so much better this morning. They had a marvelous menu today, did he like eggs Benedict?

"I do, but my stomach's feeling a little jumpy—"

"That's too bad. How about some creamy oatmeal?"

"Do you have a corn muffin?"

"Oh, yes. Sit down, dear. Coffee?"

"No thanks. Just juice."

HE broke off a piece of muffin, looking out at the course. Sparkling in the sun now, it had a magical, beckoning quality, and he couldn't wait to play—he would be damn disappointed if Gordon didn't show. But he was also a nervous wreck thinking about the match. Augie finished his juice and stayed at the pink table with fresh-cut flowers, trying to be philosophic. If he lost to Plumber, he lost. In the great scheme of things, what difference did it make?

Plenty, Augie thought. I don't want to lose to him. I want to beat him, I want to bury him.

I want to *kill* him. And he wants to kill me . . .

He stood and went out. Before he could ask Jimmy if he had seen Mr. McSweeney, Jimmy said, "He's on the range."

"Mr. McSweeney is on the range," Augie repeated.

"It's a first."

Augie inhaled deeply.

"Your bag's on the back of the cart, Mr. Wittenbecher. Mr. McSweeney drove it out."

"OK. Thanks."

Augie walked on, angling across the lot. When he got to the practice tee he moved behind twelve or fifteen golfers— then, there he was. Sizing up a teed ball with his unique head tilt, like a bird eying a bug.

"—Dr. Hathaway, Mr. Senz, to the first tee, please. On deck: Mr. Benedict, Mr. Delpizzo—"

At the announcement, the player hitting balls beside Gordon—a twenty-five-year-old towhead in khaki trousers— picked up his loose clubs and left the tee, and Augie grabbed a 9-iron and a 7-iron from his bag and walked out. A wire pail, half-full, sat on the ground. But he didn't immediately start in. Thinking it best to clear the air, he waited for Gordon to look up.

He didn't look up. He kept hitting. Finally Augie said, "How they going for you?"

Gordon lifted his head, his expression straight, cold. "Can't you see when a man's practicing?"

"I'm glad to see it. I only—"

"Then let him fucking practice."

Augie toppled the pail and began knocking out balls.

"Shit," Gordon said.

Augie hit several more balls.

"Fuck," Gordon said.

And a few more.

"Piss."

Augie ventured a half-turn, watched Gordon swing lustily and the ball sail away in a big slice. Gordon glanced up, catching Augie. "Yeah?"

"Nothing."

238

"When I want your advice I'll ask for it."
"I wasn't going to give you any advice."
"Good."
Augie stood there, just looking at his old friend.
"So turn around, *OK?*"
"No problem," Augie said.

SOME forty people were gathered around the first tee watching teams from the different flights tee off. Then it was time for Flight 12 to go at it. Augie pulled his 3-wood from his bag and Gordon took out his battered driver. Carrying their weapons, they met Dr. Flannery and Gil Plumber in front of the tournament chairman's table. McMahon said that the course was basically in good shape in spite of the heavy rains. They might encounter some soggy conditions, though. Players were entitled to a free drop, not nearer the hole, if water squished up under their shoes while taking a stance. McMahon paused; his eyes passed over the four players' faces and he spoke seriously. Second-round play had generally taken too long, he said. Slow play in today's round would not be tolerated. The tournament committee had appointed a full-time ranger who would be driving around checking on individual teams. A penalty of *two strokes* would be assessed to a team after the first warning. Were there any questions?

There were none.

"John, your team will be leading off."

"Thank you, Steve," said Dr. Flannery.

There were no handshakes. The players simply separated. Augie put the shaft of his 3-wood behind his back, then hooked his arms around the shaft and twisted and turned his upper body. He thought he might see Azy in the gallery but he didn't see her anywhere and he kept loosening up. Plumber was doing knee bends and Dr. Flannery, holding a club fully extended, was rotating his wrist and forearm quickly back and forth. Gordon was yawning. The golfers ahead hit approach shots, and when both carts crossed the little bridge leading to the green, Steve McMahon announced, "All right, gentlemen. Play away."

Gil Plumber picked a spot between the markers and teed a ball. He had on bright red pants and a rose golf shirt with a white collar; his cardigan was white and so were his shoes. He was an all-business kind of player. Tee ball, take stance, swing. His swing was very compact—extremely aggressive—as Augie already knew. The drive went deep but curved left, though not so far as to catch the swale; his ball lay in open rough—probably an 8-iron in.

"Good hit, Gil," said Dr. Flannery.

Plumber moved to the rear of the tee. He wasn't smiling but he wasn't displeased. Dr. Flannery's turn. He was deliberate, very precise in his movements; he had the golf swing perfectly worked out. If you did the same thing each time your ball would go the same way each time: for John Flannery, that was straight. When you were sixty-eight you were bound to lose distance, but that didn't mean you had to lose accuracy. His backswing was slow and herky-jerky; once he reached the top, however, the program kicked in. Dr. Flannery's downswing was neat and precise. The ball flew out in a pretty arc and dropped dead in the middle of the fairway some one hundred ninety yards away.

People gave him a good hand. He stood beside his partner and his sons, who had come by to see him tee-off, and because Gordon didn't say anything about the order of play, Augie went out and put a ball on a tee, stepped back and got his line. He didn't see anything when he looked down the fairway: just big gray space. He took a stance; his heart was thumping and his joints—shoulder, hip, knee—all felt fused. As much to end the ordeal as to hit, he brought the club back and swung down. The ball popped up high and to the right, maybe going twenty-five yards, and settled in the top of the tall hedge.

The stillness in the area of the tee was like death.

Augie stepped away, head low. Gordon was now on. He assumed his start-the-mower stance and kept moving his head until he got a bead he liked; then he made his backswing and lunged down. The shot was his old slice but didn't go out of bounds. Something. Then Augie, because his first shot was unplayable, teed a second ball. He knew what had happened the first time; he had looked up and caught the ball on the tip of his club. Nervous though he was, he could at least keep his goddamn head *down*. He swung, determined to stay with the ball through contact. But at the last moment his head rose again; the ball burned grass for thirty yards, then died.

He walked off the tee and got in the cart with Gordon, who drove to Augie's second ball without speaking. Augie said he was picking up, which he did. They drove to Gordon's ball, and Gordon commenced to whiff his second shot, dub his third and drop his fourth into the pond. He wanted to try again but Augie said no, they would concede the hole and move on.

"We're not delaying play!" Gordon said angrily.

"You're four in the pond," Augie told him, "six wherever you land next. There's no point to it."

"I need the practice."

"You've had your practice; this is the *match.*"

"If I put my next ball in the hole, we could tie."

Augie felt himself losing it. "OK, shoot—go ahead. Fuck!"

Gordon tossed down a new ball—new to him—and knocked it sweetly back into the drink.

"We're conceding the hole," Augie yelled to Flannery and Plumber.

Dr. Flannery, on the apron of the green in two strokes, lifted his arm in acknowledgment.

Silently, sullenly, Gordon and Augie crossed the little bridge, passed the first green as if they were on an express track and it was a local stop, and parked alongside the second tee behind their competitors' cart.

"OK, let's settle down," Augie said.

Gordon was silent, gripping the wheel.

"I'm sorry for yelling and carrying on back there," Augie said.

Nothing.

"Gordon, are we going to talk or just ride together?"
"Just ride together. Fuck you."

THEY lost the first four holes about as fast as you could lose
four quarters in a slot machine. Dr. Flannery played with the
deftness often attributed to one in his profession, and Plumber
was strong, determined, combative; one way or the other he
propelled the ball toward the hole. For a muscular go-at-'em
player, he also had a nice touch around the green. All Gordon
and Augie could do was hack; furthermore, because they were
both playing so poorly and didn't want to concede *every* hole,
they spent time looking for errant shots: making sevens took
longer than making fours. The foursome, as a unit, began holding up play. Having eked out a halve on the fifth hole, Augie
and Gordon went back to duffing on the sixth. They were in
the process of going five down when the ranger appeared.

Augie couldn't hear what Dr. Flannery said to Plumber
across the fairway, but he could guess. "It's about goddamn
time!"

The ranger pulled up alongside Augie and Gordon in his
official cart. "Listen, I'm sorry, you're going to have to speed it
up—you've got two open holes ahead of you." It was Curt
Kolchak.

"OK," Gordon said. He got out of the wagon and walked
over to his ball.

"How you playing, Augie?" Kolchak said.

"Don't even ask."

"Where are you?"

"Up ahead."

Gordon topped his shot and came back to the cart and
they rode to Augie's ball, which was in the rough. Kolchak
trailed along, ostensibly checking on their quickness—or slow-
ness—of play. Augie had a reasonable lie and chose a 3-iron.
The ball was badly struck. It went *clunk* and just made the
fairway. Gordon walked over to hit his next shot.

"Hey, relax," Kolchak said in low tones. They could have

242

been talking about the weather or the tournament generally. "You're tense as a drum. What's going on here?"

"I'm a basket case."

"I guess so! Smile, all right? Let me see you smile."

He tried to smile.

"Good. Now ease up all over. On your backswing, I want you to make a fuller turn with your shoulders."

Gordon came back after slicing his ball out of bounds. Plumber and Flannery both made good shots and stayed on the far side of the fairway. Kolchak tagged along after McSweeney and Wittenbecher, every now and then making a show of checking his watch. Augie was looking at a 6-iron for his approach. He pulled the iron from his bag, then walked out to his ball on foot. Kolchak, still in his cart, followed; here, to a casual onlooker, was a ranger really doing his job.

"Take a practice swing," he said. "Smile—hum a little tune. Turn those shoulders."

Augie took a practice swing.

"Better. Keep smiling. Full shoulder turn, ninety degrees."

Augie took another practice swing.

"Great. Now go ahead. Hum!"

"Hmm hm hmm hm hmmm—"

Augie stood over his ball, letting the pennies from heaven drop all around him, made a full shoulder turn on the backswing, and came down smoothly. The ball went high, deep. Instead of fading, it started to draw—and landed twelve feet from the flag.

"Next time it'll cost you guys!" Kolchak said, good and loud. "Two strokes. Got it?" He held up two fingers to Augie; it was a *V* for Victory. Then he spun off in his cart.

AFTER nine holes they were three down. Not good but at least they weren't *seven* down. Which they would have been. There was a small delay—a backup—on the tenth tee because players were stopping for refreshments at Halfway House. Gordon guzzled a beer and Augie drank a Coke. Then they were at it again and Augie unleashed a drive that went ten yards past Plumber's, who by his own admission had "put the persimmon to it." Augie had his first birdie of the day, and now, on the eleventh tee, he and Gordon were only two holes down.

Eleven was a par-3 to an isolated, elevated green, and Augie, really pumped up, bounced his ball over the green into a clump of bushes. Gordon's shot landed in a trap, short. Dr. Flannery hit the edge of the green, and Plumber muscled a 6-iron tight. Augie didn't want to go three down but it looked as if they would. Gordon played first. He took out his pitching wedge—he didn't have a sand iron—and made a vicious cut at the ball, intending to take a lot of sand. He took no sand at all. The ball came out hot and low, straight for Augie, who was on the green. He dropped. At the last instant the ball nipped the top lip of the bunker and slowed, then bounced across ten feet of grass, reached the putting surface, followed the break like it had eyes—and *fell.*

"I'm getting pretty good at that shot," Gordon said coming out of the trap.

Augie, brushing himself off, thought it was a funny comment, but Dr. Flannery looked as if he might blow his good wife's breakfast and Plumber couldn't help swearing under his breath. To halve the hole, now, would require either man sinking his next shot. Dr. Flannery's chip was short. He picked up. Plumber had seven feet to the hole. He crouched over his ball, rear end thrust out, old rock-ass himself. His concentration was intense, Augie felt certain he'd make the putt—

"Ker-choooo!"

Plumber stood back up.

Gordon whipped out his handkerchief and sneezed again. "Sorry—my feet are getting wet."

Plumber said nothing. From where Augie stood he couldn't see the man's face, just a section of his jawbone; it was pulsing, a mild crimson. Dr. Flannery was scratching his lip, perhaps wondering if such boorishness should be brought to the attention of the Committee. His partner stuck out his rear end again, drew back his putter . . . the ball lipped the rim, hung on the edge, wouldn't drop.

"Shit!"

Plumber swung his putter like a polo mallet and rocketed his ball into the gorse.

Augie and Gordon rode to the twelfth tee just one hole down.

"We got 'em worried now," Augie said.

No response.

"Great shot—it pays to be Irish."

"You're the lucky one, Wittenbecher." Gordon parked the cart beside the tee.

"Why is that?"

"I was aiming for your balls."

"Oh."

They stayed one down through twelve, thirteen and fourteen. Then on fifteen, as both teams were getting ready to hit second shots, the tournament chairman Steve McMahon came motoring down the fairway. Augie thought the official was going to assess a penalty against him and Gordon for slow play even though they weren't playing slowly. He saw himself being summarily disqualified for language disrespectful to a club official. McMahon braked. "You guys will have to suspend play. Championship Flight's coming through."

"I don't see anyone behind us," Augie said.

"Just pull to one side and wait, Mr. Wittenbecher."

McMahon turned his steering wheel and scooted across to inform Dr. Flannery and Gil Plumber, who obliged the tournament chairman by driving their cart into the rough. Gordon did the same, in the opposite rough, and set the brake.

"I don't like this," Augie said.

"Take five, relax."

"It kills the momentum."

"We're doing good."

"I guess we're talking again," Augie said.

"Don't bet on it."

Through the evergreens separating the fifteenth from the

fourteenth holes a hoard of people, mostly in golf carts, suddenly came into view. The procession then stopped, became still; approach shots were made, and the gallery rolled on.

Augie propped his feet on the front cowling and tried not to think. From the fourteenth green came a great roar; then the crowd moved to the next hole. Some of the gallery stayed at the tee but the majority rode ahead. A phalanx of golf buggies came sweeping down the fairway, then parked in the rough on the left and right. Gordon repositioned their cart so they would be able to watch the play. People were all looking back toward the tee. "Who's winning?" Gordon asked the woman in the neighboring cart who had on a white E.C.C. visor; beside her was a little girl of seven or eight.

"Donohue and Sargent, 1-up."

The first three drives were all beauties. Two bounced past Augie's ball by twenty yards; one was only a few yards farther but in the light rough. The fourth player, Larry Bisell, started his ball out to the right, hoping to draw it back in; but it clipped the branch of a tall pine, lost steam and dropped into the deep grass short of where Gordon and Augie were parked.

The players began walking down the fairway in distinctly separate twosomes. There was a good deal of laughter and chatter among the gallery, but when Larry Bisell got to his ball and examined the lie, all was silence. He conferred with Jack. Standing to one side was the opposition, Bob Donohue and Ed Sargent. Bisell's caddy handed him a 5-wood.

As he was setting up, Augie let his eyes wander over the many faces in the gallery. On foot, looking on with her brother and sister-in-law Kate, was Azy.

Bisell swung; there was a *click* and people shouted, "Great shot, Larry." The caravan advanced. Azy walked by with Dennis and Kate, and for a moment her eyes met Augie's, but what were they saying? What was she telling him? He saw himself going out and walking beside her for a few steps to find out. But didn't, wisely; it was killing him, though. Three separate irons flew toward the green, and Azy angled across and spoke with Gil. Augie, taking practice swings to keep loose, watched them kiss. She came in close—Gil squeezed her hand—she smiled and walked on. Augie swung furiously at an imaginary ball, cutting a swath in the deep grass. On the green it took forever for the Championship Flight to finish. Jack lined up his putt this way, that way. From one side, the other side. He examined the cup, leaning way over and peering in, as if maybe there was a toad inside that was gonna jump the fuck up. Augie kept swinging, trying to stay loose. Knowing he wasn't loose. Knowing he was up-tight and bleeding. Finally Jack putted, there was a loud cheer and he pumped his fist. The four men walked to the next tee, and *now* Flight 12 could resume.

Dr. Flannery and Plumber both hit solid approaches, though neither ball was dancing. Augie took too much divot and left himself thirty yards short. He then proceeded to stub his bread-and-butter shot, the pop wedge. Gordon managed to get a 9-iron on the back fringe in three, then two-putted for a bogie, which earned the halve. Still 1-down. They rode to the sixteenth tee.

"Come on, partner."

He gave Gordon a look but he was just steering; it was as if he hadn't spoken. But he had, and it mattered, and suddenly he felt much better. On sixteen he lofted an 8-iron from the right side over a series of bunkers, then canned the putt for a birdie. *All-even.* Seventeen was the long par three. Augie faded his tee shot into a bunker, and Gordon yanked the string on his mower and spun his ball to the back of the green, right side. Plumber missed left, but Dr. Flannery, using a driver, dropped one smack in the center.

Augie left his first explosion shot in the trap, put his second into the tall grass at the top of the bunker, and picked up. Plumber made a neat chip, Gordon putted to seven feet, Dr. Flannery to one—and Gordon, needing the putt for the tie, knocked it in. Augie didn't say a word as they drove to the eighteenth tee. He was too grateful to talk.

"Three days in a row," Gordon said, parking.

"That's right."

"Come on, partner," he said again.

But Augie didn't hit one of his better drives, pulling a shot high and to the left, shy of the swale. He gave the tee to Gordon, who sent a routine banana ball into the rough. Then Dr. Flannery walked out and, showing he was human, hit a terrible drive—the ball ducked left and dove into the marsh. Now it was up to Plumber, who readied himself over the ball and hit it right on the screws. It was his biggest drive of the day. Grinning, he stepped in his cart and Dr. Flannery said, "It's your hole, Gil. I'll pick up." In the driver's seat, Plumber took off with his partner.

Gordon cruised along with Augie. They came to his ball and Augie got out and looked at it, studying the lie, trying to figure what he had to do. It was similar to yesterday's shot—he had to clear a fir and really couldn't see the green. It was a 4-iron, but he needed more elevation and decided to go with a 5. He would have to put something extra on it; maybe he'd catch a flyer. "Go ahead, I'll watch your ball for you," Gordon said.

Augie made a couple of practice swings. Thinking positive. He could, he would, put this ball on the green—and close. He began humming, not "Pennies." Another oldie he liked . . . "It Had To Be You."

"Hmm hm hmm hm hmmm—"

Full shoulder turn, nice and loose. Augie took a big rip, looked up. The ball flew away, cleared the tree, straight, deep, slight draw—it was the sweetest, the truest shot he'd hit all weekend. Any weekend. Ever in his life. Gordon was already yelling and Augie was thinking it's in the hole and the ball started coming down—dead to the stick—his heart was pounding—then the ball just—he didn't know—vanished. There was no bounce. When a ball hit a green it bounced. This ball—disappeared. Had he possibly holed out on the fly?

"Shit!"

"What?" said Augie.

"You're in the trap."

"The *trap?*"

"Three more inches, Augie! You were there!"

He stood, staring dumbly, in shock. Then he said, "I'll take my wedge and putter."

He yanked them from his bag. Gordon rode away and Augie walked mechanically toward the green, thinking maybe it wasn't meant to be, after all. He couldn't hit a shot any better. And where was he? In a goddamn hazard! Where was the justice? In the right rough, Gordon swung vigorously—but no miracle shot on eighteen today. The ball never came up. He whacked at it again and it still didn't fly. Finally he quit and drove over to where Augie was now standing, waiting for Plumber to hit. A 7-iron, straight in. When the pressure was on, what shot would you rather have than a little 7-iron straight in?

Plumber swung. It was nicely hit but—Augie saw in a second—wouldn't get there. The ball landed squarely in front of the green some five yards short of the fringe. He would have to chip and sink his putt for the par. Augie didn't get in the wagon with Gordon, just continued walking. Then he was at the bunker and saw his ball was partially plugged. He'd have to loft it six feet to clear the bank. He stood there, looking in, staring down. Azy was sitting on the grassy edge of the trap. No one else was watching. Who cared about Flight 12? Plumber came over and stood close by; he didn't say anything to Azy. He just wanted to watch. Augie dropped his putter on the bank, went down the grassy incline and walked across to his ball.

From in the bunker he could see the flag and a third of the stick. He opened the face of his wedge and twisted and turned his feet to get a good solid stance. He glanced up, then back down. He figured he had to hit the sand two inches behind the ball; from the trap on seventeen he had figured the same thing. Fuck. He opened the heavy blade another degree. Steeply up, he told himself, then steeply down. And don't peek. Augie made the swing. There was a burst of sand and he had to step back. The ball jumped up, cleared the lip and landed on the fringe. Augie scampered up the embankment. The ball rolled across the green and stopped three feet from the flagstick.

Gordon went crazy. Hootin' and hollerin'. Augie was grinning—

"Sorry, you lose the hole," Plumber said.

"Excuse me?"

"You grounded your club."

"What the hell are you talking about?" Augie said.

"The penalty for grounding your club in a bunker is loss of hole," Plumber said. "That's the rule."

"I'm lying three," Augie said, "right there." He pointed.

"I saw your club touch the sand."

"You saw wrong," Augie said.

"What's the problem here?" Dr. Flannery said, coming up.

"His club made contact with the sand," Plumber said.

"That's bullshit."

"Augie, stay cool," said Gordon, also coming up.

"I'll stay cool, but you're either blind or a liar," he said to Plumber.

"We'll settle it later," said Dr. Flannery. "Play out."

"There's nothing to settle," Augie said. "I'm lying three next to the flag!"

"You're lying nothing, you're lying zilch," Plumber said. "When your club touches the sand in a bunker you lose the hole in match play. End of discussion—"

"Gil, fuck you—*end of discussion.*"

He was ready to rush Plumber, and Plumber looked perfectly ready to rush him, but Dr. Flannery and Gordon both stepped in, holding back their partners.

"Play out, guys—come on," Dr. Flannery said.

"That was a great shot, Augie—just relax now," Gordon said.

"Sure, sure . . ."

But his hands were jumping as he marked his ball. Plumber chipped and left his ball four feet short; still away, he read the break from both directions, putted. The ball skimmed the cup. He tapped in, picked it out of the hole and walked off the green.

"OK, Augie," Gordon said.

Augie replaced his ball and put the coin in his pocket, still shook up. His vision was fuzzy, his hands were shaking. He hated this game, why in hell did he play it? He took the putter back on a line resembling a cardiogram. He wanted to stop and try again, hoping to make a smoother stroke, but it was too late —it was all guess anyway, one stroke was as good as another when your hands were jumping like his. Sure as hell they were going to sudden death. He came forward with the putter, hit the ball. It rolled, miraculously held the line—and went in.

Gordon ran up and grabbed Augie's hand and hugged his old friend, pummeling his back. "Augie, we did it! We *won.*"

He was too nervous to reach for his ball in the hole.

"I'm taking this up with the Committee," Plumber announced.

"Gil, a player has to call a penalty on himself," Dr. Flannery said. "If he doesn't, you need a witness."

"Is he doing it? Do you hear him doing it?"

"No. So you'll need a witness."

As one, the four men looked across at Azy, still sitting on the back edge of the trap. It was her father who spoke. "Did you see anything, Azy?"

She hesitated. Augie seemed to see her struggling—with what he didn't know. But he could imagine. "I didn't notice," she said.

"You were sitting right there!" Gil shouted.

"I didn't see."

Plumber's face grew redder. His host led him away before he said anything else, talking to him quietly. They got in their cart. Plumber looked over at his fiancée. "I'll see you at the house." He stomped the pedal and they drove off.

Augie picked his ball out of the hole and replaced the flag.

"Come on, partner," Gordon said.

Her head was against her raised knees. Augie wanted to say something, but what? What was there to say? Especially if she didn't look up. He and Gordon walked across the green. Augie picked up his wedge, and stowed both clubs.

"We *did* it, partner," Gordon said in the cart.

Augie slid beside him, momentarily looking back to where Azy was sitting, head still lowered. "Let's go get a cold one," he said.

"**Y**OU GUYS MUST feel real proud." Jimmy was unstrapping their bags for what would be the last time.

"We do, Jimmy," Gordon said. He was standing on one side of the cart, Augie on the other.

"Want to check your clubs, Mr. Wittenbecher?"

Augie flipped through his woods and irons. Just then Curt Kolchak came down the storage-room steps. "Did I hear right?"

"If you heard we won," Gordon said, "you sure did."

"I speed you guys up, look what you go and do."

"Did you actually nail anyone," Gordon said, "or just roar around all morning like Attila the Hun?"

"That was about it."

Jimmy laid Augie's bag against the low fence, then picked up Gordon's by the handle. "Here you go," Gordon said, stretching out his hand with a tenner in it.

"Thanks, Mr. McSweeney," Jimmy said, and went inside.

"So, congratulations," Kolchak said. "How did it go?"

"Just now on eighteen," Gordon said, "Plumber lay two off the green—we're all even. Augie lay two in the big trap on the left, blasted out to three feet! What does Plumber do? Tells Augie his club touched the sand."

"Oh, boy." The ex-pro turned to Augie. "Then what?"

"I told him he was wrong," Augie said. "He kept saying I'd done it—loss of hole, loss of match. I blew my stack."

"When you went to putt, I bet it looked like twenty feet."

"I don't want to even think about it."

Kolchak grinned, then gave his head a little shake. "As cons go, that's one of the better ones."

"It damn near worked." Augie expelled a huge breath.

"When you leaving?" Kolchak wanted to know.

"Later today."

"Well, take care of yourself, Augie."

"You too . . ." They shook hands.

"Regards to Dean and Hannah."

"You bet. And Curt"—he held up two fingers—"thanks."

Kolchak smiled and retired to his cavernous room. Gordon ambled over to the wall and scanned the postings. "Flannery and Bisell won—1-up."

Augie couldn't care less.

AFTER they washed up in the locker room they went into the lounge and sat at a corner table. A couple of cold ones arrived and Gordon lifted his mug. "Good playing, partner," he said.

"You too."

"I contributed some, anyway."

"Your contributions got us here."

"Do you know what really got us here?"

"I sure do. Your 4-iron yesterday."

"No. When you told me to keep looking for your ball on the first hole, Friday's round."

"What was so good about that?"

"Savvy. That you knew. I would've never kept looking."

Augie made a head gesture toward the eighteenth green. "I'm so savvy I took Plumber's bait—hook, line and sinker. They would've beaten us in sudden death."

"You think so?"

"I know so."

"Some guys will do anything," Gordon said.

"I once played in a tournament with a guy who wanted me

to raise the topic of *Roe v. Wade* on the seventeenth tee," Augie
said. "The way he figured it—"

"That would've worked—it was good strategy."

Augie laughed, they both laughed and they drank. "This
will be my first piece of tin ever," Gordon said. "I'm going to be
real proud of it."

They were quiet for a minute, looking around the lounge
at the other golfers. Jack Flannery and Larry Bisell were con-
spicuously absent, which didn't mean they weren't celebrating.
They were probably popping champagne out on Ocean Drive.
Winners, Championship Flight. Their names would go on the
big varnished plaque. Augie rubbed his left hand at the base of
the fingers—no blisters, just sore. He wanted to say something
to Gordon but was hesitant because, in a sense, it was behind
them—and in another sense it wasn't. Something was still un-
settled . . .

"Listen, Gordon, about what happened yesterday afternoon—"

"What happened, happened. It's over."

"Then you want me to shut up," Augie said.

"Say what you want. I'm telling you it's history."

"I just don't want us hiding anything, that's all. Covering
up bad feelings. That was heavy shit we went through."

"It was very heavy shit."

"I didn't think you'd show up for today's round, to be
honest with you," Augie said.

Across the room two young golfers—Augie took them for
hot players in one of the low-handicap flights—were standing
on their chairs in stocking feet singing an Irish ballad. There
was a pleasant, a relaxed atmosphere in the lounge. "I wasn't
going to," Gordon said, "but then I changed my mind."

"I'm damn glad you did."

"Kelly told me what happened."

Augie, having a taste of his beer, slowly put down his
glass.

"That's what it's all about," Gordon said. "The other isn't
so much, not really. I mean, I wanted to kill you but we were

255

drunk—people do crazy, fucked-up things when they're drunk. Then when Kel told me later on, things sort of took on perspective. That told me something, Augie. What friendship really means. Do you know what I'm saying?"

Augie felt as if he'd caddied double all day and had just set down the bags for the last time. "I'm glad I was there."

"I'm glad you were too. So is Kelly."

Gordon finished his beer. Augie thought he was going to suggest another, but instead he glanced at the big clock on the wall. "The awards thing starts in forty-five minutes," he said. "We should get going. I've got your luggage in my car."

"You do?"

"I know you've been using the facilities here, Augie. Don't blame you, either."

AUGIE picked up his golf bag at the low fence and carried it out to his wagon, where he changed his shoes on the tailgate. Gordon stopped his car as he was exiting the lot. Augie's luggage was in the front passenger seat among accumulated newspapers, candy wrappers, an old T-shirt and a pair of dirty socks. "Listen, I almost forgot," Gordon said, foot on the clutch as the old Chevy trembled and jolted like a dying horse. "Your bet! Do you have the ticket?"

"Jesus, that's right! I hope!"

"We've got bucks coming our way, partner. I'd say two hundred plus."

"Terrific."

"Listen, wait for me, OK? We'll do it together."

"Sure."

"The clothes you left in the kitchen, they're in there too."

"Thanks, Gordon."

Augie grabbed up his bags and walked back to the club. In the locker room he sat down on a bench and struggled out of his sweat-soaked shirt. He checked his wallet for the betting slip, there it was, neatly tucked away. So, he'd have money to get home with. Maybe things were falling into place. From

Shufferville, mid-week, he'd give Azy a call; and if she had an unlisted number, he'd try her office. He had a feeling he knew what she'd say. It had been very nice, she was glad to have met him—maybe something better than that—but she was following through on her commitment to Gil. He would listen, wouldn't argue with her or get sore. He knew what fire was. He was a big boy. Maybe he would say it had been a wonderful four days for him. He didn't want to sound sentimental but he might say knowing her had been wonderful. Something. He would wish her good luck, then he would just say goodbye. That was what he would say. "Goodbye, Azy."

BEFORE he showered he called home, not expecting to get anyone on a beautiful summer afternoon; he didn't. So at the beep he said: "Hi, Heather, Brian. Gordon and I won. *First place.* I'm staying to pick up my prize, then I'm outta here. If Maria wants to spend the night again, fine. See you about ten. Love you both, goodbye."

He took a long shower, shaved, used all the good stuff on the shelf and went back to the locker room, where he put on the clothes he had intended to wear yesterday—blue trousers and white short-sleeved shirt. He folded Jack's clothes in a tight bundle and dropped them off at the shoe counter, telling the old man whose they were; he really didn't know how to go about returning them. Jerry said he'd take care of it. Augie wished he had a couple of dollars to give him. He made a second trip to the parking lot, tossed his luggage beside his golf bag and came back to the club.

People were already assembling on the patio as he approached, the women in pretty dresses, the men in bright trousers and shirts. Some members and guests were walking about on the trampled grass where the pari-mutuel tent had stood. The clam bar was in business again. The setup was exactly the same as the opening cocktail party, with one exception. A long table stood on the far end of the patio, and on it were some thirty boxes, beautifully wrapped in white paper and green ribbons. Two sizes: the large, some seven inches high; the small, about four. Augie stepped onto the patio and looked around for a waitress.

One came by, a well-endowed college girl in a green-and-white uniform. He ordered a vodka and tonic and signed Gordon's name when she reappeared with it. Every minute more and more people arrived. No one spoke to him, came up and asked him how he had played, how his team had done. He stayed near the edge of the patio, where the tent had stood, directly across from the wide doorway leading into the main bar. A handful of golfers hadn't changed, still had their spikes on—the younger players, winners of their flights, who obviously were enjoying the image. Victorious gladiators. Augie drank his vodka and tonic, looked about—

—and saw her coming through the doorway in a stunning silk jumpsuit. Plumber, at her side, wore a white blazer with a pair of mint-green slacks. Also a straw bowler with a matching mint-and-white band. Dr. Flannery and Mrs. Flannery, who had preceded the couple by a step, immediately saw and joined son Jack and son Jack's partner, Larry Bisell. Azy and Gil went up, and the six stood in a loose knot ordering drinks, talking. Almost everyone who happened by gave Jack and Larry a congratulatory handshake. Augie wondered where Janet O'Roehrs was. It was her celebration too—when your future husband won, you won. Right? Just then Kate and Dennis appeared in the doorway, and now the clan was at full complement, minus a fiancée.

Augie couldn't speak for the Donohues. If they were here they hadn't assembled like the Flannerys. Maybe they were all at a local bar somewhere pounding down Buds. He had another taste of his drink, the while looking across at Azy—and feeling a dull ache in his chest. He would take home a prize. He had played the game and he'd won. Except it occurred to him he really hadn't won at all. It was Plumber who was standing with his arm around her waist.

He turned away, just wanting the party to end so he could get on the road. The crowd was spilling over, and many people were now on the grounds, talking and drinking. Augie decided to have a couple of clams. Al Keegan was just gliding one into his mouth as he came up. Seeing who it was, Keegan turned quickly and walked away. Par for the course, no problem. The same two men were shucking and serving the clams in big rubber aprons. Augie had several and returned to his place on the side of the patio. He managed to snag another waitress, a tall brunette, and ordered another drink, thinking, as he signed Gordon's name again, he'd spot him thirty dollars from his winnings. Augie lifted his new vodka and tonic, had a sip. Behind the prize table, Steve McMahon was checking a list of names—

"There you are!"

He turned, recognizing the voice. Angling toward him on the grass was Gordon, with wife and daughter. When the Mc-Sweeneys stepped up to the patio it was like boarding the already overcrowded deck of a ferry. "Hi, Mr. Wittenbecher," Kelly said. "Congratulations!"

"Thank you. Your dad told you all about it, I bet."

"He sure did."

"See you have a little drink for yourself," Gordon said.

"I signed your name. Twice."

"Getting ahead of me. Big mistake, partner."

"Hello, Augie," Catherine said.

She did not seem upset or even embarrassed. She only seemed her public self—glittery and brittle. She had on a rose-pink cocktail dress with a big white bow on the waist in back, and a short hemline; also pink heels. Catherine extended her hand at a formal distance. "I'm really, really happy for you."

"Thank you."

"I heard you hit an incredible shot on the last hole, from a sand pit."

"Trap," Gordon said.

"Pit, trap—who cares? You won! Can we have a drink?"

"Let me shanghai a waitress," Gordon said.

He did, getting the tall brunette: 7-Up for Kelly, Scotch sour for Catherine and a vodka and cranberry for Gordon.

With a work day tomorrow, maybe they were both easing off. When the waitress went away Kelly gave Augie a little smile, for no reason except—he thought, smiling back—that she wanted to. The tip of her nose was peeling and her hair had pretty blonde streaks in it. Gordon mentioned the crowd. A few guests had probably left, he said, those beaten in an early round; but most, obviously, had stayed. Catherine said with so much to *do* in Easthelmsford besides play golf, why would anyone want to leave? Augie didn't answer the question, though he could have. Finally the drinks arrived. "To you, partner," Gordon said, lifting his glass.

"To you. To both of you, many thanks."

"Tonight let's go someplace and celebrate," Catherine said. "Just the three of us."

"I really don't see how I'll be able to," Augie said. "I told my kids—"

"We'll have you on the road first thing in the morning," Gordon said.

"Oh, he's staying," Catherine said, laughing gaily. "He's just playing hard to get!"

"Mr. Wittenbecher," Kelly said, "could Heather ever come down and visit?"

"I'm sure she'd like to," Augie said.

"How about next month?"

"Whenever. Your parents haven't said anything, Kelly."

"Augie," Catherine said. "We'd *love* to have her. My goodness. Your children are *family.*"

"OK, may I have your attention?" came a general announcement.

People turned, looked at the front table. Steve McMahon was standing with both arms raised. "Ladies and gentlemen. *Members and guests.*"

The tournament chairman let several moments go by, waited for the gathering to quiet. "I want to thank everyone who participated in this year's tournament," he said. "I personally think it was one of the very best ever. A total of sixty-seven matches went to the eighteenth hole, and eleven matches were decided in sudden-death playoffs. That's a record. The level of competition this year was outstanding. I want to thank the marvelous staff of the Easthelmsford Country Club for doing such an outstanding job, from Curt Kolchak and Jimmy in the bag room to Fran Hanrahan in the dining room. I particularly want to thank our golf professional, Kyle McIntyre, for helping in so many ways, from the long hours he spent in his shop to his invaluable contributions on the Committee. We relied on his expertise time and time again on matters pertaining to the game we all love so much. Let's hear it for Kyle—and all the E.C.C. staff."

Clapping, cheering. "All right. A lot of you have to catch planes, start for home," McMahon said, "so let's get the ball rolling. *Flight 14.* Runners-up are Bill Swenson and Don Cleary!"

Two men—one in his early sixties, the other about forty-five—made their way through the crowd. McMahon gave each of them the smaller box, shook their hands. The older man raised the box above his head, grinning proudly, and to applause he and his partner rejoined their group.

"OK," said McMahon. "Now—the winners of Flight 14. Randy Kiernan and Sam Etter."

The cheering and clapping were louder. Again two men, both about fifty, dressed in polo shirts and slacks, went forward. Each was given the larger box. One of the men, the taller and perhaps younger, said loudly, "It was all Sam!"

"Randy carried me all three rounds, don't believe him!"

"Until you guys agree, maybe you should leave your prizes with Steve," someone shouted from the crowd.

People laughed. McMahon laughed. "OK, *Flight 13.*"

He read the names of the runners-up, who stepped forward, then the winners, two men standing next to Catherine. When they came back one of the men—the guest, Lou Holtz—couldn't restrain himself. He reminded Augie of a kid opening a Christmas present. Off came ribbon and paper. "Oh, it's from Tiffany's," Holtz's wife said, seeing the box. Holtz slid out an exquisitely crafted solid brass clock. *Ooohing* and *aaahing.*

"Ready, partner?" Gordon said.

"I'll follow you."

"I'll probably trip and fall on my face."

"On we go," said McMahon. "But first, a small announcement. Flight 12, unfortunately, is under review. These things happen occasionally. We never like to see it but in the heat of competition infractions do sometimes occur. We're in close touch with the USGA. We'll keep you posted by mail, those of you who have Flight 12 tickets. We should have the problem adjudicated in a week—"

"Son-of-a-bitch," Gordon muttered.

"This isn't *fair,"* Kelly said.

"Damn it, partner, we *won."*

Augie was silent. He could feel the blood surging upward, but at the same time his throat was very dry, tight. He glanced toward the doorway leading into the club. Plumber's head was bent toward Jack Flannery, and he was saying something . . .

"I'm going to lodge a complaint," Gordon said.

"Now, *Flight 11,"* McMahon said. "Runners-up are Don Turner and—"

"Wait a minute."

People looked over. "I don't like this," Augie said, taking a step forward.

"Mr. Wittenbecher, this is in the hands of the USGA," McMahon said. "Whatever you have to say, put it in writing. We'll certainly take your comments into consideration—"

"I'd like to make my comments now, in person," Augie said.

"For God's sake, stop him," Catherine said to Gordon.

"Go for it, partner."

"This is so embarrassing."

Augie was now at the long table. An angry voice: "That's that troublemaker, get him out of here—"

"Mr. Wittenbecher," McMahon said, "this is not the time and place. If you don't cease immediately—"

"This is the perfect time and place."

Shouts for him to shut up, hit the road, came from several

corners of the patio. He looked out at the crowd, chest thundering. "Gordon McSweeney and I won Flight 12. If it's under review, it's because a couple of players who *didn't* win it are rotten sports."

"Drop dead, Wittenbecher."

"Call security."

"Mr. Wittenbecher, you're *way* out of line," McMahon said. "I'll give you one last warning—"

"I say let him speak."

Everyone looked over. From a spot near the clam bar, André Gilliam had his arm outstretched, finger extended. "Wittenbecher and McSweeney beat me and Tom Hrazanek yesterday—it was a terrific match. They beat us fair and square. The man has something to say, let him say it."

"Hasn't training camp opened yet, André?" someone shot back.

"Go ahead and talk, Augie," said Gilliam.

The crowd quieted down some. "In Friday's match there was a dispute on the first hole," Augie said. "So I played the hole with two balls, leaving it to the Committee to decide. When we walked off eighteen the club professional was there with the decision—which went against Keegan. He didn't like that one bit and—"

"I'll kill that bastard."

"Shut up, Al," someone yelled.

Augie, taking deep breaths, went on. "In yesterday's match Gordon and I beat Gilliam and Hrazanek. As André just said, it *was* a terrific match, and they were, and are, gentlemen in the real sense of the word. Today in the finals we played Dr. Flannery and Gil Plumber, and we beat them on the eighteenth. Plumber accused me of touching the sand in the bunker—"

"You *did* touch it," Plumber called out.

"I didn't—and you know it," Augie came back. "You just didn't want to lose. So you accused me of grounding my club to get a rise out of me, because I still had to make a putt. Well, you got a rise out of me, I'll say that. But I made the damn putt."

Augie looked out at the people seated and standing on the patio. "What's going on here is just lousy politics. I made an enemy of Steve McMahon on the first tee of the first round when I told him he didn't know the rules of golf—"

Laughter from a few isolated spots. Standing behind the table, McMahon's face was tight, cold.

"I should've said it more diplomatically," Augie said. "But it was pretty heated and that was the way it came out."

People were listening now. "This whole review business is a pretext to keep a couple of guys from winning their flight. We played the game and we won. And do you know how we won? On the strength of a shot yesterday in our match with Gilliam and Hrazanek, when we were looking defeat straight in the face. Gordon McSweeney, a novice compared to a lot of you, looked into his heart and found the courage he had to have, any golfer would have to have, to reach the green from the o.b. stakes on eighteen. Arnold Palmer's iron out of the gorse at Royal Birkdale when he won the British Open in '61 wasn't any greater—and that was one of golf's greatest shots. Then Gordon sank the putt for a birdie and we won the match. That was the beauty and thrill of this game—a miracle can happen to anybody with guts. It's the reason we play it, and I'm going to give the man who hit that 4-iron and made that putt his piece of tin, because he won it and he deserves it. I suppose Mr. McMahon, or others, could try and stop me, but there's going to be one awful fight if they try. I don't want that to happen," Augie said. "Listen, I never meant to disrupt your party today or to step on anybody's toes during this Member-Guest—it was just the way things worked out. You have a beautiful course. It's a great course. Just remember on seven, hit one more club than you think . . ."

He picked up a first-place box. McMahon just stood there, watching. The crowd opened up for Augie and he gave Gordon the box and some people actually started cheering, clapping. "Thanks, partner," Gordon said.

264

"Thank you, partner."

He gave Kelly a kiss on her cheek and pushed by Catherine, then cut across the patio—and behind him was a sudden hubbub, loud voices, shouts and someone was grabbing his arm and he had a terrible feeling it was Plumber or Keegan or one of the Flannerys. He spun around. It *was* one of the Flannerys.

It was Azy.

The expression on her face—he couldn't say what it was. It wasn't joy or excitement or love, although he thought he saw love in it. Then he seemed to know. It was the look that said she'd done it. Finally. And she was saying, Augie, help me. Help me now. And then Gil Plumber was pushing through, and Augie thought, It isn't over yet. We're going to sudden death after all. He stepped in front of Azy as Plumber made to swing. But Augie, not worrying about honors, swung first. He saw it as two hundred twenty yards—a 2-iron if he could catch it. He caught it. Clean—a low vicious shot drawing to the pin. Plumber's nose exploded and he fell back, blood covering his face, transforming it into a gruesome flag. Then there was screaming and yelling and confusion everywhere, and Augie left the patio, Azy's hand in his.

"Come back here, Azy—"

Brother Jack.

"Let's run, Augie." She tugged on his hand.

"No. We're doing fine."

Then again: *"Azy."*

"Augie—"

"Just keep walking. I love you."

They moved on past the pro shop and practice green and first tee, around the high hedge and out to the auxiliary parking lot and his car. He was in, she was in, she slid across the seat and came into his arms and they kissed, her hands all over his face, his hair, and she was crying now. He searched his pockets, unable to find his keys, but then he remembered where they were—over the visor—and he started the engine and drove out of the lot and down the street that paralleled club property. He looked in the mirror to see if anyone was chasing after them, no one was. His heart started beating normally again, or closer to it.

"Are we dreaming this?" she said.

"I don't know, are we?"

"If we both are it doesn't make any difference, does it?"

"No. None."

She slid closer and he put his arm around her. They were traveling on a county road, seven miles out of Easthelmsford. "Driver, 5-iron, Augie."

"Driver, 5-iron?"

Azy's hand was in the V of his shirt, on his chest. "The distance to Shufferville," she said.